NIZPATCHES

VOLUME ONE: CRIME STORIES

NIZPATCHES

NIZ THOMAS

COPYRIGHT

Nizpatches
Volume One: Crime Stories

Made in the USA
Published by Throughplace Publishing
throughplace.com
Text copyright © 2024 by Michael Nisivoccia
All rights reserved.

Cover and Layout copyright © 2024 by Throughplace Publishing
Cover design by Michael Nisivoccia / Throughplace Publishing
Cover art copyright © breakermaximus / Depositphotos

"The Omega Diner"
Published by Throughplace Publishing, 2023
Text copyright © 2023 by Michael Nisivoccia
All rights reserved.
Cover design by Michael Nisivoccia / Throughplace Publishing
Cover art copyright © savi88 / floor perspective / Depositphotos
Cover art copyright © pwollinga / man walking / Depositphotos

"The Two O'Clock Killer"
Published by Throughplace Publishing, 2023
Text copyright © 2023 by Michael Nisivoccia
All rights reserved.
Cover and Layout copyright © 2023 by Throughplace Publishing
Cover design by Michael Nisivoccia / Throughplace Publishing
Cover art copyright © feblacal / Depositphotos

"Call Me Betsy"
Published by Throughplace Publishing, 2023
Text copyright © 2023 by Michael Nisivoccia
All rights reserved.

Cover and Layout copyright © 2023 by Throughplace Publishing
Cover design by Michael Nisivoccia / Throughplace Publishing
Cover art copyright © breakermaximus / noir illustration / Depositphotos
Cover art copyright © DELstudio / train / Depositphotos
Cover art copyright © sozon / aged paper / Depositphotos

"The Bad Guy"
Published by Throughplace Publishing, 2023
Text copyright © 2023 by Michael Nisivoccia
All rights reserved.
Cover and Layout copyright © 2023 by Throughplace Publishing
Cover design by Michael Nisivoccia / Throughplace Publishing
Cover art copyright © jmeka_m@ukr.net / Depositphotos
Cover art copyright © HorenkO / Depositphotos

"Lane Change"
Published by Throughplace Publishing, 2023
Text copyright © 2023 by Michael Nisivoccia
All rights reserved.
Cover and Layout copyright © 2023 by Throughplace Publishing
Cover design by Michael Nisivoccia / Throughplace Publishing
Cover art copyright © summercandy / Bright pastel pink swimming pool / Depositphotos
Cover art copyright © anilin / Sunbathing young woman on a floating mattress/ Depositphotos

"Thin Air"
Published by Throughplace Publishing, 2023
Text copyright © 2023 by Michael Nisivoccia
All rights reserved.
Cover and Layout copyright © 2023 by Throughplace Publishing
Cover design by Michael Nisivoccia / Throughplace Publishing
Cover art copyright © isampuntarat@gmail.com / Depositphotos

"Burn Off"
Published by Throughplace Publishing, 2023
Text copyright © 2023 by Michael Nisivoccia
All rights reserved.
Cover and Layout copyright © 2023 by Throughplace Publishing
Cover design by Michael Nisivoccia / Throughplace Publishing
Cover art copyright © Loraliu / Depositphotos
Cover art copyright © mpavlov / Depositphotos

This book is licensed for your personal enjoyment only. All rights reserved. This is a work of fiction. All characters and events portrayed in this book are fictional, and any resemblance to real people or incidents is purely coincidental. This book, or parts thereof, may not be reproduced in any form without permission.

COPYRIGHT

Family Tree

Made in the USA
Published by Throughplace Publishing
throughplace.com
Text excerpt copyright © 2023 by Michael Nisivoccia
All rights reserved.

Cover and Layout copyright © 2023 by Throughplace Publishing
Cover design by Michael Nisivoccia / Throughplace Publishing
Cover art copyright © Robert Adrian Hillman / Shutterstock

This text excerpt is licensed for your personal enjoyment only. All rights reserved. This is a work of fiction. All characters and events portrayed in this book are fictional, and any resemblance to real people or incidents is purely coincidental. This book, or parts thereof, may not be reproduced in any form without permission.

CONTENTS

Also By Niz Thomas	xi
Introduction	xvii

THE OMEGA DINER

Intro	3
Chapter 1	7
Chapter 2	12
Chapter 3	18
Chapter 4	24
Chapter 5	27
Chapter 6	32
Chapter 7	35
Chapter 8	38

THE TWO O'CLOCK KILLER

Intro	49
Chapter 1	53

CALL ME BETSY

Intro	65
Chapter 1	69
Chapter 2	100

THE BAD GUY

Intro	105
Chapter 1	109
Chapter 2	111
Chapter 3	117
Chapter 4	120
Chapter 5	121
Chapter 6	126
Chapter 7	129

LANE CHANGE

Intro	139
Chapter 1	143
Chapter 2	160
Chapter 3	165
Chapter 4	178

THIN AIR

Intro	189
Chapter 1	193
Chapter 2	196
Chapter 3	200
Chapter 4	204
Chapter 5	207
Chapter 6	210
Chapter 7	213
Chapter 8	215
Chapter 9	217
Chapter 10	218
Chapter 11	221
Chapter 12	222
Chapter 13	225
Chapter 14	227

BURN OFF

Intro	233
Chapter 1	237
Chapter 2	244
Chapter 3	250
Chapter 4	255
Exclusive Sneak Peek	257
Afterword	259

FAMILY TREE

Chapter 1	265

Join the Mailing List	273
Also By Niz Thomas	275
About the Author	279

ALSO BY NIZ THOMAS

For a full list and links to purchase, visit: nizthomas.com/books

Nizpatches

Volume One: Crime Stories

Volume Two: Twisted Crime

---

the Ledgerman series

The Omega Diner: A Ledgerman Story

Razor's Edge: A Ledgerman Novel

Thin Air: A Ledgerman Story

Last Ride: A Ledgerman Novel

---

the True Name series

Call Me Betsy

Call Me Gertrude

Call Me Aileen

Novels

Family Tree

Door Number Five at the Memory Motel

And The Moon Is Full And Bright

Election Day

Short Stories

A Refraction of Kind Light

A Void of Ascendant Light

Becalm This Mighty Sea

Burn Off

Burn Together

Cheers

Elder Hunger

Fiona's Mercy

First Light of Every Morning

How to Commune with a Futurist

Lady Death

Lane Change

My Bleeding Kansas

No Control

Paint It Thrice

Rail Music

Ray-Ray's Stoop

Recidivist History

Red Tempest

Ships in the Night

Songbird

The Bad Guy

The Climb and The Glory

The Forever-ish Flame War

The Imminent Fire

The Impassable Way

The Light Alone

The Two O'Clock Killer

The Voice of Rage and Ruin

Upon Your Dreams They Prey: A Lullaby

Vanguard

Vida's Sixth Trip Around the Sun

When Sheds Talk

NIZPATCHES

INTRODUCTION

What you are holding in your hand, not to put too fine a point on it, is truly a miraculous thing.

I don't mean the writing–though if, after you read this collection of short stories, you feel the writing *is* miraculous, please feel free to tell anyone and everyone you come in contact with (and don't hesitate, in that scenario, to come in contact with a lot of people; get yourself out there!).

What I mean is that, until very recently, everything that follows this point was nothing but a kernel of an idea that was floating in some kind of subconscious deep sea within which I swim–half-submerged, half-treading above the surface. Most stories do not come to me fully formed. Most stories do not really *come* to me at all. They are much more a process of discovery. Of uncovering something that intrigues me. As Stephen King alludes to in his seminal craft book *On Writing*, it's almost a process of archaeology. The stories are *there*. But it is incumbent upon me to go in, dig out the dirt, dust off the gentle parts, avoid the booby traps, and escape before the rolling boulder finally catches up to me.

As you read through the stories, each one has a little bit about what inspired it, or how I worked to bring it to fruition, but you will see there are very few flashes of great insight which had me rushing to the nearest keyboard in a feverish fit to record these Great Ideas before they floated away with the tides. Unfortunately, that just isn't how it works for me.

It would make things a whole hell of a lot easier if it were.

But I suspect, like most things in life, that *easier* would simply translate to *boring*.

And then you wouldn't be holding anything in your hand at all.

At least nothing quite so miraculous.

So let's talk about it. What you're holding in your hand, I mean. This is the first of what I suspect will be many volumes of *Nizpatches*–what I intend to be a frequent and semi-regular collection of stories all centered around a theme. All original fiction. All mine.

Well, yours, too.

There are two competing concepts that occur in fiction reading and fiction writing (which, after all, are two sides of the same coin). When you read, your eyes scan across tiny black marks on a page (or a screen). Those black marks–what we experts call *words*–have a certain meaning. A meaning that we share. An agreement, if you will. That is probably the simplest definition of language. When strung together, those words tell a story. And while you are the one reading the stories in *Nizpatches*, and I am the one who wrote them, there is a question of whether they are *my* stories, or *yours*.

There is the saying, credited to Fitzgerald of Gatsby fame, that "the test of a first-rate intelligence is the ability to hold two opposing ideas in the mind at the same time, and still retain the ability to function."

And so that is what understanding reading and writing necessitates. Holding two opposing ideas in the mind at the same time.

(But since you are the one reading this, I'll leave it up to you whether you'd like to retain the ability to function or not).

When I put these little black marks down on my computer screen, they have a certain meaning to me. But I must also be aware of what they might mean to you. It does no good for me to *think* I mean one thing when most people would read what I've written and think something else. And so in that regard, writing is an exercise in great control. It's the art of mind control, really. For not only do I need to interpret what it is someone on the other side of the page might think about what I'm writing, so too must I recognize that perspective for someone in Morristown, Arizona and someone in Oyster Bay, Mauritius (yes, I checked, and Mauritius–beautiful island–is on the opposite side of the world from Arizona. Fun fact that I just found by checking that out: the exact opposite of something else is called an antipode, as in, *Oyster Bay is the antipode of Morristown*. Who knew?).

But I digress.

So, we've established that for me to tell a good story, I must get very good at mind control.

No big deal.

But–and here's where the opposing ideas part comes in–*you* are here, too. And do you not bring to the reading page a wealth of experiences, history, secrets, sins, guilts, weaknesses, and strengths? (You do. Don't sell yourself short).

So, then, how can I control your mind, while your mind also runs free with all that makes you, you? And with all of that, would your mind not then be far more than a passive spectator to these here stories? I daresay it would. It would no longer be mind control on my part. It would be more of a mind-meld. Both of us working together.

Given the topic around which all these stories sit–crime–I daresay it makes you an accomplice.

Something to ponder ...

And, unfortunately for any truth seekers among us, that's all the allotted space I have for this introduction.

Well, almost ...

Because inside this inaugural volume, you'll find a collection of stories that all delve deep into the criminal underworld in a number of strange, exciting, and surprising ways. There are thieves, killers, cops, robbers, lowlifes, thugs, ne'er-do-wells. There's even a boxer. And a kid. It's a mixture of the wrong people in the wrong situation–some of whom are intent on doing the wrong thing.

I do hope you enjoy it.

In fact, if you buy into the mind control theory, I *insist*.

And if not, well, you do with it whatever you please.

These stories are many things to me. And they can be many things to you, too.

I told you this was truly a miraculous thing.

Niz Thomas
January, 2024

THE OMEGA DINER

A LEDGERMAN STORY

INTRO

This story was born from the character's name imprinted into my mind. I was flying across the country, minding my own business, crammed into a modern airplane without much of a care in the world (oh, how naïve I was).

Ledgerman.

I wrote the name down. What did it mean? It was a name, at least. That was very clear to me. But whose name?

Ledgerman.

Sounds like ... a superhero? What would the superpower be? Bookkeeping?

I needed to write that day and I figured a cross-country flight was enough time to get a good session in. I hadn't planned to write *about* anything in particular. I was in between projects. Should I write about this mysterious character that rose to the fore of my subconscious? I had learned to trust that little messenger that lives inside all of us, the one who whispers directly into the center of your brain, who says things you need to hear, or don't really want to hear, or sometimes the truths that we have all been avoiding.

But I didn't have the faintest clue what a name like this might mean. That damned messenger never really takes the time to explain itself.

Ledgerman.

So I did what any self-respecting artist would do.

I feel asleep until they brought the drink cart out.

Later, when I awoke, I still had no idea who this Ledgerman character was. But as is often the case, the writing was a way to find out. This particular story was my first introduction to the mysterious man who–after a lot of discovery–seems to fit the name rather well (if different from my original thought–don't worry, this isn't a story about accounting).

What resulted from that plane writing session, and several more thereafter, is a series of stories about a man trying to do his best in a world he doesn't fully understand–one where danger and dread seems to always be looking just on the horizon of his ken.

Oh, and one other detail which seems rather poignant in hindsight. The date of my flight.

February 4, 2020.

A few weeks before the whole world shut down in what I can confidently say was a new experience for everyone–one we didn't entirely understand at the time.

Am I a psychic? Some kind of prophet (Niztradamus!)? A writer capable of bending the fourth dimension so that I might report back with that which I see?

¯_(ツ)_/¯

I sure hope you enjoy the story. It was a great entry point into my understanding of this character and the circumstances in which he finds himself. The first of many such stories in the Ledgerman universe. Some of which are finished as of my writing this introduction, and some of which are still forthcoming (and remember: Niztradamus!).

Plenty more to explore.

INTRODUCING
LEDGERMAN
IN

THE OMEGA DINER

NIZ

AUTHOR OF THE *TRUE NAME* SERIES

THOMAS

ONE

Ledgerman takes a long pull from his diner coffee, the scalding liquid and heavy, bitter aromas waking him up like a sparring match against Mike Tyson. He didn't much believe in heaven, but if he did, this would be his idea of it:

A nice table (nice as you could get anyway) at the Omega Diner—your typical New Jersey greasy spoon.

Big windows displaying an icy thoroughfare of hard-pack snow, rock salt, concrete, and passing cars going too fast on a road that wasn't quite a highway but not a municipal street, either.

A mouth-watering aroma of strong coffee, sumptuous, creamy eggs, and the silky sweet hint of pancakes and syrup. But mostly, enough bacon to keep cardiologists in business for the rest of eternity.

In front of him, paper placemats with Omega Diner written right in the middle—the symbol for omega in place of the letter O—so it reads Ωmega Diner. Not that clever or original, but it shows some effort at differentiation. It contains advertisements for everyone from the local newspaper delivery to a video rental store to a shady lawyer to help you when you fell down on an icy sidewalk and weren't already trying to con somebody (else you would have called the lawyer first). It seemed the diner placemat was the last holdout from the internet's encroachment on modern life. For crying out loud, how could a video rental store still be in business, if not for something *just a little bit off* going on there?

And then of course, there was the feel of the diner.

It was a place of refuge for Ledgerman. A safe, calm place where the world's problems didn't dare creep in past the big windows.

A place where time seemed to stop. Welcome relief.

Not just this one, either, as it was almost indistinguishable in so many ways from the multitude of others he had spent time in. More, the genre of diners appealed to him. He read a magazine article a while back (in another diner somewhere) about how children often created strong emotional connections to foods and places their mother visited when they were forming in the womb. Ledgerman knew nothing about his mother, but based on his own feelings about diners, he would have put a tenner down on her sitting in a booth like this one, Disco Fries and a nice greasy burger on its way while *he* was getting cooked to the right temperature. *Ding, ding, order up.*

Place like this, you could sip coffee, read a magazine, the paper (or just the ads on the placemat). Ruminate. All without time rushing in on him.

In this case, he was reading a local paper, taken from a pile by the hostess stand. It was an area paper (not confined to just this town, but not covering the entire state, either).

He'd been flipping through, mostly scanning the articles: the measure to increase property taxes had failed (of course it had); the approval to cut art and music classes had been given the go ahead (who needed culture); the mayor of the next town over would break ground on a new, state-of-the-art police station (despite crime being down, he boasted); the boy's soccer team would host their end of season dinner, celebrating their county championship (good on them); Bethanny Ebbells, aged 94, died in the loving arms of her family after a long battle with old age.

Not exactly the Watergate scandal, but this was what you got. He wasn't complaining. The news had become a rough, nasty thing these days. Reading a paper like this heartened him somewhat.

And he wasn't a man who could be easily heartened.

Aimless reading, of course, wasn't the only thing he liked about diners.

This one, especially, allowed him to watch as cars sped by outside (being Jersey, that was all of them). Wonder what destinations lay ahead for them and their occupants. What winding roads and dark pasts lay behind. You could watch people of all sorts and play the same mind games.

Games Ledgerman didn't get to play, really. The rest of his life was situated a lot differently than that. More rigid in its construction.

The diner allowed for him to sit and bask in the temporary facade of a man with nothing much to do.

Mostly, let it be said, you could eat. And diner food suited Ledgerman just fine.

"What'll it be, hon?" A teenage waitress stands next to him at the table. Pad in one hand. Pencil in the other. Ostensibly attending to Ledgerman but not looking at him—eyes on table twelve, the one with four kids in letterman jackets playing a game where they put every ingredient within reach in a glass of water, make the loser drink it. And this was a diner not short of available condiments.

Ledgerman watches the waitress watching them. Wondering if she does so longingly or in anticipation of a problem. Are they classmates, maybe? No, she looks older—by a hair, not by much. Former classmates, maybe. They don't seem like bad kids. But in today's day and age, can you ever be sure?

She has shoulder-length blonde hair pulled back in a ponytail that reveals one side of her head shaved short, perhaps with a number one buzzer blade. Punk rock, maybe. If kids still were into that sort of thing.

Already speaks like she's a veteran in the service industry. *Hon.* She has sad eyes.

"Three eggs, scrambled with cheese. Extra-large side of bacon. An order of French toast. Orange juice. And," he holds up his mug, "more coffee, please."

"Toast?"

"Heaps. You have Texas toast?"

"Afraid not. You want, I could scrounge up some challah in the back. They're using it for the lunch special today."

"What is it?"

"What is what?"

"The special, for lunch."

"Oh. Right. Fried chicken club sandwich."

"How's that work?"

Mandy—according to her nametag—gives him a winner's smile that almost reaches up to those sad eyes. "Big, beer-battered fried chicken pieces—boneless thigh, not any of that lean breast stuff," she rolls her eyes as if to say, because who would want to live half-assed when you can live hardcore, to which Ledgerman would simply nod in agreement, "—and let me just say, the head cook knows how to fry a mean chicken. Top those honkers with a thick slice of melted cheddar cheese, add our thick, applewood smoked bacon on top. One—and only one—piece of iceberg lettuce atop that, a slice of tomato, and a nice heap of fresh avocado. Stuck between two pieces of untoasted challah."

Ledgerman makes a mental note to come back for lunch if he can.

"You had it?"

"Last week, first time we made it. Been dreaming about it ever since."

Describing that sandwich was the first time Mandy's eyes almost turned up. She wasn't a heifer, was actually skinny. Long, too-young legs. Might have been a middle-distance runner. Eight hundred meters, maybe. No less than that. But nothing more than a miler, either.

"Tell you what, have the cook use the challah in the French toast and we'll call it even."

She smiles, making him believe she means it this time. "I like your style, Mister."

Without hardly more than a glance, Mandy makes the appropriate notations on her pad (though Ledgerman feels maybe she was just doodling, 'cause it ain't too hard to remember a breakfast order) and makes the pencil and pad disappear into the front of her apron like a magician performing a long-practiced trick. "Coming right up."

She disappears for a second, not even enough time for the letterman jacket boys to pour three dabs of tabasco into the cup, and gives Ledgerman another steaming pour of the coffee.

He thanks her, though she's already gone to fill someone else's coffee, and he watches the steam rise up from the cup, twisting and twirling in on itself. Creating shapes akin to watching the clouds roll by on a sunny day. Each one a puffy white Rorschach test of the viewer, though he doesn't see anything much in them.

One of the letterman boys is half-standing, half-squatting now, feet up on the patent red leather of his booth, squeaking up a storm. Taunting one of the other kids as he pours a packet of one of those fake sugars into the cup.

Ledgerman turns away from them, content to just watch the cars fly by and disappear into their distant, imaginary nowheres while he sips on his go-go fuel.

His watch vibrates on his wrist, stopping him as he lifts the mug to his lips. He could almost taste the brown elixir. Has a moment of sheer panic that he won't ever taste it again.

But when his watch vibrates, it means it's time for him to do what he was put on this earth to do.

It's a smartwatch—which is about the most ridiculous notion he ever heard. But he's gotta admit, it *is* pretty damn smart.

For a watch.

The screen lights up with the time when he looks at it (but never when he doesn't). Tells him how many steps he took (none since he sat for breakfast), how long he sat down for today (all the minutes between sitting for breakfast and now).

But perhaps most consequently, when the watch vibrates, it tells him he needs to do one of two things to somebody:

Save them.

Or kill them.

TWO

Ledgerman has an insane notion that he should ignore the watch.

It only vibrates the one time, so far as he knows. He never really ignored it before, though. So maybe it would vibrate again, in a minute. Or five. Ten at the outside. Enough time, anyway, to finish his breakfast.

He could probably just ignore it, go about enjoying this moment inside. Sip his coffee. Fill his belly. Mind his business.

Of course, there's always the chance that ignoring it would mark him for some unknown fate, the same way it does to others.

He wonders these things in the split second it takes to place his steaming cup down atop the paper placemat, the brown coffee ring forming already where he sets it down. Right on the symbol. The omega. In place of the O.

It seems fitting, now that the watch has vibrated. Omega. Last letter of the Greek alphabet.

The end of the line.

Ledgerman raises his wrist, his black wool button-down shirt lifting helpfully enough so he can see the face.

He knows he won't ignore the vibration, silly as it is to imagine he would.

As it always does, the watch lights up with three pieces of information:

A name.

A picture.

A time.

Ledgerman sees all three pop up in order, just like always.

Mandy Beaudreau.

A picture that looks like it was taken thirty seconds ago, when Mandy the waitress was ringing his order into the ordering system.

10:05 a.m.

In the upper corner of the watch, rendered in tiny font because of the notification, Ledgerman sees that it is now 9:55 a.m. That leaves ten minutes before he needs to either kill Mandy or save her.

Sometimes he wonders why the watch doesn't tell him the fourth piece of information he needs: which of the two options it is (kill or save). Seems like it would be more likely to result in the correct outcome. Though of course, *correct* is in the eye of the sender.

And Ledgerman has no idea who that might be.

No idea how any of this fits into the larger puzzle that is his life. Not even sure why he knows—knows on a cellular, *molecular* level—what he must do with the information provided to him. There simply is no thought to ignoring it.

And while it might be simpler for him to know which choice—death or salvation—the person in question has been ordained to receive, that would take all the fun out of it. Somewhere deep down inside him, Ledgerman enjoys the challenge of figuring out right from wrong. Putting the scales of justice back into alignment.

Nobody dies without a reason. And nobody gets saved without one, either. At least not when he's involved.

Mandy Beaudreau places down three steaming plates (one of which she holds with a toweled hand). One plate of scrambled eggs with cheese. One with a heaping helping of freshly cooked bacon (he can tell because it doesn't have that re-heated sheen to it that so many diners fall back on). One with fluffy challah French toast, doused in butter and powdered sugar that looks like freshly fallen snow. That's the hot plate.

The time is 9:56 a.m.

"How you fixed?" Mandy says, doing her best octopus impression—somehow topping off his coffee, despite having just set down three plates.

Ledgerman looks at his food, the aromas rising up, grabbing hold of the primitive areas of his body and soul, the way they probably had back when he was in the womb.

"I'd be fixed just fine if you sat down and joined me for a cup of coffee."

Mandy freezes, obviously not expecting that. "Sorry, Mister, but I got a ... like ... a man. A boyfriend, I mean."

Ledgerman smiles. "I'm sure you do. And I didn't mean it like that. No offense."

"None taken."

"Just was hoping for some company. I'm just passing through. Sometimes it's nice to talk with a friendly face."

Mandy let out a little laugh. "First person to ever say I was a friendly face."

Ledgerman notes the time. 9:57 a.m. He picks up his fork and knife and nods across from him. "How about it? Not many tables left in here."

Mandy looks around, gives one last look at the letterman jacket table (who have found a squirt bottle of yellow mustard for their concoction), and seems to agree.

"Coffee?" Ledgerman reaches across the aisle to an empty table and grabs an upturned coffee cup. He takes the pot from Mandy's hand and pours her a cup.

"Thanks." Her eyes are half-here and half-looking around the restaurant. Maybe for her manager. Maybe for an abusive boyfriend. Ledgerman isn't a sentimental fella, but he sure hopes she isn't looking around for a partner who's looting the register or getting ready to rob the place blind.

Ledgerman starts in on the eggs, knowing they will get cold the quickest. Bacon isn't bad if it's cold. Neither is French toast, especially with and powdered sugar that looks like freshly fallen snow. That's the hot plate.

The time is 9:56 a.m.

"How you fixed?" Mandy says, doing her best octopus impression—somehow topping off his coffee, despite having just set down three plates.

Ledgerman looks at his food, the aromas rising up, grabbing hold of the primitive areas of his body and soul, the way they probably had back when he was in the womb.

"I'd be fixed just fine if you sat down and joined me for a cup of coffee."

Mandy freezes, obviously not expecting that. "Sorry, Mister, but I got a ... like ... a man. A boyfriend, I mean."

Ledgerman smiles. "I'm sure you do. And I didn't mean it like that. No offense."

"None taken."

"Just was hoping for some company. I'm just passing through. Sometimes it's nice to talk with a friendly face."

Mandy let out a little laugh. "First person to ever say I was a friendly face."

Ledgerman notes the time. 9:57 a.m. He picks up his fork and knife and nods across from him. "How about it? Not many tables left in here."

Mandy looks around, gives one last look at the letterman jacket table (who have found a squirt bottle of yellow mustard for their concoction), and seems to agree.

"Coffee?" Ledgerman reaches across the aisle to an empty table and grabs an upturned coffee cup. He takes the pot from Mandy's hand and pours her a cup.

"Thanks." Her eyes are half-here and half-looking around the restaurant. Maybe for her manager. Maybe for an abusive boyfriend. Ledgerman isn't a sentimental fella, but he sure hopes she isn't looking around for a partner who's looting the register or getting ready to rob the place blind.

Ledgerman starts in on the eggs, knowing they will get cold the quickest. Bacon isn't bad if it's cold. Neither is French toast, especially with

As it always does, the watch lights up with three pieces of information:

A name.

A picture.

A time.

Ledgerman sees all three pop up in order, just like always.

Mandy Beaudreau.

A picture that looks like it was taken thirty seconds ago, when Mandy the waitress was ringing his order into the ordering system.

10:05 a.m.

In the upper corner of the watch, rendered in tiny font because of the notification, Ledgerman sees that it is now 9:55 a.m. That leaves ten minutes before he needs to either kill Mandy or save her.

Sometimes he wonders why the watch doesn't tell him the fourth piece of information he needs: which of the two options it is (kill or save). Seems like it would be more likely to result in the correct outcome. Though of course, *correct* is in the eye of the sender.

And Ledgerman has no idea who that might be.

No idea how any of this fits into the larger puzzle that is his life. Not even sure why he knows—knows on a cellular, *molecular* level—what he must do with the information provided to him. There simply is no thought to ignoring it.

And while it might be simpler for him to know which choice—death or salvation—the person in question has been ordained to receive, that would take all the fun out of it. Somewhere deep down inside him, Ledgerman enjoys the challenge of figuring out right from wrong. Putting the scales of justice back into alignment.

Nobody dies without a reason. And nobody gets saved without one, either. At least not when he's involved.

Mandy Beaudreau places down three steaming plates (one of which she holds with a toweled hand). One plate of scrambled eggs with cheese. One with a heaping helping of freshly cooked bacon (he can tell because it doesn't have that re-heated sheen to it that so many diners fall back on). One with fluffy challah French toast, doused in butter warm syrup (which this definitely was). But cold eggs could ruin a meal before it started.

As it was, they're heavenly. Cooked to perfection. Fluffy without being dry.

"So what do you want to talk about?" Mandy says.

Ledgerman sips his coffee. "How long you been working here?"

Mandy reluctantly sips her own coffee, having put no cream or sugar in it. "Three years."

"Three? You barely look eighteen as it is."

"Nineteen. You can start waiting tables about sixteen, usually. Gotta be older if you're at a place that serves booze."

"That what you want to do?" She has a look on her face like she's a minor league baller talking about the show.

She nods. "Bigger bills, better tips."

Ledgerman studies her. In his experience, there are people you could see had a rough upbringing. Whether it was the way they talked, the way they walked, or the things they did—tiny mannerisms that mostly go unnoticed—he had a sixth sense about that sort of thing.

"Why do you need money so bad?" Seemingly a dumb question. Directed at some people Ledgerman has come across in his work, it would be akin to asking what you needed oxygen for.

Something about Mandy tells him it wouldn't seem quite so strange to her.

"Everybody needs money. What kind of question is that?"

"Sure, people need some," he says in between forkfuls of eggs, him having to lift the fork damn near above his head to break the stretching cheese, "You're working here three years already. But you don't like it. Why not find something else?"

As he says this, he checks his watch.

9:59 a.m.

Six more minutes until something must be done.

Mandy takes another sip of coffee, not taking her eyes off him now. Squinting at him as she sips. Curious. Or annoyed about this intrusion on her personal life.

"You think I grew up pretty easy, huh? Like why's a girl my age not in college?"

"College is for thinkers. Pontificators. You're a doer, clearly."

"Meaning I'm stupid?"

"You know I don't mean that. You're dancing around it now." Ledgerman stabs his knife and fork at the French toast, careful not to drip any syrup onto his eggs. Even though lukewarm French toast isn't terrible, no sense letting it get too cold.

"Dancing around what?"

"Whatever it is you need three years' worth of off-the-books cash to pay for." He nods to the shaved spot along the side of her head. "Clearly it's not for trips to the salon."

That was probably either the thing that would make her split or get her to open up like Hoover Dam.

Ledgerman watches her reaction, slipping a piece of thick, fatty bacon into his mouth to mix with the ecstasy that was challah French toast. No matter what happened here, he would always remember Mandy Beaudreau for introducing him to this wondrous creation.

The thing about his line of work—if work was what you wanted to name it; *calling* might be a better word for it, but damned if he even really knew why or how he got into this in the first place—was that the *calling* involved a certain measure of violence. Violence was, by its nature, unpredictable.

So each time his watch buzzed, Ledgerman never lost sight of the fact it could be the last time. One day there was bound to be a person he flat couldn't kill, because that person would kill him dead first.

That's why he always enjoys a meal. Each and every one.

24/7/365, his watch could vibrate, giving him minutes, hours, days until he was supposed to step in and settle some score. One he never saw the bigger picture for, nor did he learn the final score at the end of regulation. Probably he never would. And maybe that was for the best.

To someone or something, Ledgerman was simply a pawn with which the score could be manipulated.

"Mandy!" A voice from somewhere behind Ledgerman. Back toward the hostess stand, which also doubles as a cash register. Three cameras were perched in view around it, all of them pointed straight at the cash machine. Ledgerman notices two others, better hidden, pointed at the same place.

They didn't, apparently, trust the waitresses with cash.

Mandy shot up straight like she'd just been stuck with a cattle prod. Before Ledgerman could blink, she was gone, back toward the kitchen like a dog who just pissed on the rug.

Ledgerman scoops up another fluffy serving of eggs, tops it with a piece of bacon, and washes it down with a thick pull from his steaming mug of coffee.

The time is 10:00 a.m.

He wonders if he is going to have to kill Mandy Beaudreau.

THREE

Ledgerman stands up from the table, walks himself around to the seat Mandy had just been sitting in. The patent leather is warm, the way leather gets when someone's been sitting on it. It squeaks as he slides into the booth, his back to the group in the letterman jackets (who have finally found the Tabasco, though you'd think they would have started with that). As he sits, Ledgerman sees the cup is a putrid brown color.

The loser will have his work cut out for him.

Ledgerman's new seat has two distinct advantages from his previous one:

First, he can now better see Mandy—where she went, her interactions with the rest of the Omega's staff. If she needs to be saved, the threat it more likely to come from someone she knows, rather than a stranger. And he hasn't flagged anybody seated in the diner as a threat. Meaning any threat would come from the back of the house.

Second, his new seat affords him a better angle to eat his challah French toast, having now finished the eggs. He can do so with less fear of burning his hands on the plate, which has somehow kept its heat despite being out of the kitchen now for almost six minutes.

He puts another piece of the sumptuously sweet and cinnamon-y

French toast into his mouth, this time adding a sprig of bacon so he may enjoy the flavors together, and he thinks about what he knows so far.

Mandy does not appear to be a criminal. The first obvious tell is that criminals typically cannot hold jobs long term. They also typically do crime for one of two reasons: for the rush or for the money.

If Mandy *was* a criminal and she did it for the rush, working at a diner would seem an odd choice. You get about as much rush working here as from returning a book to your local library.

If Mandy did crime for the money, the diner represents an even weirder choice. Not much to be made here. Probably not even enough to cover basic expenses without another job. And when do you do crime if you have to hold down *two* jobs?

So probably criminality is out.

Meaning Mandy must be saved.

Saved ... but from whom?

Ledgerman ponders this as he hears one of the letterman jacket kids (now behind him) say, "OK, last one. This milk."

"Dude, no," another one says, "that smells gnarly!"

"Shut up, Pirchman. Don't be a bitch."

"Yeah, bitch," another chimes in helpfully.

Ledgerman takes a honker of a bite from his French toast and stands up. Wherever Mandy has gone—and he assumes it was the kitchen—she has not reappeared since.

He steps to the table of the four letterman jacket boys. Immediately spots Pirchman, a slim kid swimming in his jacket. Face clear of freckles but pockmarked with pimples. Glasses, light skin, and hair that could best be described as sand-esque in color. As sad as it was to say it, being called *bitch* might have been the best-case scenario for Pirchman. He was smiling, though Ledgerman could see that behind that smile lay multitudes of quiet, agonizing pain.

Kids can be cruel to one another.

And he knew cruelty. Had been cruel to many people, though none of them children. And every one of them deserving.

Another boy, the biggest and most muscular of the group (this clear from the industrial bucket of a neck protruding out from the jacket's collar), was pouring the milk into the glass. It turned the putrid brown into something resembling coffee with milk splashed in it. If Ledgerman drank his coffee with milk, this sight would surely have convinced him to stop.

He said nothing. Not at first. Mainly because he still chewed on the French toast, his bite having been taken with the understanding that once he stood up, anything could happen. So it had been large, enough to remember this breakfast by, should one of these kids be carrying a gun or something (unlikely, but unfortunately these days, not outside the realm of possibility).

After a moment, a third kid at the table, sitting on the far inside seat away from Ledgerman—a kid who could simply be described as forgettable—said, "C ... c ... can we help you, sir?"

At least he was polite.

Ledgerman finished chewing as Big Neck put the glass of milk down.

"Actually," Ledgerman said, "I think I can help you."

Four confused looks (though one mixed with that deep emotional pain) stare back at him.

"How do you plan to choose who is going to drink it?"

Bless their hearts, the answer to this question had clearly not occurred to them yet. They all look at Big Neck, obviously the leader of the group. But nobody says anything. Despite their somewhat rambunctious behavior, they were quite obedient. Perhaps they were good kids after all.

"I have an idea," Ledgerman says. "I'll choose."

"How would you do that?" Forgettable asks, finding some confidence.

"Three simple questions. I ask them, you answer. The loser is the one left at the end."

Open mouths. Confused, short-circuited looks.

"Each of you put your pointer finger on the table. Go on, now. This won't hurt."

They each comply, slowly, the commands registering in some part of their adolescent brains that hasn't yet formed to completion. It is the one that adults access to control children as much as they can, before said children start to realize they don't have to listen.

Ledgerman checks his watch.

It is 10:01 a.m.

Four minutes until something needs to happen.

The last few minutes are always a jolt of energy and action. This time, amplified by the helpful aid of about five different kinds of sugar and several cups of coffee.

"Each question I ask, if your answer is yes, you remove your finger. You are safe. If your answer is no, you leave your finger on. You are still in the game. Got it?"

Three heads shake yes.

"This is on the honor code," Ledgerman says, giving them the same look he's used to quell fighting instincts in stronger men than these. "Don't lie. You won't like the consequences."

They all nod like good boys.

"Good. Question one: Do you know the waitress? Mandy?"

All four of the letterman boys look at each other, clearly confused at this seemingly random question.

Pirchman, however, removes his finger. Big Neck glares at him. Pirchman says, "What? She used to babysit my neighbor."

Perfect.

"Question two: Have you ever won a county championship game?"

This, of course, is a cheat. The fourth kid at the table, the one who had yet to say anything, wore a letterman jacket with a giant soccer ball patch on it. He smiled, pumped a fist, and removed his finger like he just won the World Cup. Apparently the track and field team (Pirchman) and the lacrosse team (Big Neck and Forgettable) weren't quite as accomplished programs.

"Two of you left." Lederman looks at Big Neck, looks at Forgettable. He honestly doesn't care who wins, doesn't know enough about either of them to goose the results.

But he can make an educated guess.

"Question three: Are you still a virgin?"

Pirchman giggles, the word virgin itself striking some comedic chord that runs even deeper than his pain, breaking through it like a fat boy standing on thin ice.

Big Neck removes his finger and pounds the table. He points at Forgettable. "Ha! You're still a virgin, Freddy! Probably always will be. Pussy."

Ledgerman puts a firm hand on Big Neck's shoulder. This would feel good. "I think you've misunderstood the rules. If Freddy over here is still a virgin, he answers *yes* to my question. Meaning he removes his finger."

Big Neck looks up at Ledgerman, uncomprehending.

"Meaning you lose."

Big Neck does not take this well, some color draining from his face. Ledgerman imagines that Big Neck had perhaps been the one to dream up this game. That he might lord the notion of drinking this disgusting concoction over his tablemates for as long as possible, asserting his dominance over the group (who would never expect that he be the one to ultimately drink it).

Not that Ledgerman cares much, but this intervention over the small-scale terrorism of bullies might very well make a nice feature story in the paper tomorrow.

"Haha, drink it!" Freddy says, relishing the fact that he has yet to score with any of the ladies. Probably once the concoction is gone, he will come back down to earth about this particular boast.

Ledgerman is now done here, with the exception of one other thing.

He points at Pirchman. "Tell me about Mandy. She's in trouble."

He blinks, glasses bouncing around on the bridge of his nose as he does so. "Trouble?"

"Someone wants to hurt her. Who might that be?"

Ledgerman knows he is taking a long shot here. There are perhaps three, three and a half minutes left until he needs to do something. If he cannot determine for sure that Mandy must be saved, he must kill her.

But this town seems small enough that Pirchman the bitch will know any possible suspects.

"Um ... uh, I mean,"

"She has a boyfriend."

"Brent?"

"Sure. What's his deal?"

"Good dude, man. Used to run track, too. Two years older than me. But we hung a little bit." Pirchman says this with neither disdain nor pride.

"What else? Where can I find him?"

"Well, I mean, I guess if you knew what dorm he was in ..."

"He's in college?"

"Yeah. VCU, down in Richmond. Hear it's a pretty cool party school."

Ledgerman clenches a fist. The boyfriend is most likely out as his target.

"He's not around much?"

Pirchman shakes his head.

Ledgerman nods, thinks. Turns back toward the kitchen.

The time is 10:02 a.m.

Three minutes left.

And he doesn't have answers yet.

FOUR

As Ledgerman passes his table, he picks the largest piece of bacon off the top of the pile, folds it, and pops it into his mouth.

Goddamn. That's good.

He marches toward the back of the diner, passing an elderly couple being shown to their table by a presentable hostess of about thirty (one who is not fooling Ledgerman, though).

Despite being presentable, Ledgerman can see within her what he could not see within Mandy. A hard life, etched into her like a someone writing their name in wet concrete. If you really thought about it, that was pretty much what a hard life was.

Behind her and the old couple, another elderly group of four wait. Three others, all moving like glaciers, are behind them coming through the diner's entryway.

The lunch time rush.

In front of Ledgerman is a long bar top counter with fixed stools in groups of two, each covered with the same patent leather as the booths. All empty at this time of day. Condiment caddies containing salt, pepper, ketchup, mustard, and napkins dot the counter—one between every two-top that the barstools create. A soda machine and several glass dishes showcase various pies, cakes, cookies, and muffins. The Omega Diner does not serve liquor, but with a little sprucing up, this wouldn't be a bad place for a beer.

There are two doors fixed into the wall that runs behind the countertop. One that leads you out from behind the bar and into the restaurant. Another that goes back into the kitchen.

Ledgerman puts a hand on the bar top and hoists himself over. His boots touch down on the squishy non-slip floor mat behind every bar and kitchen in America, a nice brace against the weight of his frame. His knees were once flexible, spry things. They are less so now.

Ledgerman imagines himself working here, what that might feel like. He turns away from the door to the kitchen and looks over the restaurant. Sees himself picking up the damp towel hidden just out of sight on a shelf under the bar. Wiping down the counter after a spilled milkshake. Big smile. "That's alright, Champ," he's saying to a kid who isn't far away from tears. "How about a refill, huh?" The kid nods.

Ledgerman, with the order coming up.

He slides it halfway across the counter, connects right with the palm of the kid's hand. Smiles all around now, as the kid gets back to slurping his shake, the sprinkles and whipped cream getting slowly sucked down into the vortex created by the straw.

Another happy customer.

As this reverie fades away, Ledgerman notices the elderly woman staring at him as the hostess puts serious distance between them. Practically already to their table—the corner booth that sits seven (which they presumably requested). Desperate to avoid congestion at the door, she is. Probably needs this job, maybe is even already on thin ice from being late or flaking out early before. Today, though, it's the letter of the law. Get 'em in, get 'em out. Diners make their nut on volume, not a fine dining experience.

The old woman seems confused by Ledgerman jumping over the counter like he owns the place.

He gives her a thumbs up and turns away, confident that if she does tell anyone about what she saw, he'll already be long gone.

Behind the doors, the kitchen air is humid enough to swim through. It has a musk, one that can be either pleasant (bacon, pancakes, eggs) or off-putting (unwashed dishes, food scraps) depending which whiff you get. The humidity carries scent further and more intense than dry air, so that doesn't necessarily help much either. Otherwise, though, the place is clean.

Two chef looking guys are working in the back of the area to Ledgerman's left, behind a few shelves and racks of kitchenware. One is scrambling up a storm—using a whisk the size of a baseball bat on a bowl of eggs that could fill a moon crater. The other is knifing strips of chicken like they killed JFK or something. He can't see either one besides the outline of their figures.

Or, like the lunch special today was the fried chicken club sandwich.

The kitchen is bigger than Ledgerman expected. Most he'd been inside were the opposite. It's separated into four quadrants.

Back left is a prep area, where Scramble and Chop are doing their thing.

Front left is all the hot stuff—ovens, stovetops, and a flat top grill that has a sheen like a glazed donut. A window out to the diner sits empty, save for the completed tickets pierced through the center of an upright metal pin like shrike food. Twin heating lamps, directed at nothing but the metal surface where finished orders are placed.

This placed really died down during this time of day.

The two right quadrants are for storage—jars, spices, extras, all went in front on wire shelves. In back is the walk-in freezer.

The door isn't fully closed.

Ledgerman checks his watch. 10:03 a.m.

Two minutes left.

FIVE

Before Ledgerman opens the walk-in freezer door, someone comes out. He can't actually see who. They are hidden behind five frosty boxes labeled PAPAS FRITAS. To avoid a confrontation, Ledgerman steps out of the way.

Just not in time.

The man tumbles. The PAPAS FRITAS tumble. Luckily none get free from their captivity. Would be a shame to lose good fries.

"Hey, which one of you dipshi—"

The man stops mid-cuss. Ledgerman is not whoever this man was expecting to see. "Who the hell are you?"

Sizing him up immediately: wrinkled, slightly frumpy collared button-down shirt, collars curled in on themselves.

Khakis not made by Dickie's or Carhartt.

An externally jangling key chain with plain white swipe cards for voided mis-orders or 86'ing an unsatisfactory meal.

This was the manager of the diner.

And his first reaction after anger (then confusion) was fear.

"Hey Freddy!" he says over his shoulder. Then to Ledgerman, "You can't be back here, man. Right, Freddy?"

Chops (apparent real name: Freddy) steps out from his prep station. He's a bad looking man—dirty bandana wrapped around his hair, low on his face so his eyes are draped in shadows. At least three fuzzy dark blue tattoos poke out from beneath his kitchen jacket collar.

The massive chef's knife in his hands doesn't help much, either.

"Who are you?" Freddy says, voice instantly dropping any pretense of politeness. Dropping into the clipped tone of a guy who'd done time.

Ledgerman thought back to the extra cameras around the register. The fact the waitresses weren't allowed to handle money. The reaction from these guys made him think that maybe this place had been a robbery target recently. Maybe more than once. Was close enough to enough feeder roads, leading to everything from major highways to smaller three-lane county roads that led you in pretty much any direction you wanted to go. Not easy to throw a police blockade around, that many methods of egress. Made sense as a target, you were desperate enough to risk arrest for what was probably only a couple thousand bucks, max.

All these things coalesced into a single, flashing red neon sign inside Ledgerman's mind:

PROBLEM.

PROBLEM.

PROBLEM.

Freddy steps fully away from around his station now, standing in the middle of the four quadrants so it wouldn't be easy for Ledgerman to get out in any particular direction.

The knife catches the glint of the bright fluorescent overhead lights like it's being lit for its movie closeup.

"Easy now, Freddy," Ledgerman says. Puts both hands up to show the guy he isn't any threat. Freddy takes another step closer as the manager slides a body length back away from Ledgerman across the floor, knocking PAPAS FRITAS boxes out of the way as he goes.

Freddy smiles. Is unusually chipper for someone who is about to get into a knife fight. But then again, if you are getting into a knife fight, always better to be the guy with the knife.

Probably that was the reason that Freddy Neck Tattoos got this job in the first place. Enjoyment of violent confrontations. Saved from having to pay for a security guard.

"C'mon now," Ledgerman says, flashing his winningest smile. "Surely you don't think I'm here to rob you." As he said it, he saw that the back exit from the kitchen—probably leading to an alleyway of dumpsters and maybe an employee parking lot, or the back of another small business backed up against this one—was unlatched.

"Last three guys who robbed us said the same thing right before they pulled their pistols," Freddy says, taking another step closer. Relishing this moment.

"If I had a pistol, wouldn't I have pulled it by now?"

Freddy takes a half-step forward but hesitates, this question leading to something a guy like Freddy—who *definitely* looked like he grew up hard—hasn't come into much contact with in his life:

Logic.

"Uh—"

Ledgerman takes this moment of confused hesitation for the opportunity that it is.

In less time than it takes to blink, synapses inside his consciousness fire, pushing unseen levers and connecting electronic currents that even the most modern of science did not yet understand. Millions of years of evolution all merge into one single, glorious moment of savage violence.

Ledgerman's left foot plants, his boot finding purchase against the squishy non-slip floor mat on the floor of every bar and kitchen in America. His weight shifts there, slightly to the outside of his left foot, about equally spread between the ball and the heel. Slight bend in the left knee.

From this position, Ledgerman could punch, jump, balance, or tap dance.

Instead he unleashes a hellacious roundhouse kick, letting his right leg fly like Cristiano Ronaldo letting loose a corner kick.

He likes a kick for this situation for many reasons:

A prison brawler like Freddy is used to fighting a certain way. Hands-centric. Punches, elbows, grappling. That's prison fighting, mostly, if you include stabbing. Holding a knife makes Freddy even more likely to focus on the hands, a smart move when that is the likeliest source of death you might be facing.

No one in prison ever got a shank from someone's foot.

Not to mention, I'd you're going to throw body parts around in space, there is precious little on the body that weighs as much as the leg. Couple that with the sheer size of the muscles in the lower body, and a kick is impossible to beat when trying to generate maximum force.

To say Freddy's jaw was unprepared for the impact it received would be like saying a toddler was unprepared to get blind side sacked by Lawrence Taylor.

Freddy was undoubtedly a tough guy, in the sense that he'd probably been in plenty of scrapes and he never walked away from a fight. But even tough guys get knocked stone cold on their feet every now and again.

This was the now for Freddy. He does one of those zombie shimmies that you see every now and then in the NFL—the one where it seems you might have just witnessed a death on the field.

The knife lands silently on the rubber flooring. Approximately five seconds later, Freddy lands there, too, though with a considerable thud that will reverberate around his body for some time still.

The manager has hardly had the chance to back up another body length away from his fallen bodyguard.

Scramble has since put the whisk down, his eyes bulging from his head like a cartoon character.

If Ledgerman were a vindictive person, these remaining two members of the (apparently) dangerous Omega staff would be in trouble. They might end up in worse shape than their buddy Freddy.

They might even find themselves at the end of the line.

But Ledgerman is not that sort of man.

And even if he were, he is now running out of time.

It is 10:04 a.m.

"Where is Mandy?" he says to the manager, not bothering to soften his words.

He needs to know this information.

And he needs it now.

The manager's face twists into confusion. Then something else comes over it, something Ledgerman can't yet identify.

Never a hint of defiance, though.

He simply points toward the unlatched back exit.

One minute left.

SIX

Ledgerman rips open the door and storms through, a gust of late winter cold wind as sharp as knives pushes back against him with all the might of Mother Nature. He stands and takes it.

Eyes scan the immediate vicinity outside the door.

There is a small alleyway to his left, one narrow enough so that no car could travel down it. Littered with trash bins, puke-inducing puddles filled with liquid that looks like the letterman jacket boys' concoction, and the random, rusted appliances that was too often forgotten and discarded in out-of-sight places like these.

To his right is a collection of green industrial dumpsters. Black plastics lids closed, not overflowing.

Straight ahead is a five-car parking lot, partially blocked off from the street by a fence which now stood open just enough for a single person to slip through.

He is basically in the parking lot now, the exit not having much to it besides the door and a single step down to the pavement.

Beyond the fence is a red Oldsmobile about ten years older than it should have been, brown rust spreading out from the edges of the tire

And he needs it now.

The manager's face twists into confusion. Then something else comes over it, something Ledgerman can't yet identify.

Never a hint of defiance, though.

He simply points toward the unlatched back exit.

One minute left.

SIX

Ledgerman rips open the door and storms through, a gust of late winter cold wind as sharp as knives pushes back against him with all the might of Mother Nature. He stands and takes it.

Eyes scan the immediate vicinity outside the door.

There is a small alleyway to his left, one narrow enough so that no car could travel down it. Littered with trash bins, puke-inducing puddles filled with liquid that looks like the letterman jacket boys' concoction, and the random, rusted appliances that was too often forgotten and discarded in out-of-sight places like these.

To his right is a collection of green industrial dumpsters. Black plastics lids closed, not overflowing.

Straight ahead is a five-car parking lot, partially blocked off from the street by a fence which now stood open just enough for a single person to slip through.

He is basically in the parking lot now, the exit not having much to it besides the door and a single step down to the pavement.

Beyond the fence is a red Oldsmobile about ten years older than it should have been, brown rust spreading out from the edges of the tire wells like gangrene. Black exhaust spews from the back pipe like it's giving the EPA the middle finger.

Inside the car were two people. From this distance, Ledgerman can't make them out exactly because the passenger side window is fogged up.

But he sees the outline of a girl that just has to be Mandy. How the hell could she have gotten farther than that in the last few minutes?

He wasn't about to fail this mission. He never failed before. And given the swift and exacting justice he meted out—the omnipotent watch on his wrist choosing targets, deserving or not—Ledgerman did not want to find out what would happen *should* he fail.

He sprints across the lot, not bothering to slither through the fence. Scaling over it instead. Uses two smooth movements:

One—left hand grabs the top of the fence, right foot plants about waist high.

Two—left foot explodes off the wet, salty sidewalk. The momentum from the run and jump makes him weightless as he clears his hips and chest over top.

He lands with something between grace and a thud on the other side of the fence.

Give him a 7.2 on the dismount.

He is at the passenger car door in a second. Rips it open.

Mandy's startled face meets him, cheeks red from the car's heat, which blasts out of the open doorway like he just got to the mouth of hell.

Based on what he saw, that wasn't too far off.

Mandy's face looks like a kid just got caught sneaking in the house at night.

Two men sit in the car—one in the driver's seat and one in the back, directly behind Mandy.

Two-on-one. Bad odds for such a young girl. And one more than he saw from the doorway.

The man in the driver's seat has a thick, hairy hand out, touching Mandy's lithe upper thigh where her uniform rides up. Not touching in a good way. Clearly making her uncomfortable. His dark skin and the forest of hair on the back of his hand and wrist are a stark contrast to Mandy's innocence.

The other guy in back is squirrelly, slits for eyes, face cast in shadow from the dome light. His hand is also out, though it's small and feminine. It has a stack of wadded up bills in it. Mandy's tips. Ledgerman can tell because Mr. Squirrel dropped one as he reached for it inside the pouch of Mandy's apron.

Whatever's going on here, Mandy isn't making out on top.

"Who the hell are you?" the hairy man in the front seat says.

Ledgerman says nothing. Knows it's time. Or just about. Not official yet.

One second later, his watch beeps, punctuating the quiet that has befallen all four of them. The quiet before the storm, or the calm before the boom. However you wanted to say it.

Either way, the beeping meant only one thing.

10:05 a.m.

Time to finish the job.

SEVEN

There are a million ways to play this scenario. None of them involve kicking, though, so Ledgerman uses his fist.

He levels a left roundhouse punch through the back window, careful to punch toward the top so no shattered pieces of glass fall down on top of his arm.

Most people couldn't punch through a car window. But this is an older car, not yet using the improved shatterproof technology created in the past two plus decades.

Also, Ledgerman punches damned hard.

Besides, this plan of attack carries the element of surprise with it. And takes Mr. Squirrel off the board almost immediately.

Ledgerman isn't sure how, but he knows Mr. Squirrel carries a gun. Not a conscious thought, simply the intuition in the heat of the moment. Maybe because Mr. Squirrel is the one grabbing the money. Or because he's the one in back, where bosses usually sit (or at least guys who want other people to think they are bosses).

His punch has an additional agenda item embedded within it, other than simply surprise.

It flies through the shattered windshield and connects directly with

Mr. Squirrel's right temple. Ledgerman doesn't even bother to go for the gun that scatters across the backseat. Mr. Squirrel won't be able to grab for it again soon. His time in this fight is ended.

Ledgerman removes his fist from the back window, careful not to catch his forearm against any of the jagged glass, and centers his attention on the hairy man in the front seat.

The man's hand is still settled atop Mandy's thigh. This guy didn't move too fast, though he was beefy. A punch or a slap from him would certainly intimidate a girl like Mandy.

Just not a guy like Ledgerman.

The next half-second is a poetry of movement. More impactful than Shakespeare. More elegant than Henry James.

Ledgerman pulls Mandy out from the passenger seat. So fast that her body doesn't slacken or tighten. It simply goes. Effectively, he replaces her body with his own. This requires both a violent efficiency of movement and a graceful touch, so as not to send her staggering down onto the sidewalk where she might hurt herself.

So there he is, in the passenger seat of the Oldsmobile, the interior a funky combination of stale chips, cigar smoke, and one of those cheap gas station air "fresheners," which Ledgerman always thought should have been called air stranglers, since their scent didn't so much freshen the air as it suffocated anything else that lingered.

This switch happened so quickly that the hairy hand of his next target was still stretched out in the same place. Now touching Ledgerman's decidedly not-innocent thigh.

Easy place to start.

Ledgerman uses both of his own hands to take hold of the thick, hairy one. With a violent wrench, he pulls the pointer and pinky fingers in opposite directions, both away from the center of the hand.

There are two crunches as bones and tendons shatter into mere memories of working parts. But it would be easy to miss both crunches, as they occur with the sort of timeless precision you only see on high end wristwatches.

Before the hairy man can scream—or frankly, react—Ledgerman

reaches across the ash covered center dash, his left hand placed behind the head, his right against the temple.

He slams the head forward onto the steering wheel at first, the janky ass car's horn not even blaring at the impact. As the head bounces back, Ledgerman catches it, slams it again. Not necessarily aiming for the steering wheel this time (without the beeps, it hardly seems necessary, or fun). Content to make impact with his new bouncing ball on anything hard inside the car. The radio serves as an acceptable target. And the dash above it. And the stick shift, too.

It is over quickly, at least for the men on the receiving end.

For Ledgerman, each movement is part of a fluid symphony of pain and violence that comes so naturally to him that he does not even question its source.

To do so would be like someone questioning their desire to drink water.

The time is 10:06 a.m.

Ledgerman has once again completed his task.

EIGHT

Ledgerman needs maybe two seconds to catch his breath. His heart rate returns to normal almost immediately, a fact that the watch will confirm for him later when he checks it.

The scent of burgers, bacon, and grilled cheese permeates the fresh air pouring in from outside, the scent wafting out from the massive industrial vent on the back side of the diner. However, in its toe-to-toe battle with the stench of the inside of the Oldsmobile, it is losing.

He checks unnecessarily on Mr. Squirrel sprawled out cold in the backseat. Ledgerman reaches for the gun on the floor and places it inside the glove compartment, turns off the car, removes the key from the ignition and locks the gun inside the glove compartment.

He steps out of the passenger seat and stands above Mandy, who has not even moved in the second or two since he placed her there.

Then he winds up like Orel Hershiser and launches the keys onto the roof of the building across the alley.

Mandy reacts unconsciously by putting her hands in front of her face, nearly immediately realizing Ledgerman intends her no harm. She lowers them, eyes darting toward Mr. Squirrel, then to the hairy man and back again in a crazed loop.

Having experience in this situation, Ledgerman allows her to retrieve her wits, not pressuring her to do so on any timeline.

This way, actually, always ends up being fastest. It is not even 10:07 a.m. when Mandy finally speaks.

"You're bleeding," she says first, her eyes breaking the loop of knocked out scum bags and catching on the red mess all over Ledgerman's hand and sleeve. There is also blood on the shoulder of his shirt, the moisture from it clinging to his skin. Mandy doesn't see that, though, because the black of the shirt masks it.

She reaches for his hand, her eyes glazed over, still in the dreamlike state that so often follows violent action—at least for those who are not experienced in it.

"It's alright," he says, meaning it. He's had plenty worse before, undoubtedly far, far worse still on the horizon. He doesn't need Mandy's help to mend this wound.

She squeezes his good wrist and forearm, though. Her mind clings to the opportunity to help this man—this stranger—in any way she can. A concrete, tangible task that can be done before wrestling with the far more vague and obscure arithmetic that Ledgerman has just done, irrevocably changing her future life.

"You're bleeding," she says again. This is, Ledgerman knows, a common symptom of what was once called shell-shocked, but is today called PTSD. It is perhaps too soon for Mandy to be experiencing the true dangers of the disease. But in the moments immediately following, those in its wake often present themselves as people on a loop. Repeating themselves, stuttering, unable to focus on the reality that is present in front of them. Their brains not moving as quickly as the real world around them, trying once again to anchor itself onto some stable shore.

In the movies he might smack Mandy across the face to get her attention, center it on the present moment.

In real life, he simply allows her to gaze at his hands, her soft and innocent fingers holding him like a buoy in a dark and churning ocean.

When the fast-forward button in her mind is finally pressed OFF, Ledgerman sees coherence return behind her sad eyes.

"Oh, no ... God-G-G-God," she stutters. "What's happened?"

Ledgerman puts a hand on either shoulder, a gesture intended to both center Mandy's attention and put her at ease that she is now safe.

"The scale has been set back to equilibrium, Mandy."

"W-w-what?"

They never got it on the first try.

"Ours is a world of disparity. Differences exist between the haves and have-nots. Inequality abounds. The scale, such as it is, is not evenly distributed."

Mandy looks at him, blinks those sad eyes once, twice. Still not quite getting it.

"I am an agent of change. A counterweight, as it were. I'm an instrument by which the ledger can be balanced. You understand?"

Mandy stares.

"What happened here, Mandy. The scales have been—if not balanced—adjusted closer to an equilibrium. These animals won't hurt you anymore. You can go on with your life, free and clear of this monkey on your back."

Mandy nods, though her eyes don't belie understanding.

Snow starts to fall atop them, the back alley and street behind the diner completely silent now that the Oldsmobile is turned off. Seems to Ledgerman like a hidden, private place where only Mandy and he share this moment.

He lets go of her shoulders. Goosebumps crop up on the skin of her forearms. She is a picture of innocence, though one that has been tainted by the corrosive air of the outside world.

But Ledgerman thinks she'll be alright. Mandy is a fighter, a tough girl in a world that mostly just got a bit easier for her. He's not a sentimental fella, but this particular outcome suits him just fine.

"Here," he says, and turns back toward the Oldsmobile.

"No!" Mandy shrieks, the words careening off the brick and stone and concrete all around them like a SuperBall.

She grabs his forearm, sending a temporary shock of pain up into Ledgerman's armpit and shoulder. He'll have to take care of the cuts from the broken window. Could maybe have gone about that better. But the pain is little compared to the aura of relief that Mandy now exudes.

"It's alright," he says, extracting himself from her grip.

He turns to the car, reaches through the broken window, and manually unlocks the back passenger side door. He leans in the doorframe, putting his hand on the headrest of the driver's seat to hold his weight (to avoid the broken glass strewn about), and uses his other hand to grab the cash fallen from Mr. Squirrel's grip onto the floor.

Before he gets back up, Ledgerman rifles through Mr. Squirrel's pockets, finding a wad three times as thick (and ten times as valuable) stuffed into the back pocket of his dirty jeans.

He hands the cash to Mandy. "This doesn't fix everything, but I hope it at least goes towards making things right."

Mandy stares at the cash now resting in her palm. She hardly reacts, just blinks at this newfound revenue.

Because he isn't sure if she'll do it, Ledgerman uses his good hand to fold her hand around the wad, hammering home the thought that it's now hers.

"Thank you." The words still ethereal. The actions all around her not yet real. Ledgerman knows this, but it doesn't much matter. Perhaps there are other factors that will come into play later. Maybe this isn't Mandy's only experience with the Ledger, as he's come to call it. The entity (whether it is man, woman, computer technology, or deity) that delivers to his wrist the information upon which he is compelled to act. To save or end a life, without hesitation or remorse.

Ledgerman is not privy to other entities acting toward the same aims as he—the rebalancing of the moral fiber of society. Probably he is not the only instrument, he thinks. Probably there must be others—social workers, bankers, information gatherers, technical people.

At least he hopes he isn't the only one. What a depressing notion that would be.

But those are thoughts for another time. Right now, Mandy requires his undivided attention.

"Listen here, now," he says, using the same quiet yet firm tone he so often deploys once he gets to the end of things. "There shouldn't be any blowback on you from this. These guys, far as I can see, won't have people snooping around, looking for them."

"What about Aidy?" Mandy says.

"Who?"

"Uh ... Devillo's girl."

Now he gets it. "Front seat or back?"

Mandy doesn't look back to the car. But a shiver runs through her body, raising a fresh round of goosebumps. "Front."

Ledgerman nods. "I'll take care of Aidy. Don't fret another thing about her." He can put potential collateral damage in a report, something required of him after each of these missions. They'll be looked after.

Mandy seems to accept this.

"What happens when the police find them?"

"No reason they'll think you're involved, is there? No cameras back here. No witnesses. I'm certainly not telling anyone. Neither are they. As long as you don't answer any questions that you—an employee, and *only* an employee, of the restaurant—shouldn't know, they won't have reason to suspect your involvement. Then they'll move on. They won't be pounding the pavement too hard looking for suspects. Anybody could see these two don't deserve more than a cursory glance at the facts, if that."

Ledgerman feels, but ignores, the strong desire to ask Mandy just what in the hell was going on in that car. The answer to that question is almost entirely meaningless right now.

Instead, he simply says, "My advice to you is to treat this like what it is: a bad dream. One that you're now awake from. But rather than continuing on your day, forgetting the darkness the moment your eyes open, keep this entrenched somewhere so deep yet so far away in your mind that you both never think of it directly, yet also cannot ever truly forget it, either. That way, you'll carry forward in your days appreciating this gift you've been given. And you'll pay it forward. Not tomorrow, nor on any particular day. Just in drips and drabs along the way."

Mandy nodded but Ledgerman sees she doesn't understand. Not yet, anyway. How could she? He just needs to make sure she hears him. It would all settle in later.

Mandy lets out a cry, then another. Tried unsuccessfully to hold a third one in. Ledgerman pulled her close to his chest, warm tears and hot breath soaking into the front of his shirt. He didn't mind.

"They just took and took, you know?" she says, holding the sobs back after a bit. "And they acted like they were doing me a favor."

"Plenty people like that out there. Just because you escaped these ones doesn't mean you won't ever encounter others."

"I just ... it was like I couldn't get out."

Ledgerman didn't need an active imagination to understand the dark times Mandy Beaudreau had gone through with those men.

"Well, now you are. Watch yourself, sometimes these things come and go in cycles."

She squeezes in harder against him.

"You hungry?" she asked after they stood there together in silence—Mandy coming down from her haze, Ledgerman basking in the aftereffects of adrenaline, which had so come to color the glow of a job well done.

Ledgerman was, having not entirely finished all of his breakfast, having to rush through the end to take care of business. Hard to believe all that was merely minutes ago.

"Fried chicken club sandwich, right?"

Mandy nodded, the familiarity of talking about the Omega menu probably feeling like divine comfort right now.

Somewhere not too far away, sirens scream out into the cold winter air.

"That's alright, I should be going. Much as that sandwich sounds incredible, I'd rather not have to finish it up from inside a jail cell."

"B-but I can tell them that you helped me. You won't have to be arrested or anything."

Ledgerman thinks about Freddy inside, still passed out cold on the kitchen anti-slip mat. Thinks about the manager, so quick to sic the dogs on Ledgerman.

"No, you won't. Remember what I said, about not saying anything other than what any normal employee might know about two guys getting beat up in a back alley. You didn't know them. You never saw me."

Mandy nods into his chest.

He gives her one last squeeze and then puts some space between them.

This is always the hard part. Ledgerman's protection, by design, ends here and now.

"One last thing. You should get out of here, this job. While these guys shouldn't bother you anymore," he points to the Oldsmobile, "they ever get a little crazy idea, they'll know where to find you. Besides, this place doesn't deserve you. Go find one of those high-end places, one that serves booze."

Mandy sniffs and wipes the tears away from her eyes.

"Ok."

"Promise me, kid." Last thing he needs to hear about is some young thing found in the dumpsters behind the Omega Diner, some violent ex-con brought too much booze in his flask and let out his aggression in the wrong place. It didn't happen often, but occasionally he helped someone who didn't take advantage of their second chance.

For whatever reason, he felt strongly that he didn't want to see the same thing happen to Mandy.

He didn't want this place to be her end of the line.

Another burst of sirens screeches through the air like an attacking band of birds.

"I promise," she says, and Ledgerman can tell she means it.

"Alright," he says. And then, because he's unable to come up with anything else, he says, "Now get back inside, it's cold out here."

Maybe it's the daze, but Mandy nods and listens.

She's gone in an instant, just like she appeared before him at his table.

He checks his watch: 10:12 a.m. Like so many of his other missions, it seems like it went by in an instant. His smartwatch has once again guided him to a target that must either be saved or killed. Typically, he has no preference. This time, however, he was happy that target required saving.

But now, his strange arithmetic completed, it's time to go.

He ducks into the wind as it gusts down the alleyway, stuffing both hands into his pockets.

Tomorrow, who knew where he'd be.

For right now, he needs to find some place far enough away to eat lunch.

THE TWO O'CLOCK KILLER

INTRO

What follows is a devious little tale of which I won't say very much for fear of spoiling anything.

Let's just say it hits a lot of topics that interest me as a reader–serial killers, police investigations, obsessions, and the hard choices people are forced to make when they find themselves embroiled in circumstances where there's really no good choice.

Other than the title, this story, once finished, surprised me as much as I hope it surprises you.

Enjoy!

WRITERS OF THE FUTURE AWARD FINALIST

NIZ THOMAS

THETWO O'CLOCK KILLER

AN ORIGINAL CRIME STORY

ONE

Stimble stretched out in his silver Chrysler sedan. Enjoying the extra legroom of the personal vehicle, having decided against bringing a station-issued one with him to this stakeout. Given he was in a residential area—small but manicured lawns, respectable-looking homes (not exactly your typical stakeout destination)—he hadn't wanted to attract any unwanted attention with something screamed cop.

His gaze had shifted away from the single-level house tucked into the corner lot and toward admiring his vintage Patek Philippe Nautilus watch, rubbing his fingers along the scuffed leather band and the patina at the edges of the round face, absentmindedly thinking about when his Daddy had given it to him all those years ago.

Thinking about the past. And about new chapters. Standard for a stakeout where your mind doesn't have much else to do but wander.

His reverie was broken when his bird—that's what he called his phone—chirped on his hip.

He sat up in the plush driver seat and took the call, keeping one eye on the house. He'd been sitting on it for the last hour, parked just far enough away and in the shadows so if anyone was inside, they couldn't see him move.

"Yeah?"

It was Teddy, his partner. Lead detective on this case. On most cases. Some people called Teddy the Beagle, on account of his eager pursuit of all things investigative. Teddy was the kind of guy that took that as a compliment. Stimble was the Robin to his Batman. It suited him just fine.

"I'm twenty-five minutes out from your location," Teddy said as Stimble glanced at his watch. "Got tied up with this creep Anderson."

Anderson was a shady guy, a lead that Stimble told Teddy wasn't worth running down. But Teddy was by the book. And so he had Stimble come out here to the suburbs and sit on this other lead—this Tim Murdoch, who was supposed to be living inside the single-level home— while Teddy checked out Anderson.

"Wasn't him, huh?" If Teddy was still coming here, Anderson wasn't the guy. But Stimble already knew that.

"Don't say I told you so."

Stimble didn't. He'd jab Teddy with it another time. Instead, he said, "It was the clock was missing, wasn't it?"

"You gonna make me put a notice in the paper: *STIMBLE WAS RIGHT*?"

"Maybe just a spot on the radio. A full thirty-second one, though. Don't get all cheap on me."

"Play your lottery numbers, you lucky bastard."

"Lucky's better than good, sometimes."

"Smartass. Anything moving on your end?"

"Doesn't look like anybody's home. But I got a hunch about this one." Stimble had done some homework on Murdoch. And he liked him for this. Seemed like he could be the guy they were after.

"Sit tight 'til I get there, huh?" Teddy said.

Stimble clicked off. Looked at the house. Nothing doing.

Lights punctured the dark street. Halogens. Blinders, was what Stimble called them. Bright white and blue like they were shining down from heaven, last thing you see before you go into the light. Whatever happened to being able to see on the road?

The car approached from the north, like someone coming home for the night. Pulled into the driveway of the house, opened the garage, parked inside next to a wall of neatly arranged power tools. Stimble's eyes finally came to. A blurry figure in the shadows went to the inside garage door and into the house, the outside garage door closing as he did so. Lights went on in the house, then off. On, off. On, off.

Like an SOS.

Stimble exited his vehicle and walked to the door. Neighborhood was quiet, not even any dogs barking. Not surprising for nine-thirty on a Wednesday night. School night. Kids were already supposed to be in bed.

As he walked toward the front door, intentionally stepping on the grass rather than the neatly placed stone walkway, he noticed the low hum of porch lights and the stronger hum of the occasional spotlight in the yards along the street, lighting up front facades with some blinding, garish yellow light meant to make the house look majestic but really just casting odd shadows around the yard.

Tim Murdoch's house didn't have any lights on outside.

Stimble knocked on the door.

More interior lights turned on. Footsteps moved toward the door. The porch light overhead went on.

"Yeah?" Tim Murdoch said, opened the door. Forty-eight. Single white male. Five-nine, one-sixty. No kids, despite the neighborhood. Shaved head. Nothing special, was how Teddy described him to Stimble after pulling his info. Stimble had said it was always the normal ones who turned out to be monsters.

"Detective Stimble." Flashed the badge, watching for that flicker in everybody's eye. The one where they inventory their whole lives, wondering what they did wrong. And why Stimble was on their doorstep.

He loved that flicker.

"Mind if I come in and ask you a couple questions?"

"About what?"

Stimble stepped in. "I'll be asking the questions, Tim."

Murdoch stepped in and out of the way. Not sure what to do.

"Let's talk in the living room," Stimble said, closing the door behind him.

Tim Murdoch obliged him.

"Can I get you anything?"

"Warm water with lemon."

Murdoch looked put off by the request, which made Stimble happy. Eventually, the suspect padded into the kitchen. Glasses started clinking.

Unlike the movies, Murdoch didn't call out over the clinking sounds. Didn't try to make small talk. Which suited Stimble just fine, since he was already checking out the living room.

There wasn't much to the house. Looked about what he'd expected after watching it for hours. Nice but not sprawling. From the living room he had a good (not great) view at twenty-square-feet of backyard, both bedrooms, the office. Only the kitchen and hallway bathroom weren't visible from Stimble's vantage point.

The vintage bulbs were the first thing that caught his attention, though. How could they not, glowing yellow-orange like a collection of dying flames?

They were positioned on a mantle above the room's lone unlit fireplace. Edison bulbs, though those were easy to come by. Just table stakes for collectors, as Teddy had told him after doing a deep dive online. But Murdoch had others. Amber-hued bulbs the shape and size of an avocado. Smoky Chandeliers with twisted, ornamental filament designs.

Tim Murdoch had quite a collection here.

Stimble checked his watch. Ten minutes until Teddy arrived.

This collection was part of the profile, oddly enough. *Obsession with vintage items highly likely—lightbulbs, radios, cars,* was what they'd gotten back from VICAP. After Teddy had found trace elements of tungsten on one of their first victims, they'd narrowed it down to lightbulbs. Was a weird obsession, Stimble knew. Twenty years on the job, never saw it in any profile before.

Wasn't particularly happy to see it in this one.

The rest of the profile—the age, sex, location details—were already hits for Murdoch, which is why Stimble was here in the first place. He and Teddy had basically been working down the list of antique lightbulb collectors since making the connection with tungsten a week and a half ago.

Since that time, there'd been three more victims.

Stimble had been busy.

He'd also been the one to suggest they split up their efforts, try to catch the killer double-quick. He'd be happy to leave this all behind him now. It was this case that had him thinking about chapters ending back in the car. And what all might come next.

"My guilty pleasure," Murdoch said from behind him.

Stimble turned. Murdoch was close, almost too close. Definitely uncomfortably close, at least. Stimble grabbed the glass of warm water with lemon from Murdoch.

"The filament bulb, Thomas Edison. The appeal of that time period. The *craftsmanship*, even on the bleeding edge of technology at the time. For some reason that just does it for me, you know?"

"Sure."

Stimble put the cup down on a side table. Gestured for Murdoch to sit down on the couch.

"So what was it you needed to speak to me about, detective?"

The guy was cool, collected. Almost too much so.

"I'm part of the task force tracking down leads on the Two O'Clock Killer," Stimble said, using the obscene moniker the papers had come up with. He didn't like doing it, but it was how the general public knew the guy, so it helped with the shorthand.

"Oh."

"And your name is next up on my list."

"My name?"

"Your name."

"I don't see how that's possible."

"Luckily that isn't part of the criteria we consider."

Murdoch sat forward in his seat. "Listen, officer—"

"—Detective."

"Detective. I don't know a thing about the Two O'Clock Killer, save what I've seen on the news."

Stimble nodded, letting his eyes wander around the rest of the living room. The strange thing about the profile was it had identified three components that likely would lead to the killer. *Likely* being the operative word. Unfortunately, a VICAP workup was as much art as it was science. Just because it said the guy was forty-eight didn't mean he couldn't be forty-six. Five-nine could be five-eleven (though not usually taller than that). It was all more a landing zone than bullseye.

"Would you be surprised to hear that our profile of the killer includes a layman's obsession with applied mathematics?"

Stimble nodded toward the corner of the room. Murdoch had a reading chair setup. Worn-in leather recliner with a side table next to it. One of those arc lamps, bathing the space in a warm, peach-colored glow from the radio-style bulb. Stacked on the floor next to it were mathematics textbooks, as tall from the ground as the armrest of the chair.

Murdoch sat back on the couch, put his arm on the rest. Looked genuinely surprised. "Just because I—"

"You're a numbers guy, I see."

"Not really," Murdoch said. "Mathematics is more than that. A way to think about the world. Logic and reason that underpins the very fabric of our reality."

It was almost as if Murdoch wanted to make Stimble's case for him.

The math stuff was strike two. VICAP said the suspect had a meticulous mind. *Obsession with numbers, logic, mathematics likely.* A mind capable of planning something all the way to the end.

Like a murder. Or ten of them, and counting.

Stimble checked his watch. Five minutes until Teddy arrived. He felt his heart flutter a bit in his chest, his cheeks warm up.

"What is it you're not telling me, Detective?"

Stimble said nothing. Kept his eyes moving around the room. The words from the profile flitted through his mind like fireflies. *Obsessive. Meticulous.*

Murdoch was a surprisingly strong candidate for the Two O'Clock Killer.

Except for one key element.

"Listen, Detective," Murdoch said as he stood up, "I wish I could be of more help."

"I don't think I asked for your help."

Murdoch put his palms up. Surrender, sort of.

Neither of them said anything for several ticks of the clock.

Three minutes until Teddy arrived. Stimble could practically hear the tires on the pavement outside.

"Wait a second," Murdoch said. "If I'm the Two O'Clock Killer, wouldn't there need to be some clocks here? I mean, I've got one over the kitchen sink. A digital one next to the bed. But check the whole house..." Murdoch's mind seemed to be working, trying to play catch-up. A logician's mind. No doubt there.

He was right, though. The lack of a vintage clock collection was problematic. As stupid as Stimble thought the name was, the Two O'Clock Killer got it for a reason. It was another thing from the VICAP report, though Stimble thought that bit of it was fairly obvious.

Ascribes symbolic meaning to time or timekeeping.

"...I hardly even know how to tell the time on a clock..."

The Two O'Clock Killer left behind some type of time-keeping device at every kill scene. A clock. A sundial.

A watch.

"...so you see, I couldn't possibly be him."

"I think you'll do just fine, Tim."

Murdoch stared back questioningly.

Stimble pulled out his service weapon and shot him in the chest.

Murdoch fell back onto his couch but missed, fell onto the floor. Gasping for breath. His hands were up near his chest, as if trying to plug the leaking air hole.

Stimble checked his watch. One minute until Teddy arrived.

He bent over Murdoch's body as he faded away on the floor.

"You almost checked all the boxes, Tim." Stimble closed his eyes, letting the familiar feeling of a job well done wash over him. Felt the triumph of death tingle on his skin.

Murdoch flailed on the ground and gasped for a breath that just wouldn't come.

"I was worried you might not have an acceptable clock, though." He raised his wrist to show Murdoch the Patek.

Recognition in the near-dead man's eyes. Then terror.

Stimble put a gentle finger to the crown and used his nail to pull it out to the second position.

Took a deep inhale, savoring the moment for a single second longer. Not knowing when he might once again feel this. The investigation had gotten too hot, too much attention. And now he'd have to adjust his process to keep this story going.

The Two O'Clock Killer was now dead. Thereabouts at least. Would be a real red flag if he kept killing people same as he'd been doing.

Stimble wound the dial around until the clock face read two o'clock. Wiped his own prints off the thing, not worrying about the DNA that would be excluded for being at the crime scene. Knelt down and slipped it into Murdoch's pocket as the dying man's eyes went wide with protest.

Death's warm embrace ensconced Stimble, smothering Murdoch for eleven more glorious seconds before Teddy banged on the front door. Stimble called him in.

Murdoch's eyes went wide one last time as he saw another officer of the law enter the room. Stimble knew those eyes were dying to scream the truth.

Dying being the operative word.

Teddy took in the scene, gave Stimble a surprisingly calm raise of the eyebrow.

Inside, Stimble felt like he'd just mainlined the high he usually felt from Death. His partner in the room as his victim died was like nothing else he'd ever experienced before. Nirvana of excitement and anxiety.

What if Murdoch ekes out one last word?

What if Teddy somehow reads the room, feels some of Death's juju lingering in the air like summer static just before it rains?

What if Stimble loses it, hops onto Teddy the Beagle like a feral jungle cat and strangled him while mawing at his carotid in a fit of crazed hunger?

Stimble turned back to Murdoch, the man's eyes recognizing the futility of their plight. It was like what Stimble figured it felt like to watch a baby be born, or one of those once-in-a-lifetime comets shoot across the night sky. He could barely contain his inner trembling, less worried now about his victim unmasking him as he was with crying with complete ecstasy at the beauty of this moment.

Stimble took two quiet breaths. When he spoke, he couldn't tell whether this voice was calm or like a ten year old's who just saw his first naked lady.

"He..." his voice trailed off. He wasn't yet ready to speak.

Teddy put a hand on Stimble's shoulder. Did he feel the energy surging through? Like a supercharged electric fence for cattle.

Stimble swallowed. "He made a move," he said again, this time confident his words sounded normal. He shrugged, gestured around the room as if to say, *can you believe that VICAP profile?*

Teddy knelt next to Murdoch and checked his pulse. "He's dead."

Stimble let out a deep, relieved sigh that he had no trouble faking.

"But look at this." Teddy showed him the watch.

"Figured we'd find at least one of them in here, once he got squirrelly."

Teddy shook his head. "Wound to two o'clock and everything. The sick bastard."

Stimble shrugged his shoulders, the high of death beginning to drain from him. Usually it lasted for a while, until it once again got too great for him to keep control over.

After this, though ...

He wasn't sure how much longer he could go through life without feeling this again.

"Wonder what it meant," Teddy said, handing the watch to Stimble to take a look at.

Stimble stared into his Daddy's old watch, memories and emotions flitting around on the dying wave of adrenaline inside his body.

"Whatever it meant," Stimble said, "I guess that chapter's closed now."

And another one would soon open.

CALL ME BETSY

A TRUE NAME STORY

INTRO

The genesis of this story was the opening few sentences, pieced together several weeks apart. I wasn't in search of the first two items, which appeared together inside my head one day, almost fully formed, while stuffed into the trunk of an SUV listening to the Beach Boys song mentioned in the story itself (that's maybe a story for a different day).

As far as a flash of Great Insight, that's about as good as it gets for me (trunk excluded).

The sound of the typewriter followed along with the Beach Boys' music.

The typewriter's percussive action was woven into her like hidden seams on a dress.

Okay, I thought, I can work with that. But no Great Insight joined it that day. I had a sentence, sure, but last I checked, stories needed more than that.

Instead, we bounced and bumped along the road with me in that trunk (hell, maybe I got knocked out from all that bouncing and bumping).

It was several weeks later when the third part of the opening salvo emerged. The sound of rushing water.

I was doing laps around the 9/11 Memorial site at Ground Zero in New York City. (I don't normally do that, I promise). With me was my baby daughter, who I was hoping might get some sleep as I walked her around in her stroller. What could be more soothing than water rushing at the site of a horrific atrocity, right? It was white noise, after all–the only white noise I was aware of around Lower Manhattan. If you've never been to the memorial, it's a somber but majestic place. Truly breathtaking in size and scale, and both a remembrance of all that was lost on that fateful day, as well as all the heroism we saw displayed. Not that I really thought any of that would rub off.

In that particular moment, rushing water, the Beach Boys, and the sound of a typewriter whacking away at a pulp fiction story all came together like a three-headed monster that was meant just for me.

Very much like my daughter, the main character of *Call Me Betsy* (the main character in all of the *True Name* series, of which this story is the first) is headstrong. Confident. Independent.

Very much *un*like my daughter (and we thank our stars every day for this mercy), the main character in this series does not necessarily use her strong will for good. In fact, she seems to relish when it gets her into tough spots. She puts herself into the spots, mostly. The places where she can stand there, look into the darkness of the human spirit, and smile back at it like, "you seriously want a piece of me?" said with enough attitude and confidence so that even the darkness of the human spirit trembles in response.

In retrospect, perhaps there *was* a lot of the location where this story was born that got infused in.

More than I ever realized until now ...

AUTHOR OF THE NOVEL *FAMILY TREE*

NIZ THOMAS

CALL ME
Betsy
xo

—— A ——
TRUE NAME
STORY

ONE

If you boiled her down to two distinct elements—the core of what she was—they would be these:

First, the steady, slapping patter of keyboard iron springs against platen on her daddy's Hermès Rocket typewriter. The sounds of fiction being created out of thin air like an alchemist turning common metals into gold. Daddy had gone another route—turning thoughts into stories. Gold always seemed to elude him.

But the typewriter's percussive action was woven into her like hidden seams on a dress.

Second, the steady, ferocious tumult of the Hudson River—known to the Native Americans as the river that flows both ways. Able to drag anybody wading in unsuspecting off into the Atlantic. They'd be halfway over to Africa before they knew what hit 'em.

There'd been a cabin upstate, just beside the banks, where the Hudson got choppy and white-capped. Where Daddy could get some peace and quiet for his writing. A place he could afford, since keeping it warm meant mostly keeping logs in the wood stove and ignoring the soot seeping into the air.

The closest thing she ever had to call home. The mix of warm milk, a rocking chair, and the open window of their one-room cabin—her only companions in sleep for those first few years.

She knew all this because her daddy had said it was so. And because she could still feel the ink-laced family yearning for myth and scrapping and danger running through her veins.

Right now, she almost had to laugh at herself for embodying all of that at once. The walking cliché that she was. Or sitting cliché, since that's what she'd been doing for the past sixty hours.

She was tucked in tight to a tin-rattling boxcar she hopped the day before yesterday. Seated directly between two crates of potatoes the size of hog pens. Surrounded by maybe a hundred more of them (though she was waiting for hour eighty before deciding she was bored enough to count). Her once-lithe body fitted in a space big enough for only a dog's crate and probably half as comfortable. It was approaching rigor mortis.

The entire boxcar smelled like raw spuds ready for slicing, dicing, and hot oil baths. The only salve was the constant rush of air as the train cut down the eastern artery of the country. The slatted sliding door off to her right provided just enough air flow to eliminate the possibility that the men unloading the car wouldn't turn up a dead body along with their delivery of potatoes. And *just* enough morning light so she could see the few feet in front of her if she needed to. Once the sun got over the horizon, the whole car would be lit up with long, strange moving shadows like a low-budget burlesque show.

Not the most luxurious mode of transportation she'd ever taken, but a free ride out of a hot and sticky situation up north wasn't something she would complain about. Not today anyway.

A steamy summer morning that only the south could produce leaked in through every crack and crevice in this slow-moving tin can. Even with the wind, it wasn't approaching cool. And the ride itself wasn't exactly a hot shot, making more stops than she cared for—and at half the speed. Beggars and choosers, though, and all that. If the freight train went any farther south, which a southern-facing train was bound to do, she'd have to figure a way of cooling herself down. At least she could gorge herself on self-combusting french fries.

By the salt on her tongue and the sticky balm in the air, she figured she was somewhere near Norfolk. Maybe headed down the coast. Or bucking inland toward the Research Triangle before hitting all points that passed for cosmopolitan in the Tighten Your (Bible) Belt. If the train banked that way, she might be able to slide into a nice fried chicken joint somewhere near Nashville. Get into some hot chicken upon arrival, extra mayo, brioche bun, extra pickles. Nothing like taking down an artery bomb your first night in a new town.

'Course it didn't matter much where she was headed. She had plenty of practice spooling up a story—hell, a whole fictional life—like a spider weaving her web. And whether she was a daddy long-legs or black widow had everything to do with her own mood, the whims of the day, and the situation she found herself in when she arrived.

Right now she was feeling just fine and alright, baby. She had that Good Vibration going—something she procured from an acquaintance back up north right before skipping town. She smoked the last of it only thirty minutes ago. The mushy mellow set in—though she never got stupid on the stuff. Not that she was doing anything on this gravy boat that a little mental distraction would have prevented.

But that wasn't how it worked for her. She just got relaxed. Zoned. A way to break a little farther into that fourth dimension. But never twice baked.

Luckily, she'd been able to slink another old school treat before crisscrossing the industrial tracks double-quick and hitching onto this slow, methodical beast. It was the sort of thing that anybody else would have looked at as trash. But it was the perfect pairing with her current state.

Get this: a cassette player. Sony Walkman. Junked, but still in working condition—white paint splattered on it like Jackson Pollock had owned the thing. A few scratches and dents, too. Cosmetic stuff. Tossed away because to somebody else, it was obsolete trash, baby. Today it was all on-demand, gimme-gimme-now. It was all *in the cloud*. Which was fine, except it took away the serendipity of the world. Put you in the vortex of information of your own choosing. Because from her perspective—chemically altered as it was—there wasn't a red cent of problem with this here Walkman.

In fact, it punched above its weight, sweeping her away to the feet up, windows down, radio blasting feeling of high school and a semester of college and all the slow-riding *drift* that came after.

All rolled into one little obsolete gadget.

Maybe that Vibration she caught back up north was a little greener pastures than she thought. Which was far out enough for her. There wasn't much else to do until they hit a place that wouldn't look twice toward the spud train riding through town, so she could hop off and spin up her new story.

Her throwback present came with an even better consolation prize: an actual cassette inside. And not just any old juked-up mix tape ripped from radio tracks, with bleeding edges where your song melded into the high-pitched-cool-dude talk of the DJ—your friend one minute and the next, he's ready to hawk you women's undies or sugar smacks or cancer sticks just to keep his gravy boat rolling.

No, no, no. This cassette was the real deal, you feel?

Unfortunately, it was only a single.

Fortunately, it was a good one.

And something about the high, the heat, the spud-tinted fresh air wafting downstream through the rattling boxcar slats up ahead of her felt like the universe designed this moment just for her. Conspired to give her precisely everything she required to fully appreciate it.

And appreciate she did.

The slow-drip crooning that opened the song was like a date's coat opening up against a cold, bleak night. It ushered her in. As natural as accepting a gentleman's hand and a crook inside his coat during a time of frosty discomfort. And sure, there might have been an ulterior motive—a little grabbing here, a little groping there. But she'd worry about that later.

For now, she closed her eyes and let the harmony bring her into the mix.

Once the sweet-molasses drip of the guitar kicked in, followed immediately by the polite-and-sincere baseline and drum parts, she was already halfway into bed with the cut—a smooth, slow jam of Americana that took her halfway around the world in the blink of an eye. But it always brought her back to the good ole U-S-A of her early days. At least her early days in spirit. She wasn't old (though she wasn't about to put a number on it for you). This song was ancient compared to her—having been conceived maybe thirty years before her. But Daddy always played records like these when she was coming up. So it made her feel like she grew up in that era, too.

This song made her feel like she sidled up to a cherry red leather stool at the milkshake counter with a nickel and a dream of chocolate vanilla swirl. Like she just put money in the jukebox and was waiting for the prom king to finish football practice and come around to ask her for a date.

It was wholesome as all get out. Not exactly her bag. But right now, for whatever reason, it was *just fine*.

All the while, the crooning continued and she leaned back against her extra-extra-large side of almost-fries in their wooden crate and bobbed her head to the beat.

The song was "Ballad of Ole' Betsy" by The Beach Boys. She didn't know the words or the meaning or the history behind the song, but she didn't care. It was just her, the Walkman, and the subtle whine and shake of the cassette tape telling her that everything was going to be A-OK, even though there wasn't a damn thing in her life to back it up.

Nothing other than this moment right here, which, despite every hardship that had preceded it, was peaches and cream, baby.

Just as the cut wound down to the end of the tape—a momentary lapse in the all-out jelly-jam she was immersed in — the player whined and shrieked on her like a guinea pig with too much sugar in its water bottle. The tone touched a nerve deep inside her ear—totally harshing her high. She spasmed, pressed pause, unable to allow herself to hear that sound for one more second. If she had, it might have been the last thing she ever heard. And wouldn't that be a damn shame?

When she paused the music, she heard two things.

Strange, since she hadn't heard hardly anything since she hopped this joyride. Though loud trains and pumped-up music in your headphones tended to drown out other noises.

The first sound: the intermittent low-power mode of trains across the country. Switching tracks, taking a catnap. Whatever you wanted to call it. They were like half the men she'd been with—if you don't count the other half. All bold-faced youthful exuberance until you asked them to change course. *Then* they hit the pillow like a thousand pounds of bricks just got read a bedtime story. Only thing they ever did faster was head for the door—though they only tended to do that much later on, when things got the way she liked them.

Complicated.

The second sound—which was only possible because of the quiet provided by the slowdown: the rumbling scrape of metal-on-metal. An industrial metal rocker's dream, maybe. But not the sort of thing a freight hopper wants to hear. It meant either the train was ready to head off the rails or there was somebody coming. Maybe somebody already here. A maintenance man, maybe. Or a coal-shoveler. Looking for a place to lay his head.

Or worse: there was a 'bo-rustler afoot.

If the train went off the rails, there wasn't much she could do. C'est la vie.

If it was someone who worked on the train, it wouldn't be an issue. Probably they wouldn't see her, even. She was tucked away behind and between crates big enough to hold a full-grown tiger. Most people milling about the train were either people like herself or workers looking for a spot to lie down. Preferably one that wouldn't end with a massive crate to the forehead.

The rustler, though. Kind of a wildcard. They didn't always work on the train, proper. Sometimes they were independent contractors, paid direct by the train company's owners. Men (always men) that had a vested interest in keeping things neat and orderly on their precious metal prize ponies. And they didn't care if that meant a few hobos or down-on-their-luck hustlers needed to pay the price to keep them that way.

So a rustler...that could be trouble.

Which meant it could be interesting.

Rustlers these days—much like herself—were a throwback to an older, simpler time. Back when hobos were a "scourge" on the American train world. Daddy had written a few pulp stories about the hobo life way back when, after trying and failing to sell the same stories to the slicks—which branded him everything from a communist to Satan's red-headed stepchild. Those fated attempts all but ensured he never made a single cent off the glossies. That was how she got so enamored with the lifestyle.

Unlike so much of the modern world (certainly the world of music, as the dilapidated guinea pig screamer in her hand so aptly proved), a rustler's job hadn't changed all that much. It was still: find hobos, get rid of them. Not rocket science. And none of these big venture capital funds that dominated headlines were particularly interested in introducing cutting-edge tech in the space.

Something creeping up the back of her spine told her that being able to hear what was coming would be important. And she was pretty sure it wasn't just her butt having gone to sleep.

She pulled off the headphones. Eager to assess the situation. Only the left headphone had a pad on it, so the tip of her right inner ear still ached from where the bare plastic dug into place. But it would be easier to hear her surroundings without them in. And until she could get a fix for the demented squealing, they weren't doing her any good.

Her eyes immediately darted to the single closest point of entry to her: the open grate sliding door off to her right. Luckily, it was easy to see if anybody was coming from that direction. Their outline would be visible against the silhouette of the morning light. If she were playing the odds, someone coming at her from that angle wouldn't be a friendly. Conductors and coal-shovelers and maintenance grease monkeys were more likely to use the simpler and safer option of stepping between cars. Less likely to end up a pile of mush and crunched bones, stopping up the rail wheels because of an overhanging tree branch.

Rustlers could come at you from any angle. And they didn't always have the same penchant for mundane safety considerations.

But she detected no movement from the side sliders. Just the ever-present *whoosh* of the wind, the constant flowing companion when you were just letting yourself fly free as a bird. It was the sound she'd been jonesing on recently, before lighting up and putting on the headphones. And a strong case could be made it was the sound she'd been jonesing on her life entire—in one way or another. Because she always found a way back to the road.

Or, more often than not, the tracks.

The road and the tracks had their problems, sure. But they always provided the *whoosh* of movement and adventure. Sometimes it was so loud, you didn't even notice your whole life fly by with it.

She closed her eyes and listened closer.

The lazy-bones train was drifting through its dead zone. High-stepping, like. Keeping an eye out for land mines, like she witnessed during a strange period overseas where she traveled through Laos. Methodical men with marbles for eyes and no more than eight and a half fingers. Looking for historical artifacts that just happened to go boom.

Didn't they all?

Here, the train's hundred-plus tons shifted on four-inch thick slabs of steel. The slightest problem with either one spelling little else but doom and gloom for her. Her, and America's proverbial blood supply of groceries and grain and cattle and who knows what all else this beast carried. If the feeling creeping up her back was a derailment, there wasn't much could be done about it now. But how would the supermarkets sell their sugar-bombs tomorrow?

Somewhere far off was a whistle—either feeding time or another cargo heading back up north, doing the dance the way this one would be doing pretty soon.

Nearer, there were seagulls screaming out. Probably circling the train line as it rolled down the coast, hoping it might drop off some scraps they could swoop on down and scavenge. There wouldn't be anyone rooting for derailment more than the damn gulls.

It wasn't the gulls that worried her, though.

A second crank of metal told her she hadn't just been imagining things. That her wacky tobacky wasn't in control of her.

This time, the sound became clear: doors sliding around on the other end of the boxcar. Got her back tightened up against the spud crate. Telling her which muscles could use a stretching. Which ones had plumb given up already. Up in a hackle, like a cat being sprayed with water. She'd ridden a lot of trains in her day. And that sound wasn't a normal part of business.

It was the part that made things interesting.

Somebody was here alright. The real question was: who?

She didn't get nervous. Didn't ball up and start sweating. In fact, she took a deep breath and closed her eyes again. For a brief moment, she wished for the chance to go back to only minutes ago, when she was enjoying a mellow moment alone.

Only then she remembered who she was. And that mellow moments —while nice—didn't quite do it for her. Otherwise she'd be holed up in a suburban enclave somewhere, sipping down her first dirty martini of the day and locking the kids in the basement (*with toys*, Alma, don't go calling protective services).

Yet her whole life had been an avoidance of that in one way or another. So it seemed that something deep down inside her was telling her that wasn't the life for her.

The door she just heard was near the other end of the car, anyway. Nothing else around her to indicate trouble. No reason to get all riled up just yet. That would only make the situation worse. This wasn't an ambush—if it was even anything at all.

So this rustler, if that's who it was, would have to rustle a fair bit to find her squished into the back like she was. If it was a coal-shoveler, he'd shove off and get to napping. And if it was a conductor who was back here, well, it was as likely he had a lady friend with him as that he, too, would be looking for a nap. Possibly his lady friend was even some other hobo picked out from on up the line. And this might be his lunch break. And they might just be doing what grown folks who find themselves with a little too much time and a little mischievous bug in them do.

And she certainly didn't have any issue with that. So long as they didn't tread on the road she was bumping on. Just two horny, lonely folks trying to find some closer connection with the universe. She could dig that. Could *grok* it, as she might have said if she'd gone down a different path in life. One that had been more in touch with nature, *man*.

But she hadn't. She'd hoed her own road—and never had to hoe in the process. And her road, if it could be defined by anything, was defined by what she did next.

Like a cat, she gracefully went from seated to crouched. Like she flipped a switch. She arched her back and stayed low beneath the top crate of Idaho golds to her front, somehow staying clear of the opening between boxes on her left. She ducked to her right beneath a cantilevered crate that served to block anybody passing through the car from seeing her, bending and swooping around like she was Catherine Zeta Jones breaking into the laser vault.

Despite the safe play of simply not moving—just going statue-still and riding out whatever was coming—she couldn't help herself.

That was the thing about her—she liked the danger. Got a little dirty. Just like these spuds had been, before they were scrubbed clean and made presentable the way society expected of them.

She crossed behind an extra sturdy stack of boxes, stopped, then peered out around the left edge. Looking on down the somewhat open vantage point of the boxcar now. Not open enough for a full-on panoramic view of the place. But enough to see who it was coming in to disturb her blissful one-ness with the ole Universe.

It was a man, of course. It was *always* a man.

His back was to her, knees bent, both arms up in front of him as he slid the boxcar door into place with a grating *thunk*, keeping his arms on the iron door handles, bracing against the inevitable back-bounce of the door. These trains were made before the days of hydraulic lifts and pin dampeners. These were the roll-up-your-sleeves, grease-up-the-wheels doors. The coal-on-your-face-when-you-crack-open-a-punch-can-of-beer-after-the-day's-done doors. This wasn't no Amtrak, baby.

And this man—dressed in a long, brown leather duster, tanned, and worn in like he'd had it on since taking it from a Native American a hundred years ago—he knew how to operate in this sort of environment.

Outside, the train must have been going around a long bend because as the door bucked back, she got a glimpse of longleaf pines and thick, mosquito-infested hovels taken root amongst the shrubbery. Beyond that was a hazy morning, obscuring the lazy waves slapping against the seashore with as much enthusiasm as a trick at her last appointment for the night.

The light against the enclosed darkness of the boxcar blinded as the train ambled along its loping bend without any power. For a moment, it was serene and peaceful.

The rustler handled the bucking door with ease. What she imagined were big strong muscles beneath his duster. They absorbed the shock of the door without so much as a jitterbug backwards. Strong hands for that. Strong back and legs, too. Not muscles, even. Just live wire sinew and repetitive stresses—probably a lifetime of them. This was a hard man. Like steel and iron melted down into a single bullet, loaded in and fired off straight through your heart. Before he even turned away from the door, she knew she was in for more than she'd bargained for a few minutes ago, laced-up and face out to the meandering wild wind of the road.

It might be a fun adventure, anyway.

Or it might be the last one.

The rustler got the door corralled in his easy, strong way. Then he turned away from it and back toward the boxcar. He had a thick chin and nose like a boxer who never learned to duck out of a punch. Cauliflower ears that suggested his love for getting punched in the face was maybe only outshined by his passion for getting choked-out in street brawls. She couldn't see a lick of definition through the duster but knew for certain now that his shoulders, arms, and hands were as thick and sturdy as an unused catcher's mitt.

His beard was easily the least surprising thing about him. And despite the fact she couldn't see below his waist, it was obvious that he wore decade-old shit kickers who had seen their fair share of action out on the road. Maybe he'd even replaced the soles with something like rubber. Better for traction when he patrolled the cars. Never a great place to fall, especially when rolling through humid country so close to sea.

But all that went in and out and through, not more than a half-second. Three quarters, tops.

What she was really watching after were his eyes. Those two soul-windows that would tell her more about this fella than if he were wearing a pair of ballerina slippers and a pink tutu around his waist.

Only she couldn't make out his eyes from this far away. Bad light in here, now that the door was closed again. She squinted, sure. But his face was part-blocked, given the angle and the boxes stacked haphazardly between the two of them, obscuring her view. The part of his face she *could* see was all shadow beneath his Stetson hat brim.

Did she need to see his eyes, though? Instinct said no. That this man was exactly what he appeared to be: trouble for someone like her.

Still, the eyes would tell her for certain. Seeing them would determine her next move. Seeing them would get the measure of him. She'd seen killers and thieves, priests and saints. And everything in between, all colors of that morality rainbow. She always knew where they fell from one long glance into their eyes. She needed to see this man's before figuring what to do next. Only she didn't want to give up her location. She might have danced on the edge of safety, but she wasn't a chump. It was possible he didn't suspect a thing. No telling what he was doing here. Maybe he *was* just coming in for a nap.

Only that tingling sensation up her back told her otherwise. This fella being here for a nap didn't feel right. Not now that she'd seen him.

He probably didn't even nap as a baby.

She watched him a moment. He didn't move—not his head or his hands or his chest. Like he wasn't breathing. Until he made a strange clicking sound with his tongue, the way someone does when they just realized they left something behind, like their keys or their wallet.

She spun around, moving silently behind another stack of boxes farther toward the outer edge of the boxcar to her right. Careful not to silhouette herself against the slatted doors. But there were two nice stacks of spud crates that she nestled between where she could watch this man in the relative security of being hidden.

Not that there was any real security here. Not anymore. Only a fool in her position would see a man like this and think security still existed.

Not to mention the fact that getting found out by a rustler could mean all sorts of bad things.

For one, there was the trouble with the law. That wouldn't be *so* much trouble to her, since she didn't plan to stick around long enough in whatever state this was to see the judge. Plenty of bad eggs in the basket once you tangled with the boys in blue, though. Or in or black, depending on which branch—federal or state or county—you ran across. Any single one of them could spoil your omelet. Getting caught and finding yourself in the hands of Johnny Law could be bad *before* you ever saw the inside of a courtroom.

But then there were the other troubles. The nitty-gritty, as one of her marks back up north might have said. It was poor-person for "fine print," only—bless their heart—they never had enough money to even be fine-printed themselves. There wasn't any profit in hoodwinking those without anything to take.

Nitty-gritty in this case meant the bad stuff that could happen to you that wouldn't occur to most people.

Rustlers, by their nature, were tyrannical. Their train, their rules. Their kingdom. The potential troubles for matching wits with a fella like that were legion. And very much contingent on the particular rustling bastard. It was just as easy to get taken into the railroad company's equivalent of the school principal for a slap on the wrist as it was to find you were in the hands of the wrong rustler. One who determined justice in an altogether different way.

One road led to a slap on the wrist (or the bum) by a bespectacled ivory-tower-sitting-cross-legged man who was more concerned with pinching pennies than he was with justice.

And the other—well, that led you down an altogether different road. That led you into the private throes of some sick, deranged, and often very specific childhood fantasy gone horribly wrong.

That was a place that even someone as addicted to the thrill and the burn as she was simply didn't want to be.

Of the bad men that rustled boxcars, some were out for cash. Fiendishly stealing anything and everything a hobo might have on them. Not the best target to rob—banks, for one, would be more lucrative. But what banks had in spades—namely: security, institutionalized federal protection, guns, and big buildings with locked cages to keep you out or keep you in—hobos tended to lack.

Some were out for bruises. Wouldn't be the first profession that attracted that certain kind of man. A pugilist. A flesh pounder. Someone who liked to work on their glove game—only they usually left the gloves behind. Fellas that too often got too rough. Schoolyard bullies who never really left the schoolyard.

And who knows the reason? Maybe it was too much to drink. Maybe it was too much anger. Or maybe he was just a sadistic sonofabitch. But either way, rustlers like that just lived to find conflict and mete out justice against the relatively weak and powerless in such a way that bruises and blood were assured. They just wanted the chance to inflict and witness.

'Cause that's exactly what they liked. And why they got into this racquet in the first place.

Then there were the ones who were out for something else. Clothes. As in, they'd make you take yours off, hold them out 'til they caught a breeze coming off the coast. Let go, watch them whip away on the air like Canada geese come wintertime.

As soon as the clothes were out of sight, of course, the game changed. The appetizer course was finished.

For dinner: pain and humiliation.

Not so different from the bruising rustlers. There would still be blood. It just came as a byproduct. Because this sort of rustler was out for the squeal. The breathless plea of a choking throat. A spanking that veers off from disciplinary and deep into the Core Inferiority Range, where the sick and the sadistic play.

These, of course, were the rustlers she needed to be most wary of. That any woman alone did. The kind of predator who wanted nothing more than an easy, vulnerable, and voiceless lay. The lay, frankly, was probably the least important part. They took it one step farther than the bruisers. And some liked to take a leisurely stroll beyond even that.

These were men that needed to feel *power*—total, unbridled. To exert it. To dominate. And nowhere better to hunt and take your rightful tribute than within the untamed wild confines of the boxcar train.

The main question she needed to ask her: which one was this fella?

The train kicked back into gear. Scraping wheels and creaking metal swaying this way and that, all picking up steam and moving as one multi-thousand-pound unit. Power was back, meaning the wind would be whipping away the smell of potatoes, now thick in the air from a reduction in airflow. Soon, the boxcar would turn into an orchestra complete with a screaming industrial string section and the guttural, heavy baseline of side rods, crank pins, and pistons *chug-a-lug-lugging* their way down the track. Pretty soon, she wouldn't have a guess as to the rustler's location if she lost sight of him.

And if he caught her—and he was one of the bad ones—nobody would be able to hear her scream.

She peered around a beat-up stack of boxes filled with earthy red potatoes. The rustler was right where she last saw him. Didn't appear to have moved an inch. From here, she still had trouble seeing his eyes. If they were open, the whites weren't visible beneath his hat. His whole face was shrouded in shadow. Like a demon ready to start wielding his power in the new dark.

He swayed with the train. His only movements. Like he was part of it. Comfortable. It really picked up steam now, the sounds of the passing wilderness now mere afterthoughts. The mellow Beach Boys cassette hardly more than a distant dream.

On the precipice of turning into a nightmare.

She didn't want to act all damsel in distress. She'd been in bad situations with bad adversaries—both men and women, and sometimes the women were worse.

But this man seemed different. Not in a good way. She didn't yet quite know who he was, other than the fact that he could handle himself and looked to have a particular penchant for fighting.

The train screamed along a bend in the tracks, enough so she almost lost her footing and had to place a hand against the stack of spud boxes beside her. The box shifted, teetering in the direction of the turn.

For a breathless second, she watched as the box tumbled over and slammed onto the ground with a thud that might as well have been a GPS ping. Spuds spilled all over the floor, making some McDonald's franchise manager in Bowling Green or Biloxi or Knoxville supremely unhappy. She wondered if he'd keep her awake until she cried, or if whatever he was here to do would be quick and final so he could move along. And hopefully she could, too.

But the box didn't topple over. It shifted just enough to scare her. Not enough to alert him to her presence, the scraping wood drowned out by the sounds of train on track, steel on steel.

The train righted itself and kept on going.

Crisis averted.

She thought.

That was, until he said, "I can *smell* you in here."

She froze like the train just plummeted into the Arctic Circle.

Mainly, she wondered: do I smell?

"And it ain't because you stink. This here car is one hundred percent starchy Murphy's. You smell like a nice lady. So why don't you come on out and we can do this thing the easy way."

The way this man operated titillated and confused. But mostly, it scared.

Still, she wasn't sure saying anything was a good idea. Her mind raced through all the available possibilities, jumping from one eventuality to the next and back again. The only other sound in the whole damn car was the regular *tit-tat-tit-tat* of the train cruising south.

Finally, she got her head back about her. Too much Good Vibration, maybe. She wasn't one for long-term plans or processing through every eventuality. That just wasn't her at all.

"Easy compared to what?" she said, loud enough so he could hear it over the train. She didn't dare move from her spot. His small sample size of communication didn't tell her much, but it definitely didn't rule out danger. It could have ruled out any other eventuality. But not danger. Anyway, from where she stood hidden against the side of the boxcar, she could watch his reaction.

It was something that could have been a smirk or grimace. Pain or pleasure, baby.

She still couldn't see his eyes, though.

"So this isn't the first time you've played this game." This through either the smirk or the grimace. His voice didn't give away either emotion.

"I don't know *what* you're talking about."

"So it's the hard way, then?"

He still hadn't moved from just inside the boxcar door. She got a strange feeling in her gut—in her everywhere, really. Something was off here. No rustler she ever tussled with had ever been so slow to act. So... methodical.

He said, "It's alright, you know. If you want to do it that way. Seems like you may not know any different."

"And what do you know?" she felt a bit bolder now. Like this whole train was riding straight off the rails. And she was fixing to go down with it. Better to lean forward and put your arms out like a bird.

Enjoy the ride on down.

The train jerked right. She was lucky. Had the rusted steel of the slatted door to lean into, stop her from getting tossed. She hit the side without any parachute, though. The slatted siding would leave a mark. Maybe draw blood. But she was lucky not to have made any noise.

The rustler, though...he didn't move at all. And he had nothing to hold on to or lean against. He just stood stock-still. Like he had magnets in his feet or something.

The train righted itself and he said, "I know about what I'm doing right now. Know all about it, in fact."

"And that's it?"

"That's about it. Yeah. No need to know much else."

"So you're ignorant, then."

"Never claimed anything else, did I?"

"Never claimed that, either."

"Say, I never met a lawyer hobo before. What's your name, counselor?"

She thought about this, how he was a smartass. What did that tell her about him? She couldn't be sure. Right now, he was just a witty rustler who seemed awful confident in himself. Either he was experienced, good, and a sporting fellow, or he was downright sick in the head and liked a complicated situation as much as she did.

He liked the chase, maybe. She could dig that.

But did he like the kill, too?

He still hadn't moved a single step from his position near the door. Like he took up roots.

She figured to hell with it. He wants to be a smartass, two can play that game.

"Call me Betsy."

"Obliged to meet you, Betsy. But I didn't ask what I should call you. I asked for your name."

How could he have known it wasn't the real thing? A shiver that defied the odds ran up and down her spine like the Tasmanian Devil after a long night down in a Colombian whorehouse.

"What's your name then, hoss?"

Another smirk. Or a grimace. Pleasure or pain.

"You can call me Genghis Khan, Betsy. Because no matter if you're running, hiding, or fighting, the full force of my epic dominance is coming straight for you. And there ain't nothing you can do about it."

Pain, then. Though for this guy, was there even any difference between the two?

"A history buff, I see. So much for ignorance."

"Objection. Asked and answered."

Betsy's heart crept up into her throat. Sweat pooled around her lower back. The breeze seemed impotent against the heat. The car had only gotten hotter since this fella rolled in. And not hotter in a good way. More like it was reaching a broil. The sun baking the outside of this, the last of the tin cans she might ever see. The smell of uncooked potatoes was overwhelming, just a hint of ocean air mixed in. It got any hotter in here, there was a good chance this car would at its destination full of enough boiled potatoes to keep all of Ireland fed for the next year or so.

Betsy pictured the rising sun outside burning an orange hole through the ozone like a blowtorch against an igloo. Pictured Genghis Khan throwing her body off this train. Her bones'd be bleached inside of a month with heat like this. Maybe less.

"Big talk for a man who roams trains all by his lonesome."

"I like being alone. Something about it that tests a man's mind. Either it hardens or it softens."

"Isn't that how it always is with men? Most men, it's the latter."

Genghis Khan laughed. A baritone chord that punctured the boxcar like a gunshot.

"Well, Betsy, I sure am glad to make your introduction. Sounds like you need some exposure to a real man."

"When you find one, send him my way."

That same strange expression passed over the lower portion of his face. He turned his head slightly, nose toward the ceiling.

"Never mind about the name. Betsy will be fine for today, I guess. Won't do you much good, anyway."

"Why's that?" she asked.

The rustler clicked his tongue again—a primal animal sound that made her feel gross.

"'Cause I got you right where I want you. And your name could be Jesus Christ Cometh and it wouldn't do you no good now."

Betsy's blood ran cold as the rustler's head turned—sudden and with an alien precision.

It turned directly toward her.

She pulled back behind the crate, though she knew it wasn't quick enough. Toward the front of the car, she heard heavy, thudding footsteps —rubber-bottomed shitkickers with either metal spurs or metal toe caps jangling against the corrugated steel floor of the car.

Her heart rate had gone from Good Vibrations and a Beach Boys croon to a heavy metal encore performance. A guitar opening like Satan's bargain. A confident, naughty thing that would have pulled a girl like her —at a younger and more naïve time in her life—onto the road less traveled. The hippie-dippie weirdo bus, Day-Glo in her eyes and on her clothes and inside her heart. Instead, her heart was filled with the detritus of a life lived on the edge and on the move. And right now, a hummingbird at a Megadeth show would be gasping for air. The first bass riff punched through the floorboards like she was the dark horse at Indy 500, waiting for the last second nut punch to propel her straight up the side wall until the checkered flag sparkled the whites of her eyes.

The drums rumbled like approaching summer rain. She felt faint, like her chest might explode.

And all the while she couldn't stop herself from sweating.

"Nothing in this world can help you now, Betsy."

She almost believed him. But she never truly believed anybody who said something like that. And there'd been plenty of bums over the years who'd tried to get one over on her and pull her down into the depressing muck that so many people got stuck in.

They always left one thing out, though.

Her.

"You ever wonder, maybe, if going looking for the sort of woman who rides the rails is a wise idea?" She said this to try to buy some time. Maybe to cause him to stop walking, consider his response.

She leaned forward to peek around the crate she hid behind.

The rustler did stop to consider his response.

But he was still looking directly at her.

Only looking wasn't the right word for what he was doing.

Maybe it was the distance, which he'd closed to about fifteen feet. Or the brightness from the rising sun streaming through the open slats of the boxcar, situated at her back. Or maybe he'd tipped his Stetson up and farther back on his head.

But she got a good look at his eyes.

Or, where his eyes used to be.

From getting a look at the whole thing now, his face wasn't marked by the cauliflower ears or the beard or the grin-grimace (and would he just make up his damn mind about it, anyway?).

It was marked by the callused pits where his eyes used to be.

He was blind.

And yet he seemed able to see her just fine.

He gave her a grin that turned her stomach inside out.

"Smile, Betsy. You're on doomsday camera."

Without thinking, she pulled back and slammed into the slatted doors behind her, then slid down until her bum found the floor. There was a single three-stack of crates in front of her.

She slinked down, head between her knees. Desperate to avoid his non-gaze. Wanting to shrink away from existence.

His footsteps continued. *Thud-thud.* Getting louder. Closer.

The same preternatural click she'd heard before followed his footsteps. Then again. *Click-click.* Quick. Rapid succession. She had no idea what it was. Maybe some weird tick he had. Like Tourette's.

"Come out, come out, wherever you are." The words rattled around this tin can car like sharpened jacks being thrown against the wall. There was something about the acoustics in here that seemed to echo the sound. And all she wanted was for it to be quiet—to leave her alone. She pressed down tighter into a ball, her whole body contracting as she did. The cassette player in her hand jammed into her palms. She was white-knuckling it. "On second thought, you might as well keep trying to hide. Maybe I *won't* find. Besides, you already forfeited your chance at the easy way out of this."

For once in her life, she didn't know what to do. Sat frozen in place. The only reason he hadn't found her just yet was the haphazard nature of the boxes, strewn about the boxcar in seemingly no order. It was the same reason she'd chosen this car to hide out in. Easy to take a nap and tuck herself away, out of sight.

Of course, she didn't account for someone looking for her who didn't have any damn eyes.

The callused pits flashed in her mind's eye again, sending a slice of sharp fear, served cold, up the back of her neck.

Wood scraped against metal. Him moving crates out of his way. How in the hell did he even see them? And how did he know which direction to move them?

Another clicking sound. Maybe twelve feet away now. Approaching from the same direction. Dead ahead. Her legs wouldn't move. She couldn't get up.

"I guess I was wrong about you, Betsy."

The words grabbed her. Shook her. But still, she couldn't get up.

"How's that?"

Another scrape of a crate somewhere behind the ones in front of her. They were now the only thing standing between her and him.

"I thought you had a little more *oomph* to you."

Hell, she used to, didn't she?

She stood up on shaky legs, using the metal siding of the boxcar to steady herself. The wind whipped behind her, just inches from the door. She didn't want to die here. Didn't want her bones to get bleached. Not here. Hell—not ever, anywhere.

If she had any tricks up her sleeve, now would be the time to use them.

The top crate on the stack in front of her disappeared and slammed down onto the ground somewhere on the other side of the boxcar.

In its place was the rustler. Only feet away now.

The crate must have weighed a few hundred pounds. He made it disappear like an empty cardboard box.

She could see him now, in all his hideous glory. Confident. Not a question in his mind he'd catch his quarry. Probably already thinking about what he was going to do with her.

She shuddered, visions of squids, spiders, worms, bats, and all other creepy-crawly things flashing across the front of her eyelids. Giving her the creeps. Sending shivers not just up her spine, but out to her fingers and toes and back again.

He was about four feet away now. Two crates—one stacked on top of the other—stood in his way. Almost close enough he could reach out and grab her. Up close, he was far bigger than she thought. Six-seven, probably. Ringing the register near three hundred pounds of solid slab. Like if someone took a steer from the refrigerated car and brought it back to life, mad and ugly as all hell. He smelled like spices—cinnamon and paprika. And up close he was even more beat-up and worn in than she could tell from afar.

But the eye pits were by far the most frightening part of him.

And he still somehow stared right at her.

She took a step left. His head tracked with her.

She went back right. Same thing.

A slow simmer of a smile crossed his face. This time, no doubt that it was all pleasure. No grimace here.

"I guess I was wrong about you, too, Genghis."

He stood up. Not quite straight. More like a bear might stand up before attacking an intruder to their territory.

"How so?"

"I thought you'd be more interesting. I'm already bored."

She backed herself up against the slatted door. Taking one last look at this pit-eyed freak, she expertly unlatched the door with one hand and slid it open.

The rush of wind burst through the door's opening like a river breaking a dam. Had she not been holding on to the handle with her free hand, it might have knocked her back into the car. Into him.

The steep drop into the deep gorge below her almost pulled her out of the vertigo.

They must have veered over a section of track that cut back inland because the ocean was a few miles away. An escape that might as well have been on another planet. Directly beneath them was a deep and raging river that stretched out east away from her, toward the sea.

All up along the edges of the river were two vertical stone faces that looked slick as glass and high as half the buildings in New York City.

The tracks seemed made of toothpicks. They were laid atop a bridge that looked outmatched compared to the weight of the train. Hardly anything beneath her to stop a fall.

Not until you hit water, anyway.

"Thinking about jumping to avoid your fate?" He said this with a smug tone to his voice.

She thought she felt his breath on the back of her neck. Spinning around, he wasn't quite that close. But he was staring directly at her like a just-returned G.I. looked at his wife.

If the G.I. hated her, that is. And meant her all sorts of unnamable harm.

"Guess not," he said. A big wicked grin cut across his ugly face.

She wasn't sure what to do. Jumping was probably a death sentence.

But at least it would be quick.

"End of line, Betsy."

"Looks like it."

He took another step closer. Paused. Clicked his tongue several times —fast and with enough *oomph* behind it that some deep and repressed memory inside Betsy's mind jarred itself loose.

It wasn't a nervous tick.

"I sure hope you don't jump."

"Why not? Ain't you planning to do me a load of harm?"

"I sure am. But it's better if I do it. Better for you, too."

"*Oh really?* Bowl me over. What luck."

He shrugged. "My way, you at least walk away." He paused a beat. "Well, you'd live, anyway."

He clicked again, pointing his mouth past Betsy and out the door. His head jerked side-to-side. Quick, almost imperceptible motions.

"That way?" he shook his head. "I'm not so sure you could say the same."

He was probably right about that. Betsy could see the gorge out of the corner of her eye.

It looked like Death personified.

"Right. Guess you're not jumping." He stretched his fingers out in front of him. "You want to say anything before we get started?"

She furrowed her brow, edging herself backwards. The wind once again whipped about, this time almost sucking her out of the speeding train car.

"You're so sure I'm going with you, are you?"

He shrugged and opened his hands wide. As if to show her that his way would be better.

"I sure hope so. Would love to hear you squeal before you start sobbing."

What a bastard. Betsy wondered how many others he'd done this to.

He pressed forward, using one arm to knock aside the top crate between them. It tumbled over, falling to the floor with a thud. Sending spuds rolling in all directions. One fell over the side.

Betsy watched it for a brief moment. It splattered into the wind once it careened off the bridge, like a bug against a windshield.

The rustler slammed both hands down on top of the lone crate left between them. Clicked his mouth again.

His empty, callused eye-pits bore directly into Betsy.

He reached for her across the crate. She could almost feel his vice grip hands. Capable of manhandling a thousand-pound door or a few hundred pounds of these crates.

What might they be able to do to her?

And for how long?

He stood up straight. Clearly ready to get on with it. He clicked his tongue one last time.

And this time, it all finally came into focus for Betsy.

In the back of her mind, she'd been trying to access the memory. The one he jarred loose a moment ago.

Before it even came rushing back to her, though, she reacted.

It was either that or jump.

Betsy pressed play on the cassette player in her hand and heard the guinea pig whine and squeal as the cassette tape rolled forward. She cranked the volume knob up to maximum.

The rustler jittered like she just zapped him with a cattle prod. His head went backward and forward. Left and right. He stepped back, uneasy on his feet. Like all that muscle and strength just got shredded up into a trash can and lit on fire.

Just to check, Betsy pressed pause. The rustler shook away the cobwebs and seemed to steady himself.

Clicked his tongue again. Five, six, seven times. Fast as all get out.

There was a time in Betsy's life—after Daddy got run out of the cabin on the Hudson—that they headed out west. Daddy looked for work in a number of menial jobs. All stuff that today they claim is done by migrant workers and immigrants. But it was the same people doing it back then. Backbreaking work. Stuff that puts you in an early grave or a late wheelchair (if you can even afford that much).

Betsy wasn't sure exactly where they ended up. She was only just old enough to remember. Young enough not to care or ask.

Daddy was picking blueberries and cherries. Somewhere in the Midwest. It was Ozarks hot and humid—like the southern morning outside the boxcar, but with less wind and more mosquito bites along your legs and arms. Coming to the end of the picking season. Mid-August dusk, with the setting sun making the sky look like a whole packet of blueberries and cherries got smushed together in a bowl and spread out across the sky.

Daddy had a mason jar with clear liquid in it. He was talking funny. Drunk, slurred. Having trouble twisting the words around his tongue, or vice versa. Whenever he got to drinking, he always spoke with a deep southern drawl that belonged more to a moonshiner than a writer. Half the words Daddy said when drunk weren't even real—you'd be hard pressed to find them in any dictionary. Even those strange almanacs that circulated the south once that newfangled War of Northern Aggression finally died down. Even the words he spoke that *were* real, honest-to-goodness dictionary members were often in the wrong order, or carried a twang so thick it might as well have been molasses.

They were sitting (or *setting*, as Daddy would have said that night) on what would have been the porch of their home. It was made of three cinder blocks, procured from somewhere, undoubtedly either illegally or at least without letting the true owners know they were getting borrowed. Atop the cinder blocks, Daddy laid a single piece of plywood. Because he only took three of them, the plywood was crooked and slunk into the mud patches all around their little shanty.

Through the purple and red darkening sky, birds flitted around. Making strange noises and flying in odd patterns.

Betsy—whose name was something different then—pointed this out to her daddy and asked about the strange noises.

"Them's ain't birds, puddin'." He paused to look up, as if to confirm a suspicion. He elaborated no further, just took another sip of his mason jar and wiped his chin with a dirty handkerchief he seemed to always carry in those days.

She watched him for a second. Perhaps realizing even at that young of an age that this man didn't know everything there was to know—the way most girls expected their daddy to. But he wasn't short of ideas about how things worked.

"Them's bats, pudding."

When she asked why they were making such strange noises—*click-click-click*—Daddy simply said, "Reckon it's their ech-o-lo-ca-t-i-on." His words slowed to the point even a geezer in the old folks' home would have told him to hurry up with it.

"Ech-no-lo-ca-t-i-on?" She could remember trying to mimic his words, just like he said them. The syllables rolled off her tongue like raindrops in a summer storm.

"Ech-*o*, pudding popper. No, no, not ech-*no*. Double, triple—No! Quad-negative—throw up some extra points on the home board." Daddy held his hands up as if signaling for a touchdown.

He took one heaping sip from the jar and made a face that even an alcoholic would've been disgusted with. The veins in Daddy's forehead and neck popped and went red, as if he'd somehow had his air cut off.

"What does it mean?"

When he spoke again, his voice came out in a hoarse whisper. Like the fire-liquor he was drinking scorched the inside of his throat.

"It means he can't see, pudding. Blind as a bat. *Blind as a bat*. They *see* with their ears. Sounds is what they see."

At the time, this made no sense to her.

Later on, she'd learn about echolocation. How bats use it, sending sound waves out from their bodies. The sound waves bounce off objects and travel back, creating a map of everything around them.

It was one thing her daddy had told her that might actually come in handy.

The rustler stood back up straight, having passed whatever ailed him like a kidney stone. He pulled down the front of his leather duster and made another series of *click-click-click* with his mouth, the sound emanating out of his bearded face just like those bats back on that night on the porch.

He was using echolocation.

He turned back to her, obviously having found her form again in the confines of the boxcar. She didn't know how it worked. But it did.

He moved faster than she did, reaching over the crate between them with his tree branch arms and grabbing her by the back of the head before she could duck. His grip was what it felt like to get caught in the back of a garbage truck just before they pressed the hydraulic lever down to crush its contents.

She tried to fall backwards, willing to take her chances with the gorge.

But his grip was too strong.

"Betsy, so nice to finally met you." He ran a hand along the front of her face, using his fingers like tentacles. Gliding them over every contour and crevice like God himself brushing the last motes of dust off his latest sculpted creation.

Her feet were half over the edge of the train car. But she couldn't get free.

His eye pits were deep chasms, as if whatever had happened to his eyes had extended beyond that. Scooped farther into his face like it was the Saturday night special at the neighborhood ice cream parlor.

He pulled her even closer and clicked with his mouth. It vibrated his lips when he did it. His tongue clucked and slapped against the inside of his mouth to produce the sound.

One last buck of her body told her that breaking free from his grasp wasn't going to happen.

"You smell like a good time, Betsy." It made her squirm and want to throw up just looking at his face. The mouth moving to talk, but no eyes. Really threw things off. Down into the uncanny valley. "Most of the time, when I get to this part, the smell needs to be overcome." He took another long sniff, pulling her so close his beard tickled her neck. "But you, Betsy. *Mm mm good.*"

He lifted her off her feet. By the back of the neck. Like a puppy straight from the litter. A move so jarring it stole her breath. She kicked her feet, but he easily swatted them away with his free hand, knocking them out over the threshold of the boxcar so that the wind whipped them around.

She lifted up her arm, desperate to hit this sonofabitch in the face, the way she'd done to so many men in the past who overstepped their bounds. Most men never stood a chance in a fistfight with her, though.

This one didn't seem like he'd much care—or even notice—if she started hitting him.

Only she didn't need to hit him at all.

She pressed the play button again on the cassette player. She'd almost forgotten it was even in her hand.

"Ah!" He stumbled backward again. "Ahhh!"

He reached his free hand to his ears. The vice grip on her neck opened, his other hand rushing to the other ear.

The rustler fell completely backward, screaming the entire time.

She landed awkwardly on the spud crate with a thud that almost knocked out her wind. She rolled off and hit the boxcar floor, not exactly sticking that landing, either.

The cassette player rolled away from her.

Her neck stung. His insane grip had left her with an Indian burn. She desperately wanted to rub it—hell, to put a cold compress on it.

But she didn't have time for that.

His screaming stopped.

Betsy rolled to her side, searching the ground frantically for it. She knew it was the only hope she had to stop him.

She couldn't see him now. Both of them were below the level of the crates. Her on hands and knees looking for the cassette.

She didn't know what he was doing.

A series of clicks emanated from the direction he'd fallen.

Oh God, oh God, oh God.

"That isn't very nice, Betsy." His voice was even keeled. The way one might speak to a toddler who just took a toy from another one.

His hulking form stood up, looking like an unfolding skyscraper to her on the floor.

Her hand brushed against plastic. The cassette player. Thank God.

She grabbed it.

"Come and get me, you bastard," Betsy said, standing back up in front of the doorway.

He was still twisting his neck, raising his nose up to the air. Getting his bearings.

Her voice seemed to jar him back to the present. He turned toward her, eye pits finding her in front of the open boxcar door. Nostrils flaring out as he sniffed the air between them.

He bent his knees. Ready to lunge at her.

As quick as he'd moved before.

This time, she was quicker.

She pressed the play button on the cassette player just as his feet left the ground.

He arced through the air like a torpedo arcing around the curve of the earth.

Betsy half-ducked, half-slid her aching body out of the way. Feeling like she got about half her flexibility back after sitting in this boxcar for sixty plus hours.

Adrenaline tended to help with that.

Instead of his quickness and strength being an asset to him, it proved his downfall. He couldn't adjust himself. An object in motion, and all that.

The last thing Betsy saw before she slammed into the corner just inside the boxcar door were his pitted eyes passing by her.

His agonized screams were only perceptible for a second or two before the gusting winds took over.

Or until he hit water below.

TWO

She wasn't sure how long after he went out and over into the void that she sat there, staring at the cassette player in her hand, or listening to the train rumble on down the tracks. At some point, she stood up and closed the slatted door, dampening the wind that seemed so intent to suck her out behind the rustler's path. It all felt like she was someone else, watching a movie projected on a screen far away from her.

Eventually, she slept.

She didn't dream.

Slowed movement finally woke her.

The train was stopping. It hadn't made any more stops until hitting the port city of Charleston, South Carolina. Chucktown. The Holy City. Home of Palmetto bugs, sweet tea vodka, and shrimp and grits.

As the train slowed its speed, approaching its final destination, Betsy once again opened the boxcar's side door. If she thought the air had been hot and humid before, she was in for another lesson in the depravity of Mother Nature. The open door poured in on her. Air awash with thick humidity, as if the entire city was stuck inside a hot-air balloon.

She stood in the open doorway looking for an open spot on the passing ground that she could jump out. Sand or grass was preferable, though she'd take woodchips or tiny pebbles. Even concrete, if she could see it was flat enough and without anything she might accidentally roll into.

She thought about the rustler. About how he'd come *that* close to getting everything he wanted. About how she'd come *that* close to getting everything she didn't. About how this was one more crazy story from a life lived on the run.

But mostly about the fact that she was in a brand new city, on a brand new day. Not a dollar in her pocket or a single possession rolling in with her.

And it was about time she became a brand new person with a brand new story.

Born again and facing forward, just like Daddy would have done.

THE BAD GUY

INTRO

The Bad Guy was an exercise in me trying to write a character with a lot of attitude. One with a distinct voice. This is sort of the writerly equivalent of an actor using an accent. For whatever reason, whenever I give myself this task of distinct voice, the "accent" I put on is either a deep Southern one or someone who is, as one editor who read my work said, "efficiently and immediately painted as an asshole."

What can I say. I've got a talent.

In this story, you will note pretty clearly that such a talent was on full display.

It shouldn't be too difficult to figure out which of the two accents I used, either.

But, I ask that you stick around. Because sometimes even jerks have redeeming qualities.

WRITERS OF THE FUTURE AWARD FINALIST

NIZ THOMAS

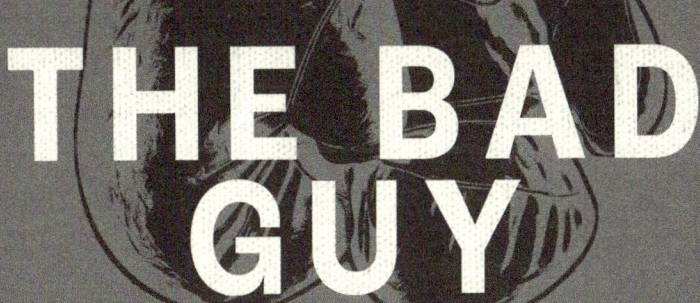

THE BAD GUY

AN ORIGINAL CRIME STORY

ONE

Usually, Teddy Pemberly couldn't even remember a passing score of the 5 Ws about one of his fights. Not Who, What, When (and sometimes), not even Where the whole thing was going down.

Just another match, another venue, another sweaty, petroleum-jelly-slicked, bruised and bloodied opponent set up before him for some predetermined number of rounds. Inside the ring, bright lights and darkness all that could be seen on the periphery. It didn't much matter usually who it was standing across from him. Fighting came natural to Teddy. The way most people breathed or ate junk food or took a crap.

Tonight, he knew more answers than most nights.

But most importantly, he knew Why he was doing it.

The crowd's chanting rained down on him like fire arrows in a medieval fantasy movie. Blocking out the sky. Fight in the shade type shit. For most people, this environment would make them crumble up. A beer can smashed against some doofus frat guy's head, trying to make the girls swoon (and allow the neurologists of the world to send their kids to graduate school). Teddy had plenty of experience with head trauma, what being a boxer and all.

He just didn't think any fancy-pants doctor was going to save his sorry excuse for a brain. It was probably most of the way to pulped blood orange by now.

And maybe that was just as well. Since nobody in their right mind would be caught fighting inside a place like this.

It was cramped. No A/C. No amenities to speak of, really. Packed-tight gymnasium, those cheap metal folding chairs that only got sold in packs of a hundred–not bad for a graduation. But absolute hell for the thirsty-for-blood spectators of tonight's fight. Hot enough to make your sweat evaporate, but too humid for it to actually happen. *Muggy*, was the word edumacated people would use.

Hotter than Hell was how Teddy experienced it. And in a church no less, Lord Have Mercy.

To most people, the sound alone would have drummed them straight into the ground. Hammer, meet nail. Here on this side of the cheap rubberized flooring (horse stall mats) beneath his boxing shoes one minute. Sleeping with the worms, or the fishes, or whatever else was beneath this church gymnasium the next (hell, it could have even been Hoffa).

But that was why Teddy was who he was.

And everybody else wasn't.

Few understood what it was to be the bad guy.

Teddy Pemberly knew what it was like to be The Bad Guy™.

He practically wrote the book.

Tonight he was going to finally show everyone just how it was done.

TWO

The walk to the ring could be long for some. Not nearly long enough for others. No matter whether it was a gym or arena or (in this case) a church gymnasium in the Bronx, if you walked the path and didn't want it to end, you were already dead to rights.

Teddy walked over the first of the black rubber horse stall mats. This was the first time in forever he felt like that. Usually he was about ready to go all rabid Doberman on whoever he might find at the end of this pathway.

Tonight though ...

Well tonight was different.

Some jabroni from seats good enough to make you wanna double-cross your mama butted into Teddy's headspace. Teddy happy for the distraction (another thing he'd never experienced).

Jabroni was either tipsy or letting out all the steam he'd accumulated over a lifetime of loserdom (except for whatever he'd done to get these seats). Jabroni spilled his beer over the little fugazi metal guardrails setup to separate the crowd and their folded metal chairs from the fighters as they entered the ring. Keeping the crowd penned in like bovine on the farm. Or maybe it was the other way around. These were the same mats they'd use on a farm after all.

Teddy's boxing shoes tip-tapped out of the way of the moisture, their soles gripping the rubberized flooring. This guy, this jabroni prick with a whisper-thin gold chain tangled up in an untamed wilderness of dark chest hair, all spilling out of a five-button shirt with three buttons undone, made from either silk or satin (but in any respect, tacky). Jabroni screamed whatever pain was inside him at Teddy, pretending like the guardrails were permanent, immovable forces instead of loosely connected pieces of scrap aluminum barricade dragged into place by a fat union crew member. Like he couldn't easily get in Teddy's actual wingspan if he wanted to as badly as he was pretending. The jabroni's face got as purple as Teddy planned to make his opponent's, just with more pressure behind the eyes. Mouth open wide enough that a well-practiced doctor could feasibly give the guy a colonoscopy. At least you figured with seats like his, he could afford the insurance.

He was unloading everything he had onto Teddy, but none of it stuck. At least *that* was the same for Teddy. It all slid off like Teflon, swept away with the rest of the boos and hisses and expletives that had turned the church gymnasium into the Devil's playground.

"We fighting in a church?" Teddy had asked his manager, Louie Bernadino, once he told him the details a few months back.

"Amen," was all Louie said.

"Is that like … legal?"

Louie laughed, chomped down on the fat cud of chewing tobacco inside his cheek. "Is it legal to beat the ever-living snot out of somebody?"

Teddy shrugged. He was never much of a legal scholar anyway.

"It's a big church, anyway," Louie B said to someone on the phone a few days later while grunting out a deal. Louie was always on the phone, working on some deal, spinning up some story about how this match or that fighter was the next train to Gravytown. He cupped his hand over the phone and leaned away from this makeshift card table in the corner of the rundown boxing gym he ran. Teddy was busy hitting the speed bag. "Big enough you can finally get that pool you been dreaming of." Teddy didn't even remember saying anything to Louie about that. Louie dropped his hand and went back to his phone call, to whatever greaseball dealmaker on was on the other end of the line. "They hardly make churches this big anymore, you know? It's practically like we're fighting in the Vatican."

Teddy continued his slow walk toward the ring. He'd read the Vatican had ceilings hand-painted by some of the greatest painters ever. This church didn't look like it had ever painted the ceilings at all. Not even with the stuff you'd use to seal in the insulation.

A faceless crowd on either side of him. In these moments, he was both here and not. The crowd was a single organism hell bent on crushing his spirit.

As if they were the first to ever try doing it.

Some small-hands, small-Johnson loser tossed a bag of popcorn over the guardrails. This from seats that would make your mama simply shake her head in disappointment at you. "You ain't made something of yourself, son," she'd say. If she was in the grave, she'd be rolling over in it. Probably call you collect, too–no reason for her to go through all the trouble of a full-blown haunting just to tell your lazy, bum ass what you already knew.

The popcorn bag hit the ground with no sound, having gotten swallowed up in the rest of the melody of malaise that Teddy had come to appreciate over all his years fighting. Had come to *love*.

If you can't make 'em feel anything, then nobody's ever going to pay to see you fight. Was what Louie had always said, anyway.

"That means *zero* pools." The spray of tobacco juice turned the coffee-stained card table into a flood zone.

"Thanks for spelling that out," Teddy had said.

Louie waved a hand. "Hey, how long I been with you?"

Teddy shrugged. He'd lost track of the years.

"Since the beginning," Louie said, screwing up his eyes and face in a *the-fuck-you-serious?* face. "And believe me, during that time, I observed you. Smarts isn't really your thing, champ. Don't start pretending like it is now, huh?"

The popcorn hit the rubberized flooring right in the spot where the ramp declined slightly toward the ring. Last mile of delivery, or something like that. The bag tumbled forward a few steps in front of Teddy. Not the first thing ever thrown at him, but what kind of idiot tosses six bucks on the floor like that? Especially one with loser tickets like his? A guy in the front row can toss whatever he wants. Even in the Bronx, even in a church gym, the door was raking in cash.

Teddy could just barely smell the butter as he stepped up to the popped morsels. His face was already covered in enough grease and sweat that smelling anything else was a true testament to butter's willpower. Belonged in some kind of Seven Wonders list. Right there next to Wonder Bread, Wonder dark beer, and the wonderful contribution to mankind that was the deep fryer.

The familiar scent of hundreds or thousands of people sweating, exhaling, spraying their noxious anxieties out into the closed-air gym. Petroleum jelly. Vicks VapoRub that his team made Teddy huff on before he left the locker room—all the better for him to breathe.

Breathing was good in the fight game.

Hard to imagine *anything* having enough sniffing power to cut through all that. But butter on popcorn did it.

"Watch your step," Wallace said, pushing past Teddy and clearing a path with his foot. He used his beefy shoulder to give the stand-back-ace to another screaming punky who'd leaned over the railing, enough spit sprayed from his mouth to grow a few weeds when all was said and done here.

Wallace was Teddy's corner man and trainer. "Don't need you slipping in the ring on that shit, huh?"

Teddy nodded.

But then he stopped.

"Hey, champ!" Wallace said, grabbing at air where Teddy's right arm shoulda been.

Here's where it happened. The big transformation. Every time, near abouts. People had wondered as time went on. Fight game writers had pontificated as Teddy progressed through his long and often arduous career. Announcers–back when Teddy was young enough to have them cover his fights–had speculated:

Was it Teddy who fell into the trap? A guy who just couldn't get out of his own way?

Or was it everybody else who got twisted up in *his* game?

Teddy honestly wasn't sure.

Like Louie said, smarts wasn't really his thing.

Teddy threw back the hood of his robe. At one point, his robes had been silky smooth. Like the jabroni's shirt, only a lot classier. Shining beneath the bright lights of Madison Square Garden, the Vegas lights. Even a few international venues. He'd shimmered beneath those flash bulbs like a phoenix out of the ashes.

Now, though, his robes were plain vanilla in a cup. No sprinkles. A lightweight cotton material. Black cloth. Woven tight so as to keep his body warm on the walk from the locker room down to the ring. Hood big enough so that Teddy's face was shrouded in shadow as he approached.

So that whoever was inside the ring felt like the Reaper himself was on his way.

Now Teddy's face was out. Glaring up at the crowd. All he saw was a single blob of shadows punctuated by white-hot spotlights. A chimera of all of man's worst things: vice, misplaced emotion, avarice. How many of these people had placed bets against him, wanting so desperately for him to finally get his true comeuppance? Laying 4-1 odds, it was the sort of boxing bet that a lot of degenerates had been waiting for. Almost too good to pass up.

Teddy glared up at the ring first before doing anything. Looked at Nate Galero. Typically, Teddy didn't care who was in the ring. Lately– due to fatigue of the grind, or age, or whatever jelly was starting to slosh around inside his noggin'–he was embarrassed to admit he just couldn't keep it straight.

Tonight though, he knew.

Tonight was different.

The past-his-prime Bad Guy stepping into the ring against the new up-and-comer Golden Boy. Everybody loved Nate Galero–even the whites who so often turned their backs against any brown-skinned brother trying to make it in the fight game (at least since Iron Mike).

Everybody wanted in on that.

But there were still a few minutes until the bets would close.

People could still lay down some cash at 4-1.

Teddy Pemberly would see to it that they did. The bad guy, making sure everybody has a good old time tonight.

He bent over, using both gloved hands to pick up the half-empty bag of popcorn, kernels and fluffy white popped clouds hovering down to the ground like snowflakes as he did so. Not an easy task to do, picking things up, with boxing gloves on.

Teddy held the bag up as if to challenge whoever it was had thrown it. That small Johnson loser. Bring it, chump. Enjoy this.

Teddy held the bag up now, higher. As if to challenge every damn person inside this church. As if it were the Holy Grail, and he was the one person to uncover the damn thing.

And now he was going to gloat about it.

Show them what they were missing.

He turned the bag up from the bottom and let the greasy, salty popcorn pour out.

Straight into his damn mouth.

He smiled as he chomped away at it, the scent of it overpowering his tastebuds. It tasted amazing. Smelled even better. The crowd's hissing and booing went from Led Zeppelin to Slayer, which heightened all of it. Made it all the sweeter.

It was nice, eating some chow before the big fight.

But most of all, it felt good to be the bad guy.

THREE

Teddy sidestepped a left jab that could have taken out a small village in Africa.

As he did so, a strange slow-motion moment of clarity: cameras flashing, blinding lights in the crowd turning every face into an apparition. The church thumped, an indistinct bass line hovering beneath the surface like Jaws. The twin-scented coppery bloodstains all over his body and shorts–his and his opponent's.

For that moment, Teddy felt in another dimension.

Despite the thrum of his heart and the adrenaline so thick inside the church that Christ himself would get jealous, it seemed to Teddy that he'd sidestepped himself out of the ring and into some other dimension.

Nifty Nathan Galero tried another attack, this time opting for a right hook. Nice try, Nate. Teddy ducked beneath it with so little space between impact that the *whoosh* of the air was like a tornado passing through a trailer park in summer. Any closer and Teddy's face would have to be picked up off the unkempt vine and weed-tangled yards.

It was the fourth and second-to-last round. Once upon a time Teddy had gone twelve rounds. Back in the title fight days. Back *before*. But when you fought in a church auditorium in the Bronx–even when it was packed to the gills like this one–people didn't have the attention span to watch twelve rounds. And nobody wanted to see the sad sight of a has-been like Teddy trying to hug his opponent to keep from tipping over.

Louie had pushed for the fight to be six rounds 'cause they could have upped the ticket price a buck-fifty at the door. But, "These fucking priests don't like that number!" Something about the Devil or something.

So five rounds it was.

Right now, Teddy was winning the fight, midway through the fourth. Probably. One of the things about boxing, you never really knew. Yeah, the scorecards were put up on the TV when you watched–but nobody was broadcasting this fight. And the judges weren't exactly the pick of the litter. They were about as shady as everybody else involved in the proceedings here, so it was anybody's guess which way they'd go.

Even still, anybody with half a brain could see it was all Teddy Pemberly in this fight. He'd had two knockdowns already in rounds two and three, respectively, and had Nifty Nathan up against the ropes for most of the fourth so far. Even if you paused everything right now, one look at their faces would sum the whole thing up.

Teddy probably still had butter around his mouth from the popcorn.

Nate's face looked like someone had just pounded a piece of steak with one of those mallets you see at the carnival. The High striker, or whatever it's called. High striker sizzling steak.

Delicious.

But Nate was nothing if not persistent. He started working his feet like he should have from the beginning. Cutting off Teddy from working his way around the ring. Keeping Teddy on the defensive. Not a half-bad strategy. Had he started it in the second round, it might have worked. Nate knew it. Teddy certainly did. So it wasn't such a surprise to Teddy when Nate tried what he tried next.

The guy needed to make some noise.

Rumble, young fella, rumble.

Nate approached Teddy from the side, sliding those young feet like Fred Astaire, if he was desperate to get the part. Teddy saw him–hell, the whole place saw Nifty Nate coming.

But Teddy saw something else, too.

Right behind Wallace's brick-wall frame was the kid. All four-foot-seven of him. Big brown eyes like saucers, the creamy whites of his eyes as innocent and pure as cats drinking their milk.

What the hell was he doing here?

"Stop wondering, start punching!" Louie and Wallace's voices both echoed inside Teddy's head. Weird catchphrase they had at their gym. Someone had even spray-painted it on the wall. It made sense though, Teddy figured. Louie always said Teddy wasn't the brains behind the operation, to leave the thinking to Louie and Wallace.

So what was Teddy wasting his energy wondering for now?

Louie was never what Teddy would consider *wise*. But maybe on this one point he was.

Because that's the thing about wondering when it comes to boxing.

It typically doesn't end well.

FOUR

The kid shouldn't have been there for a million and ten reasons. How did he even get in? He wasn't with a parent, wasn't there on some Make-a-Wish thing. Kid that age shouldn't have been sold a ticket–not to something like this. A big time fight, bright lights–if a kid his age could swing that, or get someone to bring him, then that was alright.

But not here. Here lies the seedy underbelly of the sport. Complete with every seedy character who came along with it. A fleet of clown cars full of them packed into this gym tonight.

Wasn't anybody taking care of this kid?

Wasn't anybody responsible?

No adult presence to accompany him, at least?

Those eyes–those honest, good-natured, wide eyes–were now watching the bad guy in action. They were in the bad guy's world now. This might have been a church, but Teddy didn't think it was a particularly Christian thing to do to a kid this age. He was twelve, maybe thirteen. Grew up around here. Good kid–as most are at that age–but he wouldn't be for long if he hung around places like this.

Couldn't anybody see that?

Why didn't anybody care?

FIVE

Teddy fell hard. Like tree. Like forest.

Teddy fell hard like Rome.

He did something he hadn't done much of in his career: touch the mat with his face. Having done the thing, it wasn't hard to see why you'd want to avoid it. For one: the mat wasn't forgiving. Not at all. The canvas slapped back. A woman who just found out you were sleeping with her sister. The mat was vengeful. Just another foe boxers had to face.

For another thing: falling down in the fight game meant you weren't doing it right.

Meant you might never get a chance to be the bad guy, maybe 'cause nobody ever got invested enough in your career to care whether you were good or bad.

They simply wouldn't even know you existed.

"The fight game is a fickle bitch," Louie said a million times if he ever said it once. "My first wife could tell you all about that."

"That why you left her?"

"Left her?" Louie scoffed, coughed, and brushed himself off before chomping back down on his ball of tobacco leaf. "I'd skin myself alive and let you make a jacket out of me for another night with her." He scoffed again. "*Left her.* Ha!"

Teddy didn't know what to make of that, so he hadn't said much else at the time.

Still didn't know what to make of it now, but it didn't seem so important when his brain was pounding away at the insides of his skull like someone buried alive in there.

Either his vision was going white at the edges or the flashbulbs outside the ring were blinking out like galaxies on their last legs. He didn't hear anything except for the Teddy Pemerbly's Brain High School marching band (specifically the percussion section) doing their darndest to breach a new threshold on the decibel scale inside the auditorium of his mind.

Plenty of people would say Teddy had lost a step. Anybody who just turned up would have a hard time refuting that statement, what with Teddy practically stone-cold dead on the mat and all. Hard to argue reality, that.

Only they'd be wrong.

Teddy might be on the mat.

But it was exactly where he wanted to be.

Black sneakers square-danced around to right next to his position–prone, bruised, and with a half-wit smile trying to peek through his thicker-than-a-bank-vault mouth guard. The sneaks stopped, assessing. This would be the referee. Teddy knew–from experience standing *up* in the ring while his opponent lay on the mat like a schmuck–that a countdown would be underway.

One, two.

The referee would be talking it out loud, letting the downed fighter know how much time he had before he needed to stand up or shut up.

Three, four.

For the life of him, Teddy didn't hear a damn squeak out of the ref though. Not unless the guy was talking in a single-frequency, high-pitched whine that seemed to emanate from an unknown cavern inside Teddy's skull. Teddy imagined one of those cave explorers (the kind who goes a mile deep into the darkest abyss looking for bats) taking a journey inside his fractured head, surveying the scene, and sending word up to base camp that things are even worse than they all feared. "Send help," they'd transmit up to those who might be able to do anything about it. Unfortunately for those intrepid explorers down below, base camp would get nothing coming up through the communication channels but that high-pitched whine. In fact, those explorers had been left for dead ages ago, the people up top already having mourned, performed their memorial service, and moved onto other things.

Those down below abandoned. Swallowed up my Mother Nature's insatiable appetite.

Spelunkers, was what they were called. The cave explorer guys. Teddy had looked it up once–taking care not to strain himself too bad from the effort. It even involved picking up a book. He'd learned about a cave in Vietnam that stretched almost six miles underground. Sơn Đoòng cave. Epic shit.

Five, six.

The bad guy lay prone on the mat, all of these leaching pains feeding off his energy stores. Teddy wasn't out of it, not by a long shot. The good guy in the fight–in life, hell–would have hopped right up, smile on his face, a double-glove-tap (I'm ready, Coach!) and an 'attaboy emanating from inside his soul like the chipper prick he was.

But the bad guy wanted to milk this moment.

Because in this moment, something was happening out there in the arena. Something boxers weren't supposed to think about when they were inside the ring. *Stop wondering, start punching.* These people here to see him lose smelled blood. They knew the bad guy was hurt. Was down. A little over a round left to go, too. Maybe there was still time to get in a bet on Nifty Nate? The odds were bad, but hell, it was a sure thing, wasn't it ...?

The high-pitched whine of Teddy's inner ear dissipated. In its place, another ringing sound.

A cash register.

Seven, eight.

A bunch of them, actually. Almost like a walk through the Vegas slot section.

In-match betting would be going on here. You don't wind up at a boxing match inside a church auditorium with a nightly matchup card like this one if you didn't like to gamble. And pre-fight gambling simply wouldn't cut it for you, either.

There were too many chances to lay out some more action to pass up.

Teddy got to a knee, then to his feet.

He stood up and looked the square-dancer ref in the eyes.

"I'm good," he said through the mouth guard.

"You good?" the ref asked.

"I'm good, motherfucker," Teddy said, scowl on his face, his voice loud enough so that Nifty Nate could hear. The bad guy didn't mess around.

"He's good," the ref said to the ringside crew.

The crew nodded and said something back to the ref.

Further out, the crowd murmured. So close they'd been to getting what they wanted. The bad guy had been down.

Now he was up.

Did he look shaky? Tired? Fucking concussed?

Yeah, yeah, yeah.

And maybe still, he'd go down in a heap of his own making.

Everybody wanted to see that.

Just to be sure the crowd got what they wanted and then some, Teddy figured he'd give 'em a show. Let 'em see exactly how much he valued their opinion of him.

The bell rang to end the fourth round.

Some–*most*–felt it came just in the nick of time for old ass Teddy Pemberly.

And those that didn't soon did. Because Teddy walked toward his corner and climbed the post. He raised his arms overhead and beat on his chest, giving the crowd his best come-at-me, I-dare-you stare.

The crowd roared in disapproval. Once again they shifted and swayed with unseemly aggression. They tossed a few beers toward the ring, but their pansy-ass pitchers didn't even have the arms to reach.

The bad guy was here. And he wouldn't let the people forget it.

Only one round left. The fifth.

They'd see.

They'd all see.

SIX

Jab, jab, hook, jab, hook, jab, *HOOK*.

Nifty Nate wasn't the golden boy any longer. Not when his back was up against the wall.

Now he was a savage. A caged animal. Fighting like he caught rabies.

The crowd murmured, cheered. Their collective heartbeat grabbed a quick flight down to Colombia for party favors and flew all the way back up on their own beating arms. They grit their teeth with a whine, gnawed their fingers down to stubs. Sweat and spit and vapor floated in the air like a summer rainstorm had just come through.

All the while, Teddy blocked, blocked, ducked, shifted, blocked, ducked, *ATE IT*.

Another knockdown. Another song that only he could hear. A requiem for how his brain used to be.

The mat was no more forgiving this second time. Teddy didn't just lay on it in the prone position, he melted into it. This time struggling to keep his eyes from crossing up like Iverson. He was pretty sure he was still breathing, but Nifty Nate had served him up with something nasty–ten thousand pounds of pressure on his chest.

Maybe they'd call him that after this match: Nasty Nate. The former golden boy.

Nate was now a wild, dangerous individual. Wanted in three states. Considered armed and extremely likely to make everybody a boatload of money on tonight's fight.

Could even be the new bad guy, huh? Maybe was being groomed to be just that.

Teddy–through an electrical surge of pain rushing down his spine and neck–turned slightly to look over at Wallace.

Toward the kid.

Wallace sat like an eclipse on his stool, one hand on his hip bone (like something an archaeologist might dig up), other hand on the very edge of the mat outside the ropes. He was nowhere near the action, which (so much as it even was action at this moment) was at the approximate middle point in the ring. *There lied Teddy Pemberly, former boxer, about to cross over to be with Jesus.* Wallace's eyes were still and cold. Two pits staring out from the dark side of the moon. As if he were watching his best friend betray him.

Teddy figured that was a pretty good approximation for what was going down.

Behind Wallace, the kid was barely visible. Daylight on the horizon. Peace at the frontier. The kid stood pressed up against the cheap aluminum barricade that kept the sweating, screaming, unwashed masses from charging the ring. Another few inches, the kid might get turned into string cheese squeezed through the slots.

Even still, the kid stood expressionless. Hands not even white knuckling the metal as he held it, his knuckles bruised and battered like he knew a thing or two about fighting himself.

Maybe because he did.

Maybe because Teddy had him hitting the speed bag twice a week. The heavy bag every other day. Jump rope twice each day, along with calisthenics to beef him up a bit. A way to keep some of the rougher elements of the In Christ We Believe Orphanage, where the kid lived, at bay.

Teddy heard the ref's countdown this time. A miracle on par with their current location in a house of worship (or at least next to one).

Six, seven.

Teddy didn't hear a peep from Wallace. The big man seemed to get what he was witnessing. Maybe he wasn't happy about it, but he wasn't going to say so. "It's your fight once you step in the ring," Wallace was fond of saying–less an abdication of duties than a way to keep Teddy focused during the grueling months of training.

Teddy heard Louie, though. Inside his skull, but still. "Might be your last payday before we send you to the glue factory. Let's get that winner's fifty-percent take from the door and you can finally get that pool."

Eight, nine.

Louie didn't have enough sense to recognize Teddy lived in an apartment in the city. Nothing fancy. Just enough for a guy with soup for brains to spend his days, plenty of delivery places for when his knees went to shit, plenty of ladies for when he got lonely, and plenty of floors below him in case the darkness inside of Teddy ever got too deep and menacing to flee.

There was no pool there.

No.

But there was one at the In Christ We Believe Orphanage.

Or at least, there would be, once Teddy got done being counted out.

The ref hesitated.

Teddy let himself fall into the mat. His whole career, his entire self-worth falling in with it. He was a spelunker tonight. Taking a dive, getting as far into the murky dark as any fighter could ever go.

He just hoped that in the end, it didn't swallow him up whole.

Ten.

Ding, ding, ding.

The bad guy lost.

SEVEN

Only, the bad guy didn't. Not really.

Teddy's whole body was swollen. The locker room quiet, dark. Loser-lonely. Lockers almost big enough to get stuffed into, like the weakling loser he now was.

"We should have put you out to pasture after the last one," Louie had said right after. Some people might have been able to say this kind of thing in a *mea culpa* way. *I put you in this spot, Teddy. That's on me.* Somehow Louie made it seem like Teddy had been the one at fault. Like he hadn't been the one laying it all out there inside the ropes.

Teddy didn't mind. His head hurt too much to mind. And besides, he'd done the bad thing.

Fitting for the bad guy.

Louie paced around like an aardvark on a coke binge. Teddy still had stars in his ears and ringing in his eyes, but he could see that Louie was, uh, a bit agitated. Smell it, too, the nervous sweat fuming off his manager like a chemical spill.

"FUCK!" Louie slammed an extra folding chair against a wall of lockers. Slamming it again and again and again, punctuating each creative combination of cuss words as he did so. As if the lockers were the ones who'd just lost the fight.

Yeah, he was maybe a little more than agitated. Teddy was having trouble coming up with the word. But it was a strong one, whatever word you wanted to use.

The little bit left of his mind hovered somewhere above the whole scene, detached from the throbbing pain of the rest of his body. Still feeling it, but also seeing it from somewhere else, too.

"You were expecting something different," he said. "A different outcome."

"A different outcome? The hell is this, Shakespeare? I was expecting you to come through for me! To win the damn fight against that two-ply golden boy out there."

Louie picked back up the chair and continued tapping out the beat of his anger on the lockers.

Teddy lowered the ice pack from whatever part of his face it was in contact with. He'd stopped being able to feel awhile ago. "Guess that will be something you can talk to Nifty Nate about, now that you manage *him*. Though I was thinking, you might want a rebrand. Get ol' Nifty mad, another side of him comes out."

Louie stopped mid-slam with the chair. He looked at Teddy's face, searching–probably in vain–for the fighter's eyes.

"Nasty Nate, maybe." Teddy shrugged, unable to come up with any other nicknames. "I don't know, something to think about."

A small bomb might have gone off somewhere inside Louie. But on the outside, nothing doing. Like maybe somebody hit the pause button on him.

Teddy had little control of what was going on with his face at the moment. But he hoped he smiled.

Hoped his eyes said, *Yeah, fuck you, too, Louie.*

Teddy thought they might have done just that, because Louie threw the chair halfway across the room. It broke into pieces after hitting the wall. Then he stormed out, huffing and puffing, saying something about never working again with rent-a-fighters, that he was going to finally take his talents to the big time.

Yeah, yeah, yeah.

Wallace had wandered in and out after Louie left. A mass moving through the post-fight pity party. Like a celestial body revolving around the imploded dark star of its galaxy. Wallace didn't say a single word, just tended to a few of Teddy's cuts and changed out his ice. If he knew what went down, he didn't say.

That suited Teddy just fine.

Eventually even Wallace left him alone.

So Teddy was left to think about it—all of it—by his lonesome. His conclusion (as best he could come to one with pea soup for brains): *Shit. All that for nothing.*

The kid appeared from the dark corners of the locker room. He'd disappeared into the crowd once the bell went off. Now he stood amongst the shadows thrown off from the yellow incandescent light flickering above him.

"What the hell?" was all Teddy could manage. The inside of his mouth hurt like he'd gnawed on glass. Ribs and lungs didn't feel so hot either. The rest of him would feel like shit later on, once the real soreness set in.

But the burn of the bad guy never dies. Even for a washed-up has-been like himself, something had been at stake here.

Burn, burn, burn.

The bad guy isn't so happy. "You show up here alone? Was that part of the plan, kid?"

The kid instinctively stepped back. Half-a-step. Maybe less. Even a mangled and mauled Teddy Pemberly could strike fear in a kid.

Only for an instant, though. The kid's eyes went from saucers to daggers. He balled his hands into fists.

He stepped forward into the yellow light, which seemed to flicker again. This time like it was almost cowering.

The kid said, "Dennis got into that stuff again. He could barely tie his own shoes three hours ago when I left him. How you think he was gonna do once we got here?"

Dennis was the third leg of their whole *fecocked* plan. Dennis worked at the orphanage. A social worker who shouldn't have been–too much social and not enough worker. He had a good heart, but he couldn't turn down a beer or a pill to save his life, and most of the time he didn't seem to care so much about said life to even bother trying. And once Dennis started, the rest of the night was as inevitable as death, taxes, or brain damage for a guy like Teddy. Shoe tying would seem like quantum physics compared to his capabilities.

Teddy's burning rage smoldered and flamed up. "I took a fuckin' dive, kid! You have any idea what that means?"

A smirk. Tightening of the eyes.

"Something funny?"

The kid jumped up on one of the locker room benches. The bulb above him flickered, but somehow burned brighter. "Oh, ye of little faith." Unlike Teddy, the kid was pretty smart.

He produced three betting slip receipts from one pocket of his hoodie.

A stack of folded cash as thick as an encyclopedia from the other.

"How the hell–?"

"Told some creep he better put in the bet for me."

"Oh yeah?" Teddy said with a relieved sigh. Behind his eyes, the pressure of a thousand storms was building. "Why would this creep do a thing like that?"

The kid smiled. "Told him I'd scream he was a dick diddler if he didn't." The kid was young still and couldn't help but giggle at this.

"I'll be damned," Teddy said.

Only he figured he wouldn't be. Or if he was, it would be for something else he'd done. Plenty to choose from after all.

Tonight, though, he was pretty sure he'd done the *right* thing for once.

The bad guy cashed in for the kid.

"Was hoping I might see your manager on the way in," the kid said, looking back over his shoulder toward the locker room entrance. The kid peeled a bill off the fat stack. "Maybe give him a little tip."

"Easy. Don't get so confident now." Last thing Teddy needed was the kid turning into a two-bit hustler.

"What? He was trying to play you."

Teddy sighed. Louie was definitely doing that, yeah.

"He goes down in the fifth," Louie had said on the phone after he thought Teddy had gone to the showers. It was the night before the fight, in the gym, Louie doing what he always did: talking on the phone.

It was all Teddy could do not to slam through the locker room doors and set Louie straighter than Wilt Chamberlain. If he thought Teddy was taking a dive, he had another thing coming.

Only ...

"Yeah, the golden boy will be our golden goose. Odds are opening their legs for us right now, ready for us to stick it in, baby. A bet like ours–if placed strategically at the right time–could be lucrative. More so than my first divorce was for my wife. You understand?"

Teddy couldn't believe it. His *opponent* was going to take the dive? *That* fact might have been even more insulting. Nifty Nate would hit the mat alright. But it would be by Teddy's hand.

But instead of barging into the gym and playing speed bag with Louie's face, he listened.

Listened as his little slime ball manager cupped a hand over the receiver and hunched his back forward as if he could smother the sound of his own voice.

He might have had better luck just turning his lazy ass around and making sure nobody was around to hear.

What Teddy heard from all this listening was Louie drawing up a scheme to profit off Teddy's bad guy image. "Nifty Nate is the golden boy. Young, but too green to win this fight. Teddy is old, but tough as they come. He won't let this pretty young thing take him down unless he catches a heart attack in the ring. And let me tell you, he might be shaking like an earthquake and sipping his meals through a straw in a few years, but one thing Teddy Pemberly's got is heart."

Instead of being flattered or getting angry, Teddy decided to just take the advice Louie'd been giving him for about as long as they knew each other. He'd been telling Teddy for years that smarts weren't really his thing, after all.

Well it didn't take a genius to see an opportunity like this one.

"People eat up the *story*," Louie said, taking his hand away from the phone to unleash a tobacco-soaked loogie. "Nobody wants to bet on the bad guy. They all want the golden boy to win. Early lines are coming in at three-to-one in favor of Nifty Nate, and our street team marketing in the next twenty-four will kick it up a notch. That's our chance. We bet Teddy to win by knockout in the fifth. Then we start slumming it on yachts in Saint-Tropez."

The strategy was sound. People would bet heavy on Nifty Nate because they wanted him to win. Everybody wanted to hitch their wagon to a rising star, not the aging bad guy. And whatever anybody ever tries to tell you about gambling, don't let 'em say they do it with their brain.

Heavy betting on Nate to win meant the odds would shift. Payouts for people who bet the other way, on Teddy, would grow. That was exactly what Louie was trying to tap into.

And Teddy's typical antics in the ring–even before he hammed it up tonight for the crowd–would only drive more people to bet on the golden boy, driving odds up even further.

But the bookie needs to even out at the end of the day. He wants an equal amount of money on both sides of the bet. Living off the vig, that's the bookie life.

So that same bookie would be more inclined to take an asteroid-sized bet once Louie placed his own. The way it would work was Louie's big money wager on Teddy to win by knockout in the fifth would create an imbalance. To re-balance things, the bookie would need to change the odds to make the Teddy-to-win-in-the-fifth bet *less* attractive to bettors. Meaning its opposite–a Nifty-Nate-to-win-in-the-fifth bet–would become *more* attractive.

That represented the opportunity Teddy needed. Other than betting on himself to win–something he pretty much already did with his health, life, and future welfare each time he stepped into the ring–there was no other play that would deliver big money. Betting on Nate to win *before* Louie placed the bet would simply have the same odds, which weren't great since so much money was riding with Nate. And there was no guarantee that Teddy *would* win, even if he did bet on himself. Least of all in a certain round. Boxing matches were hard enough to win on their own.

No, it had to be a bet placed on Teddy's knockout right after Louie's bet created the imbalance of money for the house. The void would need to be filled with something.

Besides, that outcome had the added benefit of screwing over Louie, who was apparently managing both sides of this fight without ever having mentioned it. Convenient.

Up until Teddy slammed into the mat in the fifth, everything had been going exactly according to Louie's plan.

It had also been going according to Teddy's.

"How much you get?" Teddy asked. "All twenty?"

The kid smiled again. This time his eyes went big. Sơn Đoòng cave big.

"What?" Teddy's mind working in freeze-frame. Did the kid not have enough dough to bring this thing all the way across the finish line?

"I got forty-seven."

"Forty-seven? Thousand? How'd you manage that?"

The kid smiled but didn't say.

"Guess you'll be getting the Olympic-sized pool, then, huh, kid?" It would be above-ground, so maybe not *quite* that big. But bigger than the zero square feet of pool the orphanage currently housed.

The kid nodded. "Maybe even a hot tub. Invite some ladies over."

"Easy, kid." He didn't need the kid turning into a player, either.

But despite himself, Teddy sat back against the cold steel of the lockers and smiled. Or tried to. His pain already fading.

He sensed his face was too swollen and tight for the smile to actually come through.

Better that way, anyhow.
Bad guys were only supposed to enjoy being bad.
And for once, Teddy did good.

LANE CHANGE

INTRO

Many of my stories are almost like fishing lures placed into that subconscious sea I mentioned in the introduction. There are far more lures bobbing up and down than I will ever have the chance to fish. Ideas for stories are cheap and easy, whereas the actual finished product requires quite a bit of time, focus, and effort to produce something I'm happy with.

But every once in a while, one of these lures bobs and catches my attention. And often times–and here is where this analogy really gets stretched to the limit–the lures crisscross on themselves and require my attention.

In the case of this story, I was thinking about, as I often do, snipers.

(Not in a weird way, of course, just like ... about them).

Okay, my lawyers tell me I should clarify that statement, given today's social climate ...

You see, I've always kind of had a thing for snipers. For sniping in general, I guess you could say. It's always been a reader fascination for me, like serial killers (both fiction and non), bank robberies, cat burglars/burgling, certain historical periods, psychological fiction, etc. You know, all the lighter sides of the world.

But snipers always seemed so ... cool. I mean, they are as stealthy as can be. They possess great patience, fortitude, focus. They are able to kill just as effectively up close as they do from a mile away. They are badass.

Other than it being a frequent topic I thought about, I can't really remember *why* I was thinking about snipers around this time. It may have been because I was–and still am–considering putting together a sniper anthology of stories (maybe *Nizpatches Volume Five: Sniper Stories?*). I have written a few sniper stories already, but still need a few more to round out a collection.

And so I had snipers on the brain.

Pair that with a location. A story set in the sunny warmth of Downtown Miami, maybe? Hm. Sure. Yeah, I think that could work.

I remember exactly where I was when that kernel of this story flowed through my fingers and onto the page–as much to my surprise as anybody else's. Another plane ride, this one returning from, you guessed it, Downtown Miami.

Sometimes it's truly a wonder where these Great Insights come from.

After a dinner seated along the water of Biscayne Bay, driving back to my hotel, I spotted one of Miami's many harbors from the highway. It seemed so darkly majestic, so intriguing, that I had to set a story there. Rather than whatever landmarks had originally caught my attention, I decided to switch things up a bit. We would be at a restaurant instead.

Well, not exactly *at* a restaurant ...

But close enough.

The rest of what makes this story what it is all developed on the fly as the words poured out, the situation got tenser, and the ending finally emerged in startling clarity.

Enjoy!

WRITERS OF THE FUTURE AWARD FINALIST

NIZ THOMAS

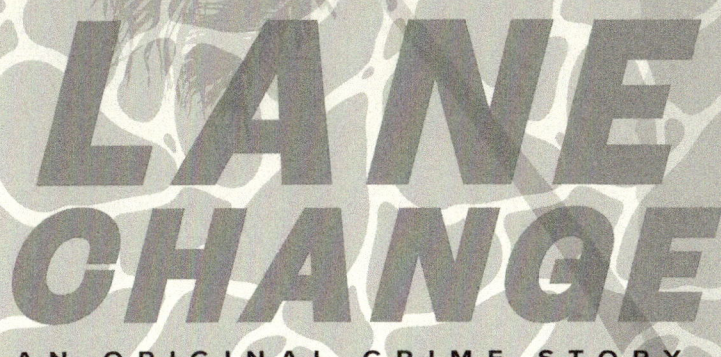

LANE CHANGE

AN ORIGINAL CRIME STORY

ONE

As far as Arthur was concerned, some things about Miami didn't feel like they'd ever change. Top of mind at the moment was the fact that the city was crawling with scumbags who deserved far worse than Fate (or whatever one believed in) seemed capable of doling out.

One thing that *was* different, though—and something Arthur could really get behind—was that snipers never had it this good.

Arthur was in the prone position on his belly, floating in opulent luxury aboard his thirty-meter yacht just offshore Downtown Miami's coast. It was late-October after the hurricanes had drifted out of everybody's consciousness and the temperature was just as perfect as you could imagine—especially now in the early evenings.

Conditions were so perfect—both for comfort and for what Arthur was there to do—that he would hardly need to account for much to ensure a smooth, accurate shot.

The veranda of the Masquiatt Grille was centered on a long cement outcropping which jutted into the dark downtown Miami water like a short chin, the waves of the unprotected shoreline lapping against the faded and erosion-smooth concrete like tired kitten paws against their owner's calves.

Arthur noted the falling sun—a problem at the moment as it descended just above the roof of the Masquiatt, a red Spanish tile slant which covered much of the veranda in a long shadow punctuated only by fingers of blinding light leaking through toward the veranda, the water, and most crucially, Arthur's vantage. The sun's light was blood orange and red as it leaked through alleyways on either side of the restaurant and a sliver of space in the roof that had crumbled long ago into the sea, never to be replaced, giving the place a certain Mediterranean flair.

Picturesque, no doubt.

But for Arthur, it was little more than a blinding nuisance. And so he settled in to do what all successful snipers did better than anyone.

Wait.

The Grille was not crowded but nor was it hurting for patrons. Ten tables on the veranda, eight full, one two-top open with a pending couple at the hostess stand deciding on indoor or outside dining. They'd be wise to take it inside, Arthur thinks (they're wearing white in an area soon to encounter a forecast of pink mist), but he just watches as the woman hems and haws and finally decides it's just divine out and why not watch the water while they dine?

That's alright. After all, Miami dry cleaners have plenty of practice with far worse stains than what's in store for that couple.

The restaurant serves fish, of course, though it has no smell to Arthur. It wouldn't fry anything—heavens no, not with this lean, beautiful clientele—but Arthur had no sense for how anything else might be prepared. He might be able to smell a fry kitchen from here, but fresh fish prepared well? No chance unless the limp wind picked up and did a one-eighty. Grilled halibut? Smoked salmon? Butter-roasted cod? Impossible for him to say from this distance. But what he was here to do didn't leave him with much appetite.

A quick scan of the tables could tell him, but Arthur knows this was not the sort of detail that would help him in this situation. Whether they were eating fish and chips or diamond-encrusted caviar mattered not.

All that mattered was what he was there for.

There, of course, was a bit of a relative term. The restaurant was *there*. Arthur was somewhere else. Four hundred thirty-three yards away on his yacht called *Terminal*, elevated roughly ten feet from the water and six feet from the front of the concrete chin (depending on how high or low the light chop of waves beneath *Terminal* kept the ship in their buoyant embrace).

Arthur lay flat. Hidden in the folds of the ship, so to speak, though not overly so. Anyone on land doing countersurveillance would likely have seen him without much trouble. Wearing clothes—white linen pants and a white seersucker shirt—on a yacht off the shores of Miami would be the first tip-off. Most wore skimpy speedos or thong bikinis or absolutely nothing at all. Even people who were as aged as Arthur, though he kept in far better shape than nearly everyone twenty years younger (often—and this was a sad fact for humanity at large, but certainly down here in Miami—the older and in-worse-shape-one got around here, the less they gave a hoot what others thought, so you got some *really* interesting clothing choices from people dressed like they weren't just angry at the rest of the world, but in fact wanted to maim and to injure the psyches of those they came into contact with by providing a free, unsolicited show that nobody wanted to see).

The other tip for the discerning viewer, aside from Arthur's clothes, would likely be the very cleverly named M2010 Enhanced Sniper Rifle steadied atop its included bipod and set on a piece of white rubber car floor mat Arthur had procured from an auto body shop that catered to the high-end cars (for most places, though not necessarily for Miami). Arthur had gotten the floor mat especially for this occasion, and bought the good stuff to ensure the rubber legs of the bipod did not come into contact with the fiberglass of his boat. Despite the bipod's rubber legs, there was always a chance of slippage against such a perfectly shined surface as this yacht. Any floor mat would have done that fine, but the good stuff—thick, rubberized, and coated for all elements—would hold better against the fiberglass, even if a storm moved through and produced humidity or precipitation. The rifle was also pressed tight against the fleshy part of Arthur's shoulder for stability when firing.

If he took his shot, it wasn't going to miss because it slipped from his grip.

So either the clothes or the roughly five-foot-long rifle would make it so anybody paying attention would know something nefarious was afoot atop the *Terminal*.

But nobody was. Paying attention, that is.

Nobody had any reason to.

Arthur glassed the veranda and the surrounding area. Countersurveillance did not concern Arthur. And not because he was careless–though a *strong* case could be made that not taking the time to properly canvas the kill zone prior to getting himself lined up for this shot was as careless as one in Arthur's position could get. The World's Strongest Man sort of strong case.

Arthur just didn't think the scumbag twenty-something kid had much in the way of funds, operational background, or lived experiences for security. Certainly not the sort of security that could deter a sniper team with the sort of experience aboard *Terminal*. Nation states and the highest levels of wealth had failed to stop them. And so Arthur didn't figure this kid–though surely privileged from birth–possessed the sort of resources to prove dangerous.

He sure had enough in the way of funds for this dinner, or for the club he would inevitably hit afterwards, or the late-night spot after that. Maybe not yet enough for a yacht like Arthur's, but from what Arthur knew of the kid, that hadn't ever stopped him from enjoying himself. *Rich thoughts, rich life.*

The prick.

Being enmeshed in genocidal geopolitical situations abroad, in civil wars, in counterinsurgencies hadn't bothered Arthur.

But something about this bastard prick kid sure did.

No–not *something*. Just the one truth that rose far above all the rest of the things Arthur knew about this lowlife scoundrel.

Sometimes it only takes the one thing before you can say for sure somebody deserves to die.

A multi-faceted existence be damned.

While his temperament was hot, the gentle breeze coming from his back did make things more palatable from a comfort standpoint. Low humidity on the day. Unusual for Miami. Arthur's hands were dry, his brow free of any dripping sweat or cracked skin. Not like most of the places he'd pulled the trigger from. He could even still smell the citrus lotion he'd applied earlier this morning, which someone managed to cling to his skin all these hours later without being even the slightest bit greasy. He would need to tell the wife that she'd made a fine selection for his birthday present this year. Fine indeed.

"You're having second thoughts?" Right on time and on target, as he would expect. The soft voice came from just beside Arthur on the ship's deck, so quiet that had he been any less keyed up, he might have thought he imagined it. As it was, when Arthur took to his rifle, his senses amplified all the way to eleven. He often felt he could hear the heartbeat of his target despite them never being closer than a few hundred feet. Out here on the water, it was actually sort of nice because the water allowed for him to more or less tune everything out as being nonessential for this shot.

"No," Arthur said, though he knew the words coming from Maggie were never spoken without purpose—especially not in a situation where guns were hot, so to speak.

Maggie did not move beside him (her ability to stay still was legendary), but Arthur *felt* her shift, emotionally speaking, as if preparing for something. "You should be, if you aren't. I certainly am."

"Well *that* is exactly what I was hoping to hear before putting my finger on the trigger."

"He's a kid, Artie." Maggie was the only one who could get away with calling him that. And even just that use of the pet name, something she'd been using since their first date all those years ago, was enough to raise the hackles on the back of his neck and arms. Back then, he'd almost walked out of the date entirely. Were it not for Maggie's impenetrable blue eyes, her amazing beauty, and the moxie to not just call him Artie, but to then double down and call him that again once he told her not to, then Arthur would have left the intimate jazz bar in Paris they'd selected as their first date venue and never looked back. In the intervening twenty-seven years, Maggie had loosened up on her use of *Artie*, but she'd never truly given it up. He could still keep steady aim and fire a perfectly placed round through this prick kid's forehead from three times as far away as he was right now, but use of the name *Artie* made that more difficult.

And Maggie would know that.

Maggie *did* know that.

"Kids are innocent, Maggie. Kids are *good*. You think this animal is either of those things?"

"Already fully 'othered' him? Impressive." There was no audible tone in the quiet of her voice, so maybe Arthur imagined it or projected it, but he felt like he heard his own wife shed some respect for him in the span of five words.

"Othering" someone was a term that he and Maggie both used, one that gave credence to something that every leader of men (and women) in combat had known since time immemorial: that it was easier to kill something who you thought of as *less than* human. It was a dark reality of the art of the sniper or the soldier or the hitman that they look at the craft of taking another's life as both a job (to be done professionally) and a service (to make the world better). Othering helped to make the latter more palatable. It allowed people like Arthur and Maggie to sleep at night, knowing they themselves were not monsters, but just people operating in an unjust and nasty world. Ridding the world *of* monsters, really.

Anybody who didn't need a little help on that front wasn't fit for this type of work. Too sociopathic, too thirsty for blood. A person like that might like this type of work, but nobody else in their right mind would want to work with someone like that.

Arthur chose to ignore her comment. "And another thing: kids are supposed to be protected from the world. By their parents, other adults, the world at large. Goddamn if everybody isn't wearing a big fat failure chain around their necks that this *kid* is walking around upright, sitting at his high-end restaurant ready to take in a fine dining experience. You think *he* needs protection, Maggie?"

Maggie said nothing.

"I didn't think so," Arthur said, pointlessly spiking the argument ball like a 'roided-up D-lineman who just picked up a fumble and took it back to the house. And for good measure: "There's someone I know who needed protection from him. That's for damn sure."

It wasn't usual that a husband and wife operated as sniper and spotter. Was, in fact, highly *un*usual. But that was how it went with Arthur and Maggie.

And sometimes that meant little spats like this one when they were out on a job.

Though this wasn't *exactly* a job, was it?

Arthur took a breath in through his nose and held it for the slightest of moments, steadying himself as the boat continued its gentle rock on the quiet ocean water. Box breathing. In for four, hold for four, out for four, hold for four. The ritual of it calmed him.

He had to focus if he was going to do this right.

And Arthur never did anything any other way.

But laying here glassing down this kid, something didn't feel right. Even though it felt *good* in this moment to think about the .300 Winchester Magnum cartridge enter and exit this prick's chest cavity, sending his innards on a mad scramble for the exit the same way an airplane passenger's body would if somebody threw open the emergency exit at thirty-five thousand feet—it still didn't feel *right*.

And that was where Arthur was experiencing a bit of dissonance.

Maggie had picked up on it. Was obviously feeling it herself. Gave voice to it, too.

Arthur, on the other hand, used his rather common male skill of ignoring this feeling, putting it away to fester and smolder like kindling.

And he plunged forward with his pre-shot preparation.

"Wind?" he asked Maggie.

Typically Jane-on-the-spot in terms of immediate response, Maggie hesitated.

"C'mon. We're not going to do this the whole time, are we?"

Maggie said nothing.

"I know you're used to being in charge," Arthur said, referring to the common misconception of The Sniper as either lone wolves or God-level force multipliers. The truth was, when they were in the field and he was behind the gun, Maggie was the team leader. Sniper teams were certainly lonelier than most other units and they could multiply the forward operating element's power (at least back when they served, before they both went private), but it was a team game between the two of them–and you could even argue it was a scale balanced in favor of Maggie. This time was different since they didn't have any kind of official (or even unofficial) mandate.

This was personal.

"Wind." Not a question this time.

"Hardly any."

Arthur nodded. Not exactly the answer he was looking for, but an answer nonetheless. He concurred with the assessment–the wind was almost negligible today, especially from such a relatively short distance. He adjusted his Leupold M5A2 scope accordingly. It was programmed and dialed-in to such an extent that it would allow him to fire at what appeared to be the prick kid, even though Arthur's rifle would actually be aimed elsewhere. Otherwise there was too much imagination involved. He'd be "aiming" at open space.

"What about humidity?"

"I don't think we should do this," Maggie said with a measure of both finality and an invitation for Arthur to share his own opinion. "Too rushed. Too reckless."

Arthur stretched his neck ever so slightly, though he did not lose visual through the scope.

"I agree with half that." It was certainly rushed. Arthur had learned of the prick target's actions only two days prior. In that time, he'd setup some very basic target monitoring–a fraction of what he would have done for a High Value Target in the field. He'd procured the weapon, which screamed Army Sniper, enough to lead the cops to the conclusion Arthur wanted them to draw. Recently in the news there was intimation that Central American narcos had linked up with a rogue element of the U.S. Army on logistics. Reading between the lines and intercepting traffic (both things Arthur and Maggie were exceptional at doing) told a clearer story: a small cadre of Army punks—dishonorably discharged due to suspicion of illegal activity while in uniform—had traded in their disgraced names for the desperado lifestyle by helping the cartels bring in drugs and smuggle out money, guns, and most likely women. The cadre was ex-Special Forces (or could at least talk the talk) because the same skills taught by one of the world's foremost tactical schools were arguably even more valuable to the narcos as they were to the Army itself.

So Arthur's use of this weapon to eliminate the prick kid would lead to suspicion of the kid being a player in some cartel drama—something the cops would certainly chase down, given the death at an upscale restaurant like this, but it would never blow back on Arthur or Maggie. Which was another skill part of the successful sniper's repertoire. Awfully hard to do the next job if you got caught on the one before.

Still ... he hadn't done the same kind of due diligence he was used to. While this prick was no High Value Target, it wasn't an excuse to cut corners.

But that was exactly what he was doing, wasn't it?

Arthur took a deep breath. He wasn't cutting corners on this one. He was just working fast. It wasn't reckless to kill this little shit.

It was street justice.

In this world, sometimes that was all you got.

And sometimes it was just enough.

"Humidity I've got clocked at fifty-two percent," he said, answering the question for Maggie. If he was wildly off base, she could tell him. But as much as he might have been rushing this, he didn't much want to lollygag through. While he was sure he could do this and not get caught (hence this not being a reckless move), there was no point in putting himself in the danger zone for longer than necessary.

The temperature was light and fresh, not unheard of for Miami in late-October, but much appreciated, surely, by all the residents on a day as beautiful as today. His Casio Mudmaster watch told him it was seventy degrees on the dot.

And that would do just fine.

Arthur, for his part, also appreciated this temperate weather. While he'd been in plenty of jungles or sandboxes or even places where it was so damn cold he had to adjust several feet in elevation of his shot because the cold bullets move slower than hot ones, he didn't mind cleaning up the world's scum in the beautiful clime of his adopted hometown of Miami. And today? Well, *today*, all he had to do was make calculations so small in nature that he almost didn't need Maggie for anything else but a confirmation of his own reads.

And part of him wondered whether that was all he *would* get from her.

"I'm not saying you're wrong, Maggie. But I still think this is the right thing to do."

She said nothing.

And after a time, Arthur returned his focus to the veranda.

Of the eight (soon to be nine) tables, Arthur was of course only interested in one–a three-top round table that housed two women and one boy-man prick kid asshole (Arthur could not think of him as simply *a man*, though he supposed that is what society called boys of this age and this level of immaturity these days). Prick kid would probably do just fine for the small amount of time until Arthur made him a *former* prick kid.

All three patrons wore stylish, professional attire (even *boring* attire, considering this was Miami), and drinking a round of rather pedestrian iced teas (or perhaps Arnold Palmers). Arthur had made sure of that much, following the waitress as she walked the order to the outdoor patio bar and then the bartender as they mixed the fresh juices together, adding nothing else that might have corrupted Arthur's job out here today.

Or from corrupting any of the patrons seated at the table with the prick kid (Arthur noted, trying to keep the hot-acid bile from circulating through his body and mind and composure).

In the foreground out over the water that lapped against the veranda's front chin, seagulls dipped and fell, their bodies going from white-grey shapes to dark silhouettes against the light of the sun. Arthur noted their upturned wings only allowing them to coast for a moment before they were forced to beat their wings, using their own effort to stay adrift. There was no hidden wind movement here—no sudden changes in air pressure which might affect the M2010's shot once Arthur put just the slightest of pressures onto the trigger.

Perfect shooting conditions.

And not a cloud in the sky or indication that would change.

But Arthur watched for several minutes nonetheless as the wind went from a whisper to nary even a gentle out breath, the massive palm leaves on either side of the veranda sitting as still as statues in their giant porcelain planters, the water going momentarily glassy. As if the entire scene was an animal waiting, waiting, waiting for that moment when prey enters the kill zone, unaware of the dangers lurking.

A good time for Arthur to complete his task.

Do it now. Be done with it.

Even through the dying light, he could have pulled the trigger. He'd shot many a rifle in situations far more chaotic and with far less visibility than this one. The sunlight was a problem with how low it sat along the backdrop which framed this scene. But it was not insurmountable. Nor would it keep him from doing what needed to be done.

Something *would*, however.

And it was a mixture of a nagging conscience and the fact that his wife—the person he trusted more than anyone else in the world—was nestled into a fold of their yacht not more than a few feet away from him. And despite the fact she hadn't climbed over and physically stopped Arthur from yet shooting, he could tell she was considering it.

He cursed. Didn't want to hear from Maggie another comment about why they should probably not be doing this right now. But that was like saying he didn't want to eat greens or moderate his intake of alcohol. He had no choice in the matter (so long as he wanted to keep himself a productive member of society) and was only the better for listening.

"Alright fine. What do you suggest we do, then?" He hadn't pulled up on the trigger or the scope, but he felt Maggie's invisible hands massaging his psychological shoulders, easing the tension and pressure of the pre-shot reality that Arthur was about to kill someone. A reality amped up even further when considering how it was all going to go down. On a non-combatant.

It wasn't exactly that it would burden him. It was just big time stakes in a game that very few people ever got comfortable playing.

Maggie was quiet for some time and Arthur wondered if perhaps she had only been playing games. Maybe this Socratic dialogue had only been to see whether Arthur could stick to his guns and shoot this kid. Like maybe if she could talk him out of it, he shouldn't have done it in the first place.

Or maybe Maggie hadn't thought far enough ahead to answer the question. That would be unlike her.

But then again, sitting a few hundred feet from a non-combatant ready to put a round through his body was pretty unlike Arthur. You kill someone in their line of work, they deserved it. They were "in-play." Maybe they weren't shooting at someone, per se, but they were pulling strings that resulted in someone getting killed, somewhere.

Or worse.

"We'll do what we always do," Maggie said.

It was almost as if Arthur himself had been shot through with a round. Only this one was imaginary and instead of cutting through flesh and bone and arterial walls, this one cut directly to the small semblance of himself that one might have considered a soul. There were plenty of times when he didn't think that still existed–if it ever had. Maggie always told him otherwise, though. And her constant presence as his spotter brought to him a measure of safety and protection against the acid so prevalent in all men who spent their lives ridding their world of others.

The one strong enough to dissolve who one is and everything they stand for.

"I don't know if I can do that." He meant it, though it may very well have been more a statement to prop himself up than a truth.

"All of us have the chance to make things right, no matter what has come before."

"This *is* our chance to make it right." Arthur bit his lip.

"It's not our place."

"When has that ever mattered before? Was it our place to decide the fate of O'Reilly in Belfast or Harlova in Ankara? How about the ones we took out during the purges in Zimbabwe or any of the countries in the Maghreb? Was it our place when we took those shots?"

Arthur sighed. Beneath him the boat rocked gently. Above him the fading sun turned to an awe-striking evening sky. All around him there was peace.

Even the birds were quiet.

And for one long moment of the soul, so was Arthur's mind.

But still he did not pull the trigger.

"This is what we do," he said.

"No. It isn't. Not really."

"So what happens if I do it? What then?"

It was Maggie's turn to take a long hard think about the situation and all its repercussions. As she did, the sun fell further in the sky, the very last rays of its light still visible from behind the restaurant, but only just. The lights on the veranda had come on, illuminating the diners in a warm glow that was powerful enough for Arthur to see everything through the scope of his rifle. Where before he could make out faces and features, now he could see even the tiniest of micro expressions on a patron's face. Despite everything in his body telling him otherwise, he trained his scope on the two women with the prick kid all seated together at the table. All three had blonde hair and accompanying light features. All three had similarly confident jawlines and sharp blue eyes. One of the women was perhaps three years older than the target, the other perhaps three years younger. All of them were a picture of youth, health, and wealth.

Arthur realized in that moment that they were family. Siblings. He hadn't a chance to properly clock them yet–a realization that shook him to his core. To have been ready to kill without identifying those inside the kill zone was a cardinal sin of sorts. Arthur was a good enough shot to get away with such an oversight, but still ...

He was being reckless. Maggie had said so, but seeing it for himself jolted Arthur from the brink of his quiet, seething rage.

The younger woman at the table stuck her tongue out at the target, who laughed with a genuine tenderness for the apparent ribbing from his sister. The eldest sister, while the more stoic of the three, smirked, the edges of her puffy pink lips turning up and revealing not even the faintest of wrinkles anywhere around her eyes or forehead.

They were quite a picture, these three. And seeing the prick bastard target in this comfortable element only served to humanize him against Arthur's own efforts to do the opposite.

"Family affair," Maggie said, as if reading Arthur's mind.

"Nice looking family," Arthur said.

They watched for a while, only the ocean's gentle soundtrack to accompany them.

"You never answered me before," Arthur finally said. It would be fully dark soon, and Arthur wanted to have a final decision locked in before then. It wasn't so much he needed it as he sort of felt a roiling sense of discomfort inside him. Like he just ate fish and found out it was days old. The sick hadn't set it in yet, but sometimes just the knowing was worse. "What would happen?"

The waiter came to the target's table, all smiles and gentle deference.

"Don't do it, Arthur." Maggie suddenly using his proper name. "It's like that Ghost of John song."

Arthur didn't know that one and said so.

"It's a nursery rhyme."

"Naturally."

Maggie sort of hum-sung it.

> Have you seen the ghost of John?
> Long white bones with the skin all gone
> Ooh ooh ooh oo-ooo-oooohh
> Wouldn't it be chilly with no skin on?

The little tune sounded familiar to Arthur but he sure couldn't place it. Sort of like a distant memory, long ago forgotten, but not totally lost to the strange architecture inside the mind.

Maggie spoke in two ways–either direct and exacting or in metaphor.

The former was impossible to miss in the same way a bullet through your abdomen was (and Maggie's directness could often feel exactly that way).

Often, the latter was several steps removed from Arthur's ability to leap from one concept to the other. It was a quirk of his wife, something he had long ago learned to love ever since she'd explained to him that firing a sniper rifle was like paint by numbers at long distance. Since that day, for whatever reason, Arthur hadn't missed a shot out in the field—and he never once took a shot without first thinking of that tidbit. The metaphor and the way she explained it was one of those things that simply clicked for him, and he forever after *just knew* how to do it right.

"I'll bite. And what about this situation would be like that song?"

"The question of the song is very simple. It's not about the ghost, nor about his temperature. Rather, the question the song brings forth is: who, exactly, was this John? And what kind of person ends up with no skin?"

"His ghost has no skin, though, right?"

"Ghosts don't have skin anyway. Not like you and me."

"Is that right?"

"That's right. And so the missing skin isn't really a ghost thing at all. It speaks to who John was as he lived. And, very likely, how he died."

Sometimes Arthur marveled at the types of things his wife thought about. It wasn't as if she were some housewife with all the time in the world on her hands. She often did as much or more research as Arthur for their missions. She trained with all the same weapons and held all the same proficiences—better, even, in many ways.

And yet she somehow found time to philosophize about things like this, then shoehorn them into relevance out here in the field. On their first few missions Arthur had thought it was just something to pass the time. Like a way she could keep their minds sharp and focused during the interminable downtime that sniper work required. But after a while, he recognized it more as a sort of subconscious sense of communication. Like there was something inside her that she couldn't turn off, even if she wanted to—some past-life educator, maybe. Maggie contained multitudes, as the saying went. And Arthur was just happy to have her, to know her, to love her–and for all those feelings to be reciprocated back.

Maggie said, "My money goes to John being a traitorous bastard– perhaps a pirate, a real scallywag, given the likely origins of the song in a late-middle century wharf town. So let's just say he's a pirate. I think he was probably tortured and skinned alive before finally passing to the other side. And forever after, those who did the deed sang about this John, not about how he died, but about what sort of thing haunted even John in the afterlife. It's maybe the origin story of every ghost who ever … uh … lived. And it served a purpose."

Arthur was at least following now. "Uh, okay? And?"

"And, the fact that his skin is all gone is not simply some temperature control problem for John. No. It is an eternal problem. Something for which he will pay forever after, due to how he lived in his mortal life. It is not deliverance from evil, but comeuppance for it. And it haunts John. And in the singing of this song, it's a lesson to all the folk of the wharf village not to live like John did, else your undying soul will never rest."

"Is that so."

"That is so."

Arthur took a moment with that. He wasn't sure he was putting the dots together. But some vague notion emerged ahead of his thoughts. "And you're saying I'm John?"

"Not yet, hon. But everybody has the capacity to be if they don't do what's right. That's how a song survives dozens of generations. It's universal."

Arthur bared his teeth and could taste the salt of the sea spray. Did Maggie just tell him his own conscience and eternal soul was on the line here? "Quite a statement from someone who helps to put down wrong- doers for a living, no?"

Arthur was uncharacteristically bristling from that deep analysis. Ready to put all that out of his mind. Whatever scant bit of wind there had been was now gone. He could see better, though the sun was not entirely gone beneath the horizon line. And, most importantly, the target presented himself toward Arthur's position at full mast–chest forward.

Asking for it.

A better target did not exist outside of a shooting range.

Screw it. Arthur was sick of the conversation.

He didn't acquire these skills with a rifle to be more diplomatic.

He sighted the kid.

Say goodnight, you fake-tough little bastard.

TWO

"Hold up," Maggie said. Arthur had a mind to flat ignore her and pull the trigger, but something in her tone told him not to.

He also hadn't gotten this far in life ignoring his wife.

"What?"

"White elephants," she said. Their code phrase for police on the scene. "In the parking lot."

Arthur took one last look at the smug face of his target, then the broad open spot of chest on the white button-down shirt, and finally with a blooming annoyance slowly scanned right away from the veranda and toward the parking lot situated to the right and just inland beyond the restaurant. From his vantage, a police cruiser crept into the parking lot. It drove low-rider slow through the rows of cars parked enjoying their meals, but it didn't stop yet. If it was looking for something, it hadn't yet found it. Or, if it was just cruising around killing time rather than arresting the punk criminal stuffing his face with the seafood tower, they didn't seem to be in any rush.

"Not a meter maid," Arthur said, tracking the cruiser, which was half-unmarked. It was a Charger sedan in dark blue with the windows tinted darker than was legal, even down here in Miami, but it had the dash and grille lights installed and an antenna that looked like it could summon extraterrestrial messages on the back. Arthur never understood why a car would take half-measures like this. It seemed, to a sniper's mind, antithetical to all sense. One either wanted to be seen as a show of force, in which case one opted for a tried-and-true cop car–something nobody would misunderstand. Or one wanted to blend in, be hidden amongst the populace, in which case didn't it make more sense to drive something inconspicuous? Perhaps a Honda Accord or a Chevy Equinox? But no, even cops had to show off and show out. Much to their detriment, Arthur figured it.

Either way, this development put Arthur squarely back in the waiting game.

And the measure of victory in this game was, of course, overcoming paranoia.

A less experienced sniper team would find this coincidence hard to overlook. A cop shows up to the scene of an execution, you tend to wonder who else might know what is going on.

But Arthur knew that only he and Maggie had any foreknowledge of what was going to happen here.

And there was not even a shred of a question about whether she would have done anything treacherous with that information.

Besides, even if he doubted her, she was on the hook here just as much as he was.

"Doesn't seem to be waiting for anybody. So I doubt very much they've suddenly uncovered the crime that brought *us* here." No cop in his right mind would ever rush an arrest like this in a restaurant without backup. And none seemed imminent.

The Charger looped around the lot again and idled beside a walkway that connected the parking lot to the front of the restaurant. Arthur had no line of sight to see who might have been coming in or out from the front door, nor what all might have been going on there. That didn't make him feel good about the situation. It was an unfortunate reality he'd had to accept if he wanted to relative safety of the boat and the water to ensure someone didn't accidentally stumble upon their sniper hide, but it sure did suck right about now. But he didn't panic yet. He and Maggie had been in far worse situations than this and lived through to the other side. They still had plenty of time and could easily pick up and be gone from sniper prone position and overwatch in a matter of seconds, sailing this yacht that nobody would ever be able to trace back to them back into the ocean. Worst case, a trained and astute cop would radio in to the Coast Guard, but the route Maggie and Arthur would take to return would cut out that possibility like a plastic surgeon looking at a lipo patient. Ditto their anti-radar capabilities. And really worst case, they would sink this thing to the bottom of the ocean, remove all trace of themselves, and be gone under cover of darkness faster than any Coast Guard–even one with the sort of skill and training as the Miami branch– could combat.

Arthur didn't move.

Neither did the cop car. Not for a long while.

"Something feel weird to you?" Arthur asked. If it did, he was somehow missing it. In the waning light, the cop's taillights had drawn a glow around where it was parked, an almost halo, as if to say that the car itself was not subject to the same rules and regulations as the rest. It wasn't just Arthur's sniper skills that tagged this thing as cop. It was everything about the damned thing–from the way it was parked to *where* it was parked, all the way down to the windows so dark they could blot out the daylight.

Maggie didn't answer immediately. Which Arthur took to mean she didn't think anything was wrong, either–even though a development like this should feel that way.

"Can't say it does," Maggie said. "Should feel like Ramadi, but it feels like a regular walk in the park."

Arthur hadn't thought of Ramadi in quite some time. And he was happy to keep it far from his mind.

"Funny coincidence, though, no?"

That prompted a snigger out of Maggie. "Coincidence" was a bit of an inside joke between them. It was common knowledge *there was no such thing as coincidence*. But try telling that to someone who once army crawled into a nest of venomous snakes, or who got planted in-country and had to hunker down while a once-in-a-lifetime rainstorm poured down on them, closing off all possibility of assassination during the only period of time it could go down, or who found themself stuck in an airport that was suddenly devoid of planes because of an outbreak of wildfire forty miles away that threatened to overtake an entire Saharan village if not tended to immediately.

If you were in the game long enough, coincidence was an impossible acquaintance to avoid.

"Far as I can tell, they're either biding time or here for takeout."

"Keep an eye on them, would you?" Arthur asked. He swung his rifle back toward the veranda where the waiter was clearing the last of the three plates from the target's table. The entire back half of the restaurant and the water were now engulfed with the darkness, a promise of night even despite the patio lights draping just enough twinkle on the place so that Arthur could clearly see faces up close. He centered the rifle again on the target and considered whether this shot was worth taking, whether the risk was worth the squeeze and all that.

But no, it wouldn't be.

Would it?

After the dinner course was half over, Maggie finally said, "They're still parked out front, if that's what you're asking."

Arthur blew out a breath. "Wasn't what I was asking. I asked what I was asking."

"Maybe you *should* be asking questions like that, since it looks like you're scoping down a, what, twenty-five-year-old kid out to dinner with his sisters while a police car waits out front. And maybe if those things don't register any alarm bells for you, you might consider whether *any* red flags exist that might give you pause for this mission."

Arthur bristled. He kept his eye on the glass, able even to see the day-old stubble on the target's face as he rubbed his palm against a cheek and smiled at his youngest sister. He didn't need Maggie trying to throw him because they were close to the end zone now.

Even if the line-to-go might be impossible to reach.

"Let's keep our morals about us, Art. Let the authorities handle this."

"The authorities had their chance already."

"Yeah and one guy blew it. But we could talk to them. It isn't written in stone."

"We could also just take care of this. Not rely on those thumbsuckers to do their jobs. Just because they get paid double pension doesn't mean they're any good at what they do."

"That's not what we do. Not like this."

"Maybe the way we do things isn't all that important, Maggie. Maybe it's just the things we do that matter."

That seemed to quiet Maggie for a bit.

And it was a bit longer than that before Arthur felt bad.

"Sorry," he said. "Attitude doesn't belong here."

Maggie sighed. "Nobody's perfect. I accept your apology."

They waited.

And still Arthur did not shoot.

THREE

The target held his glass up, indicating to both sisters that whatever he was about to say would be wise and worth listening to.

Arthur rolled his eyes. He wondered whether either of the sisters were sick of the kid's shit, his pomposity, his know-it-all attitude. Arthur had got enough of a taste of that doing his light recon and signals intelligence interceptions. It was a study in insufferability.

It did nothing to dissuade Arthur from the course of action upon which he now embarked.

The kid didn't seem able to exist without bristling anybody who wasn't similarly situated–meaning, anybody else who wasn't a total dickbag.

Arthur was pissed now. Growing agitated with each passing second that the target lived. The growing risks as the Charger idled. For all they knew, the cops were up close waiting for the hit on the target. Maybe somewhere behind them the Coast Guard or one of the maritime police units were closing in. A snare. Pulled slowly. Ever so slowly. Until finally it was too late to remove one's neck. Had Maggie never brought this up, Arthur would have already pulled the trigger and they would have cut tail, maybe even been halfway home by now. After apologizing to his wife, he'd sat there and watched the kid eat dinner. Luckily for the kid's longevity, Arthur could not actually hear what was being said. They might normally try and drop a wire on target, or utilize either ears in the sky or some kind of powerful directional mic, but it wasn't necessary for this operation. Nor was there time to get it figured out. And anyway, there was nothing the kid could say that would change Arthur's mind. They knew he was guilty. And it didn't figure he'd be discussing the topic with his sisters, anyway.

But since Maggie had gone and spoken up–and really even before that–Arthur'd felt strange about what he was about to do.

The waiter came by with the bill and dumped it with the oldest sister. Arthur's blood boiled thinking of this prick and what he'd done. In fact, just the faint thought of it sent Arthur's finger to twitching. As if some cellular synapse inside him was firing, trying to out-will his mind into pulling the trigger and putting this piece of trash down like the rabid animal that he was. The fact he wasn't picking up the tab shouldn't have mattered. But it did. And it did.

By god it goddamn did.

The waiter came back a few moments later and picked up the check, scurrying back to the card terminal to process it so the restaurant could turn over the table and get another diner on the docket.

It was this chance that Arthur would perhaps not get again. The bastard target sat there between his two sisters in a moment of quiet conversation, no doubt basking in his acquired confidence that a criminal feels once the dust settles on his crime and nobody has come a-knocking. He'd done something illegal, wrong, befitting scum of the earth–and he had gotten away with it. And maybe–if he was the sort of scum that stuck to your shoe and never really went away, but rather just picked up imprints of all the other muck and dirt and grime you stepped near through the rest of your days–then maybe he even *liked* what he'd done.

Liked it and now knew there was no one in this civilized world who would ever stop him from doing it.

Nobody except for Arthur.

The one unfortunate part of killing the kid now would be that said kid would never know who it was had gone and rubbed him out. But that was something Arthur had always contended with as a sniper. Usually it made no difference to him. The bad guy got dead, that was the important part. But for this job, Arthur wished for a little more poetic justice.

The waiter came back all smiles and niceties, no doubt trying to leave a pleasant taste in everyone's mouth aside from just the dinner. Tips could be legendary in this town, and even though his patrons were young, they were the sort of top breed that wouldn't even think it strange to open a menu and find eighty-dollar entrees.

Everyone at the table looked up at this waiter as he set down the check with the credit card run. He had interrupted some engrossing conversation, surely full of sophisticated tastes and intellectual curiosities.

For that moment, everything in the entire world went on pause.

And yet still Arthur did not pull the trigger. He willed himself toward it. Thought of young Annabelle, the girl who lived down the street in the gated, private community that Arthur and Maggie called home. Seventeen years old now. Not hardly a girl. Though they had known her since she was roughly seven.

Arthur and Maggie never had kids—their lives, their work, did not really allow for such dependencies. Dependencies that made it so holidays, extended family, even friends had to fall by the wayside. They were married to the job, as Maggie used to say. Their kids were the operations they sometimes spent months planning, sneaking behind enemy lines, living amongst the enemy, fading into the background before pulling the trigger and putting some problem of the world to bed. For good. But Annabelle was someone that Arthur had taken a shine to. Such a beacon of light, airy goodness as a seven-year-old girl who'd someone managed to get into Arthur and Maggie's backyard, despite all the hidden surveillance and countersurveillance measures in place, without tripping all but the last alarm (Arthur thankful to have such a harmless intrusion by this little girl so they could tighten up their security; much worse to find a disgruntled brother of some former target who decided to come pay a visit). Annabelle who had unknowingly overcome sophisticated security in search of her lost puppy who had run away earlier that day. Annabelle who, when Arthur spotted her in the backyard, looked up to him with the innocent doe eyes of a little girl and said, "You have a *lovely* home," like some sophisticated old maid who'd just come for a visit.

That Annabelle.

Over the years, Arthur couldn't say he'd gotten to know her. But he'd watched her grow up from afar. He was made aware of her around the holidays (the ones he and Maggie found themselves at home alone for, anyway), one year feeling tears form at the corners of his eye watching the ten-year-old Annabelle sing Christmas carols with a few other kids in the neighborhood. Christmas in Miami was always a weird thing–no snow, no cold, no seasonally appropriate trees–but that year it had felt like the most right thing in the whole wide world. Maggie, too, had a taken a shine to the girl. One year when Annabelle was maybe fifteen, Maggie watched from down the street as Annabelle snuck back into her own property at an hour that was surely far past the girl's bedtime. Maggie had been on a midnight walk around their gated community. Something to help her sleep after a mission had left her jet lagged and a little stir crazy. And it was the recognition of something like a kindred spirit that tugged at Maggie's little heart string in much the same way as those doe eyes had done to Arthur.

The target cornered her, was what she'd told the police. It was a party, sure. But she didn't want to party *like that*. Hearing the little girl that was still very much alive in Arthur's head speaking like a mature woman was a mindfuck that Arthur had not expected. Of course the little girl was grown up. Maggie so much as found that out when they almost crossed paths on the midnight walk. Arthur had known as much. But to hear that girl's voice sounding like a woman's, using words like *drugs* and *sex* and *torturous*, well ... something inside Arthur broke that day.

He hadn't been looking for this. God no. Even someone as jaded and eye-clearingly weary as Arthur would never have dreamt to wade into those waters.

But he and Maggie kept a close eye on everyone living on their private island community. And that included the cops. Not because they were nosy, Arthur and Maggie. No, no. Just because they were careful. Certainly they were the very opposite of reckless. And because of this close eye (or in this case, ear), that was how Arthur came to hear the conversation between the sleepy detective Zack Tilson and Annabelle, as the former took down the complaint and resultant report by the latter.

Anybody who had half a brain and lived through the past two decades could have written it. A kid at a college party. A girl too young to be there but too brash and independent to realize that fact. The kid cornered her in a hallway of the house, drinks flowed. He pressed himself up against her until she opened the only door she could access, and then found herself alone in a room with said kid. Alone in a room with a closed and locked door, once the kid got through doing that. Alone in a room while he smiled lasciviously (another word that spun Arthur's head, he heard Annabelle saying it).

"He licked his lips like some sort of ... wild animal ... predator," Annabelle said to Tilson between gasping sobs.

Alone in a room while the target did what it was he'd done that eventually sent Annabelle to the police.

"T-T-There ... was nothing in his eyes ... but coldness."

Christ. If there was ever a time for Arthur to finally act like someone his age and just drop dead where he stood, it would have been then.

And maybe it would've been a mercy.

But no. No mercy on that day as he sat stunned to stillness in his office, listening to Annabelle's voice, Arthur wishing he could crawl through the thick jumble of telecommunications equipment and stand in the room with her, hug her, comfort her, do any such thing that might make the girl feel even the slightest bit better.

Instead all he could do was listen and try to keep calm enough to keep his heart from exploding.

Listen to just how alone Annabelle had felt.

Alone and scared.

When it was done—all twenty-five minutes of it to give an idea of how thorough Tilson was (Arthur having had haircuts that lasted longer). In front of Arthur there were four broken pencils in a heap and a splotch of blue India ink staining his leather desk mat from where he'd bent the nib of his Montblanc Steinway until it burst open. Arthur vowed to do the same to the prick bastard of a kid. Until Maggie patiently listened to Arthur's rant and finally talked some sense into him. There was no way even Zack Tilson could screw up an investigation like this, given how eloquently Annabelle had spoken, how clearly she'd described the assault on her. *There was just no way. Just have faith.*

It was a moment of staggering naivete from a woman who was anything but.

But Arthur had listened. Surely, something would come from the investigation.

Two days later, Annabelle was back in the station. Arthur was listening. And this time, he was watching, too. Now that he knew what to look for, he had practically been standing guard on the precinct house's surveillance and security systems, having tapped into them shortly after Maggie had pulled him back from the precipice of the scorched earth doctrine. He hadn't noted a lot of hustle up from Tilson, but maybe, just maybe, there was something had slipped through the cracks of Arthur's surveillance.

From the first moment of the conversation between Annabelle and Tilson, Arthur's blood could have boiled the oceans.

"I'm wondering, Annabelle," Tilson started off and his tone, his goddamn tone, was already more aggressive than any cop investigating this kind of crime ought to be. Ever. Unless he was speaking to the perpetrator of the crime. "What were you wearing that night? I went through my notes twice and it seems you never mentioned it."

"That's cause you never asked, you lazy sack of shit! Not that it makes any bit of goddamn difference!" Arthur was up at his desk. Luckily there were no more pencils to break. But he was about as cool and collected as a prisoner on steroids who just initiated a jailhouse riot. Arthur had been in conflict zones his whole life and could never remember raising his voice the way he had to the grainy video feed on his computer as he watched Tilson start off this follow up conversation.

Maggie entered the room shortly thereafter. She turned off the hacked video and audio feed not long after that, knowing all too well it wasn't doing a bit of good for Arthur. Not to mention the questions were even pissing Maggie off–something hard (and strictly inadvisable) to do. It was there, in Arthur's office, that they decided to take matters into their own hands.

And now here they were. Ready to do it.

At the table on the veranda, the older sister signed the receipt without hesitation–without even hardly looking at the damn bill–and they were, all three of them, through the veranda's doorway and lost in the intimate darkness of the inner sanctum of Masquiatt Grille seemingly as quickly as the round from Arthur's rifle could reach them.

"You made the right choice," Maggie said once there was no chance Arthur could confidently take a shot.

Arthur grunted. He wasn't so sure about that. What he *had* done was let a target walk when he could have been buried dead. And unlike some of the people he'd been charged with taking out, this one was confirmed to be a wrongdoer. Way wrong. Who knows? Maybe the kid had plans later to find another girl and do with her what he'd already gotten away with once. Maybe he'd take it even further this time, the way so many first-time criminals do, since there didn't seem to be any blowback for such behaviors.

The way Arthur himself almost just had, perhaps.

"Damnit." He already felt shame and that strange feeling when put up against a hard choice to only come away having selected the spineless option. "Goddamnit."

"It was right, Arthur. Just. And now we help to work it the right way."

"The right way just evaporated when that prick walked out the door."

"Now, now Arthur," Maggie said, tiptoeing on the precipice of chiding and caring. "Don't get all hung up on one target."

Plenty of husbands would have snapped at their wives after a comment like this, but Arthur was the opposite. Getting all hung up, making things personal out in the field ... well, that was the way dead men operated. Anything besides clinical, exacting, and ruthless efficiency was dangerous.

Deadly.

Besides, it was only the true lowlife husbands who did things like this, bickering with their wives, or putting them down for having something approaching an opinion. Arthur had never been like that. He liked to think of it virtuously, but it very well could have been due to the fact that his wife was just as (if not more so) dangerous than he was.

Now that the target had walked through that door and out of sight, Arthur frankly felt a potent cocktail of strange emotions surrounding this particular job. Or failed job, was how he now thought of it. First, he felt an intense pressure inside his chest–something often times relieved once he saw pink mist downrange. This wasn't so much nerves (there was likely some of that, sure), but rather the tension of a job unfulfilled having finally been completed. Snipers had a strange dichotomy to account for. On the one hand, they had the most clearly defined and consequential target known to man. Kill another. And yet, on the other hand, snipers also had the ultimate task opacity. Hardly ever was the target to be killed a certain way or from a certain place or with any specific weapon. All that ambiguity–security, approach, escape–was left to the shooter and his spotter to decide. It was pass/fail at the highest levels of consequentiality. So that undone task was what created this knot of tension inside of Arthur. He often didn't sleep more than a few winks each night until the job was complete.

And after going toe-to-toe with this prick bastard, he might not sleep right again ever.

But there was also an intense sadness inside Arthur. And he felt actually that it stemmed not from deciding against taking the shot but rather the fact that he was close to taking the shot in the first place.

"You were right," he admitted to Maggie. Plenty of husbands made it their life's mission never to say those three words to their wives, but Arthur wasn't one of them, either. Frankly, if husbands ever put their literal lives in the eyes, ears, and minds of their wives the way Arthur did with Maggie, they would show a lot more gratitude and sweep a lot more of the stupid stuff to the side of the road and just continue on.

Maggie said, "So now we just need to figure out how to hand deliver him to the cops."

Arthur swung his rifle to the right and glassed the parking lot. He wasn't done with this prick bastard yet. He hadn't considered the opportunity before him until just this moment.

The cop car still idled outside of the restaurant in the same spot it had parked when it finally came to rest.

After a few moments, Arthur spotted the blonde trio as they emerged from behind the restaurant's structure. Thye'd taken the walkway leading away from the front door, hugging the lone place on that side of the parking lot which Arthur could not see from his vantage point. These three weren't military-trained, otherwise it might have irked Arthur they'd done this. Might have spooked him, like maybe they weren't just the luckiest sonsofbitches in the genetic lottery, but also had some innate skill, too.

But no. They were just the luckiest sonsofbitches in the genetic lottery.

And for all the things that was—unfair, annoying, envy-creating—it damn sure wasn't illegal.

And as far as Arthur was concerned, it didn't justify killing.

"Damn I've gone soft," he said to himself.

As Arthur's scope found the wide, darkened void of the parking lot, he swept it from one way to the other over the sleek metal forms of Porches, Ferraris, Range Rovers. This was Miami, after all, where being ostentatious with your wealth was practically a prerequisite to going out in public.

Says the guy laying just shore aboard his yacht.

Maybe that was why Arthur had taken so much to Miami—because for all his actual work as a sniper, as the proverbial grey man, blending into the environment and being absolutely invisible through taking the shot and beyond, to the evasive maneuvers required to disappear inside a foreign country that was now on high alert looking for you, once he was off the clock, he wanted to loosen up on some of those tendencies.

Maybe he wanted to let his freak flag fly a little. Even if his "freak flag" was a bottle of Clos d'Ambonnay, a car so expensive it came with its own driver, and a boat that–while modest–still cost more than triple the average home price in this part of the world.

But there'd be plenty of time for all that later.

After a slow walking of the scope from left to right, he found the golden-haired trio approaching their car, a rather modest Mercedes G-Wagon in a matte white wrap and with tires big enough that Rommel himself would have been jealous. But here in Miami, such a vehicle was akin to driving a beater truck down in West Texas or a beater Toyota Landcruiser in the Middle East. One hardly even noticed.

All three of the golden throuple ascended into their white chariot–the esteemed target doing the driving. The G-Wagon pulled out of the spot and headed toward the parking lot's exit. Almost gone from Arthur's sight. Almost out of his capable hands.

"The cop is still there," Maggie said, notes of confusion and foreboding interlaced with one another in her voice.

Arthur said nothing.

Then with a little more fear in her voice, "This shot isn't the shot, Arthur."

Again, Arthur said nothing.

Maggie was not quite close enough to do anything about whatever it was Arthur was going to do next. But it didn't stop her from trying. There was legitimate panic frothing up like white caps along shore during hurricane season. "Arth–"

He exhaled and put just enough pressure on the trigger during his respiratory pause so that the rifle fired with the sort of precision that any expert craftsman seeks in their pursuit of the thing in which they find beauty.

And fire that rifle did. It fired at a rate of approximately two thousand eight-hundred-fifty feet per second, the round traveling the full distance from the yacht over water, over land, over the dark parking lot and directly perfect into the target Arthur had imagined as little more than paint by numbers in his pre-shot routine.

It would have been another moment until the crack of the rifle's report made landfall, rolling over the open space of the parking lot with something like a whimper from this distance, especially with the open ocean and the ambient noise of the city. Arthur had a Titan-QD Fast-Attach suppressor on the end of his rifle, which did little in this scenario, but it did provide some relief on the sound aspect of things. It still sounded like a gunshot to anybody who'd been around guns, but it would make it more difficult for a lay person to identify where the shot came from or whether the sound they heard was a shot at all.

The round tore a sizeable hole in the perfectly wrapped matte of the car's skin in much the same way a grenade stuffed inside someone's abdomen might do.

The G-Wagon slammed immediately on its brakes, giving the impression the truck had actually bunny-hopped forward. Like how a person might when walking behind someone through a doorway who suddenly stopped short. Then the G-Wagon sped up, peeling out and fishtailing against loose gravel beneath its hefty weight, before again stopping short.

What someone in the biz might call *panic*.

In the field, a sniper's job was to shoot and a spotter's job was to manage the situation. If they were there to kill someone and the sniper's first shot missed, the spotter noted the particulars of the miss–high, low, wide left or right–and called out an adjustment on the read. Out of instinct, Maggie did just that.

"Must be elevation. Kick it up a few meters. We're close enough, I'm surprised your reading was off."

"It wasn't," Arthur said and fired a second shot, this one even lower than the first. Rather than ripping a hole in the matte white, this round blew a neat hole inside the G-Wagon's front tire, instantly deflating it from the pressure and the massive weight of the vehicle above. It likely put a decent dent in the tire's infrastructure, too. They were too far away to clearly hear anything–especially with the rifle's report still clinging to the air around them–but Arthur figured the tire's sudden release of pressure and crush of steel probably made enough noise to bring anybody in the parking lot onto high alert. Followed by the gunshot's echo, anybody over there would certainly be looking around, even if they could not place the sounds.

The G-Wagon lurched but didn't go anywhere. It was now a bottleneck at the mouth of the parking lot, blocking incoming and outgoing traffic. So just in case the cop's were blasting show tunes or whatever else they got up to inside their tinted out half-incognito mobile, this would have eventually gotten their attention. Or at least the honking horns would have, from pissed off people prevented from making their dinner reservation on time or leaving the premises once done.

Well, objective achieved. The disturbance from the G-Wagon's sudden maiming curried enough attention that the red and blue check of the lights on the police car flooded the semi-dark parking lot like the first dance at the disco. Arthur pulled back from the changing colors in his spotting scope and gave the entire scene a long look, letting his eyes re-adjust to normal vision and his mind stay open to whatever was out there. This was the work of the predator who did not bring predisposition to any situation, who simply acted and reacted with lethality based on whatever they found in front of them.

The police car that had idled for the past twenty minutes was apparently interested enough to mosey itself on over across the parking lot to see what was going on.

Finally about ready to do something about a problem which had been flying under the radar far too long, if Arthur had a say so.

And while he figured he didn't have one—not really—if he wasn't willing to take his shot, it didn't mean he had to be entirely passive and silent on the situation. A man with his skill set and experiences rarely was much of either. Well, silent maybe—but only when conducting an operation.

"Just what did you do, Arthur?" Maggie's voice half-grinning.

"You said before I was rushed and reckless. At the time, even I had to agree. But now I see it different. I was quick, not rushed. And I was reckless only in my thought. Was lazy, too." Now it was Arthur's turn to use a metaphor, though his tended to be simpler and less obtuse than Maggie's. "I'd been looking to use my hammer to solve a problem that really only needed a screwdriver."

The Charger parked behind the G-Wagon. Behind it at the best angle they could squeeze in to ensure a clear approach without giving whoever was inside the broken down vehicle an opportunity to spray gunfire at them. Was a shame cops had to think about things like that, but it was reality. And it showed to Arthur two things: that these cops were evidently competent enough to know some basic tactics, which boded well for what Arthur had in mind. And, perhaps more importantly, that they approached the situation with the G-Wagon with the right eyes– eyes that saw a potential threat.

Two figures emerged from the Charger and approached the G-Wagon with guns drawn but pointed at the ground. Not a great tactic, honestly, but most cops tended to be pretty unskilled with their service weapon. So if you only went shooting the mandatory minimum amount each year to keep your licensing, it was better to point the thing away from people lest you make a mistake that was impossible to take back.

When the closest cop saw the gunshot wound flayed open on the car's exterior like a zit on the prom king, he said something over the G-Wagon's tall body and both cops raised their guns to a more serious, threat-assessment level.

"What did you do?" Maggie asked with a sly smile in her voice.

"We should probably go," Arthur said. "No sense hanging around until they ask where the bullets came from."

FOUR

Despite their relatively conspicuous sniper hides (as compared with, say, some of the woodland and jungle theaters they had operated within, with wandering countersecurity, enemy booby traps, and mortar units ready to rain down terror from the skies), Arthur shimmied himself backwards from his perch and behind the yacht's border wall. He crouched low, bringing the spent rifle with him in the process. Immediately, instinctively, he began to disassemble the M2010 with the sort of expert precision gained from a lifetime working with weapons systems. Truth to tell, Maggie was even faster and more adept than he, but she had other tasks to perform here.

She crouched behind the yacht's border wall, too, giving him a catlike look. Said nothing, though, just crouch-walked toward the yacht's captain's quarters will the smooth assurance of the operator conducting the physical movements they'd played out in their head a hundred times before the actual chance to do them.

As Arthur unscrewed the suppressor from the end of the rifle, he let out the heaviness inside his chest in the same way one might drop an anvil into the ocean. By the time he had broken down the entire M2010, he felt an even greater sense of relief, somehow, than on a mission where he'd executed on the intended target. Perhaps because this time he'd both completed the task—the *true* task—*and* avoided taking a life in the process.

It was ... nice. Almost.

"Whatever," Arthur said, using an Allen wrench to unseat the screw and bolt that allowed the rifle's stock to fold in on itself for ease of carry.

The quiet idle of the sea broke with the yacht's raising of the anchor, Maggie having made good time already as the deep-underneath engines came to life, too. Arthur went to stern and hefted the anchor into its pocket, shooting a flash of his flashlight to let Maggie know. She answered with two quick flashes of her own flashlight. As soon as the second flash was extinguished, the yacht was in motion, Maggie's expert captainship on display for exactly no one besides Arthur to witness.

At least that was the hope.

They were halfway back out to Biscayne Bay when Arthur had half the rifle chucked over the side at irregular intervals. By the time they entered Fisherman's Channel, he'd gotten rid of all of it, and with it, the last of the physical items that could connect him with firing those rounds into the G-Wagon—evidence that would put him in prison for a stint far longer than the rest of his expected life (even if Florida). Once he took a shower and wiped himself of any and all forensic evidence, he would be totally in the clear. He would do that, of course, but not just yet.

Overhead, the moon had emerged, bulbous and shining in amber in the sky. All around the yacht was the beauty that only an ocean moonscape can bring, with the waves growing larger, though still tame given the mild conditions. Arthur took a few deep breaths of the salty air as they rode farther out to sea, where at some point Maggie would navigate them through Norris Cut and toward the private island community they called home.

A light ocean breeze blew over the deck, enough to chill Arthur. It was perhaps the end of a very short window of temperate weather in South Florida. In conjunction with the loss of the flood of adrenaline which always came with a mission, he shivered, the hairs standing up on his forearms. It was nice, though, the quiet and the view of the moonlit ocean, and the few solitary moments he kept for himself.

After a time he joined Maggie in the captain's quarters. She stood at the controls, their charted course visible on one of the yacht's many control room screens. It wasn't a long journey, but it was always mapped on the GPS system beforehand, to be deleted by the computers immediately following completion of their journey, followed by Arthur taking the memory chips from the computer and throwing them into his masonry furnace, followed by a sojourn over the water where he released the ashes into the ocean. Yet seeing their charted course was a comfort to Arthur now, as the waning energy flowed from him.

"Tea?" Maggie asked. Another inside joke.

"Dirty water? No thanks."

"You planning on telling me what you were up to back there?"

Arthur grabbed an aluminum cup from beside the captain's desk and filled it with ice from the miniature refrigerator-freezer combo seated beneath the captain's desk. He then grabbed a Diet Coke and a pre-sliced wedge of lemon. He mixed both into the cup of ice and sipped long enough so that the bubbles and cold tickled his throat.

"I've been meaning to tell you," Arthur said, finding himself in a bit of a silly mood. "The lotion you bought me for Christmas? Very nice. Doesn't have any greasy feel whatsoever."

Maggie rolled her eyes. "Well your shot spread would say otherwise. I was worried your finger slipped. Lucky a little old lady didn't wind up catching lead."

Arthur smiled and the bubbles tickled his top lip.

"But seriously, Artie, don't change the subject. What was all that about?"

Arthur smiled as he took another sip of his soda. "You said before I had moved rushed and reckless." Arthur said this again and still the words felt strange to him. They almost hurt, coming from Maggie and talking about him. He wasn't any of those things. And yet he *had* acted in a way that could be construed as both or either. That stung. Because it wasn't the sort of operator he was. So it begged the question of *why*? A question now he was just beginning to grapple with.

He held up a finger from the aluminum cup. "I said you were half right. But now as I reflect back, I think you were all the way right. And also wrong."

Now it was Arthur's turn to talk opaque, apparently.

Maggie turned away from the controls for a moment and gave a look to Arthur that he'd seen plenty over the years. One that said, very simply, *you're an idiot, but I still love you, but you're mostly an idiot.*

Arthur continued, spurred on by the fake sugar and the caffeine and the sense of completion he felt.

"In my *methodical* preparation for this mission, I did something so stunningly smart that I hadn't even realized it until it was almost too late. As you know, in our pre-shot planning we had a not-insignificant problem. If we succeeded, there was the intended outcome that our target would be shot dead in the middle of a crowded restaurant. Naturally, police would ask questions. While we had no reason to fear those questions, nor was there any reason to leave ourselves vulnerable to them. And so was born the drug angle. The rifle used–determined if the police had enough sense to analyze the rifle rounds–would lead police right where we wanted: to this apparent group of defectors who worked logistics for the cartels."

Maggie swung the yacht in a wide, loping arc around Fisher Island and the southern tip of Miami Beach. The immaculate moon reflected almost perfectly in the rising and falling of the waves.

"And that was probably good enough. Or at least it would have been– for someone *reckless*."

This prompted a smile from Maggie. Despite her not turning around for Arthur to see her face, he could tell by the slight change in her posture that she was starting to get where this was going.

And liked it.

"But what I did earlier today before we set out on the yacht was take a little drive. Since I didn't know much about the target, I wanted to get a feel for him in his natural habitat. Call it one last peek before putting him down like the dog he is." Arthur was still Othering the target, but he didn't care. He'd been the angel of mercy on this job and now he could do whatever the hell he wanted with the target's avatar, that thing created solely by a sniper when tracking, hunting, killing his prey.

The chop of the oceans stayed tame as Maggie plunged the yacht forward, raising the speed until they were cruising smooth enough through the water to make even the most seasick-prone comfortable.

"What I found was the target whipping around in that same G-Wagon that just found itself with a sudden flat tire."

"And a punctured exterior," Maggie added.

"That, too. So I tailed the target on what seemed to be a morning of leisure. Coffee at some place with twenty-dollar lattes. A haircut at a membership-only men's salon. A trip to the high-end gym that's all the rage these days. Even a green juice afterwards at a place with the same branding as the coffee place but apparently no actual business relationship–I looked."

"Really dug deep, huh?"

Arthur smiled. "Am I the only one who thinks all these hip new places with their corporate responsibility schtick look the same? It's like they all ordered logos from the same company. Can hardly tell them apart."

Now Maggie smiled. Almost pitying her curmudgeonly husband. "But you digress."

"But I digress. Anyway, target goes home to shower up and do whatever silver spoons like him do for leisure after their leisurely errands have been run. And so I took it upon myself at that point to approach the vehicle."

"You're not serious."

"Serious is exactly what I am."

It wasn't necessarily out of bounds to have done this, but Arthur knew it was a risk at the time. A risk that had paid off, of course, but there was no way to know it at the time. No way to know with how little prep he'd done before putting the target in his crosshairs.

Arthur cut it off at the pass, though. "Before you get all pissed, it was always a play toward the alibi."

Of course this would only serve to piss off Maggie more.

"What did you do, Artie?"

"I put a few kilos of uncut smack in the wheel well of his car."

Maggie turned, quick and full of daggers. "*That's* what you've been doing these past two days?"

Arthur appreciated he had a wife who didn't bother to ask, "Where'd you get a few kilos of uncut smack?" but rather simply went straight to the fact that he'd obviously gone out and procured it using all the skill set that made him a good sniper. "I thought you said it was the papers and our usual ring of sources that confirmed the Army rumors."

"It was. But then I double confirmed with a little intel expedition of my own. Didn't get very far. Didn't need to, really–though it might be worth sticking our beaks back into if the cops can't tie it back to where I found it. I just figured some smack planted on our target would eventually be found upon his assassination, and then the conclusion we wanted the authorities to arrive at would be so forgone that not even the thickest local yokel deputy could connect the dots."

Maggie didn't smile but her tone softened. Because she was coming to the same conclusion Arthur had when he was on the gun. "And when you didn't take the shot on the veranda, you figured that half-marked cruiser in the parking lot could mosey on over and eventually find the same stuff you were figuring would get turned up after the fact, during the murder investigation."

Arthur smiled. "Like I said, it was a perfect, non-lethal setup."

"You're smarter than you look," Maggie said. A favorite inside joke between the two of them, something that harkened back to a certain advanced sniper tactical school they'd both gone through during their early years of training.

Arthur did a faux bow. "Why thank ye, m'lady."

"Though a truly smart person might have planned this from the jump. So we didn't have to come out here and play are-ya-gonna for over an hour."

Arthur waved an arm at the temperate outsides. "And miss such delightful weather?"

"The cop was a nice tough, though."

Arthur's smile dimmed. Enough so it was clear he'd tipped his hand.

"Oh, gosh. You didn't even plan that?"

Arthur said nothing.

"Better lucky, I guess," Maggie said and turned back to the controls. They were nearly home now and soon this would just be another mission under their belts–albeit one that went a little different than convention. "And maybe it's better this way. Annabelle can see justice was done, but without having to put herself under the public scrutiny that a case like that would bring, especially against a kid from a 'nice' family."

Arthur nodded. It hadn't even crossed his mind. Frankly putting the kid dead and gone to the next world was the only thing he'd had on his mind. Just didn't feel right. Maggie's point was a nice silver lining, though.

"Something about that kid got under my skin," Arthur said. He was a kid now, again. Twenty-something. Punk, for sure. Committed a heinous crime. But plenty of people Arthur came up with–good people, community-arch-stones–had done worse in their heyday.

It just wasn't that kind of world anymore.

"She means something to you. To us. It's understandable."

Maggie was right about that. On both accounts. Annabelle *did* mean something to Arthur. Not as much as a child, naturally. And perhaps not even in that way. Maybe she was just a reminder of all the good still in the world while he and Maggie went out and did the worst to some of the world's worst. It was understandable, wasn't it, that someone who meant that much to you would cause feelings when they were put in harm's way.

To this point, only Maggie and a select few teammates with whom Arthur and Maggie had worked with over the years would fall into the category of able-to-elicit emotions from Arthur.

Maybe he was just getting old.

Or maybe ... just maybe ... he was starting to evolve. Something he and Maggie had talked about a lot recently, as they both got older (not old, mind, just old*er*). About how to shift gears from the only life they'd ever known to something closer to normal.

Whatever that meant.

"Well it probably doesn't mean shooting people," Maggie had once cracked to him as he'd mused aloud.

Perhaps not.

But perhaps it did mean something else.

"Hey, I had an idea," Arthur said.

"Famous last words. And before you say something you'll regret, why don't you get that cute behind out there and tie us onto the dock."

Without Arthur realizing it, they were finally home.

Before the relief could settle in, he made his way toward the bow to heave over some lines onto their dock. Maggie was a pro at maneuvering this watercraft, and she could seemingly keep the thing against the dock without ever touching. Once Arthur had tied up the front, he repeated the task at the back of the boat.

Within a few minutes, both he and Maggie were walking barefoot along the fifty yards of perfectly manicured grass which stretched from the pool off the back of their house to their dock off the back end of their property where the yacht was now parked. Their glass-and-stone-encased home loomed before them, tastefully lit up, the view from the back edge of their property framed perfectly by matching rows of palm trees on either side of the grass, each side bowing ever so slightly inward toward one another. Arthur had to pinch himself sometimes, whenever they docked the boat along their own private bay space, because the home was something out of an *Architectural Digest* cover shoot (something he secretly wanted but knew would never happen on account of their anonymity being of paramount importance to things like their continued ability to live).

Both he and Maggie touched the smooth, like-new paint on "their" Adirondack chair–a quaint nod to their upbringings, both having grown up in the Northeastern part of the country. The chairs were set about three-quarters down toward the water along the lawn, close enough that if they ever sat in them, they would be able to hear the waves lapping sleepily along the sides of their yacht. This was sort of a ritual, this touching of the chair. It was the only time they *ever* touched them, since

Arthur refused to ever sit in the chairs, telling Maggie that perhaps he was paranoid or perhaps he was smart, but only someone who had never taken out a sitting duck who got too lax on security would be caught dead sitting in the chairs.

Dead being the operative word.

They held hands as they crossed the rest of the grass in quiet, their feet through the natural fibers of the earth the only sound.

As they walked around their massive infinity pool, Maggie spoke. "You said something about an idea."

Arthur had indeed. An idea about whether it was time to hang things up. Maybe use their skills for other things besides killing people. Like being a supplement to real law enforcement. Force multipliers for good.

But something inside Arthur told him it wasn't the right time.

Soon, perhaps.

But not now.

So instead he pulled up his free hand to his nose and gave it a long sniff. "Yeah I was thinking that next year, I might need a bigger container of that hand stuff. It's just divine."

Maggie looked at him for a long moment, knowing full well Arthur's thought had been something far more serious than this feeble attempt at humor.

But she didn't press it.

Rather, she slid open the back glass slider door that separated their patio from the cavernous living room. A few of the automatic lights brightened on their dimmers as she did so, welcoming them back home.

"It was a good gift," she said.

"That it was," Arthur agreed.

And he already–finally–felt a little bit better.

He just hoped one day soon Annabelle would, too.

Whatever that might mean for her.

THIN AIR

A LEDGERMAN STORY

INTRO

Another Ledgerman story. This one written within close proximity to the first (*Thin Air* is actually the third story completed in the series). That first cross-country flight I described earlier was where it started. And during the intervening weeks, I was flying cross-country quite a bit.

I guess all that air travel started getting under my skin.

Because this story is set within the cramped confines of commercial air flight–a place that is, in the first-world, notoriously complained about as if it's some medieval form of punishment (which, to be fair, it sort of is).

It's interesting to look back at the dates of when this story was written.

Started: February 26, 2020 Finished: March 24, 2020

In between, pretty much the whole damn world fell apart.

Ledgerman, however, stuck around. He became perhaps my most-appeared character in all my writing. He's great fun, if a little dangerous (okay, he is *a lot* dangerous, though he wields his danger rather judiciously).

I hope if you enjoyed *The Omega Diner*, and you enjoy *Thin Air*, you will consider checking out the rest of the series. These stories only begin to scratch the surface of what's coming–the long arc that answers the questions Ledgerman's existence raises.

There is a lot of great Ledgerman fun already down on paper.

And still a whole lot more to come.

A — LEDGERMAN — ASSIGNMENT

THIN AIR

A SUSPSENSE THRILLER

NIZ

AUTHOR OF THE *TRUE NAME* SERIES

THOMAS

ONE

Ledgerman's heart rate spikes, the adrenaline that always hits when he first reads the watch's notification—the time when the countdown begins, where the effectiveness of his next six, or twenty-three, or sixty-seven minutes takes on the utmost importance.

Ledgerman stands, forgetting to duck his tall, thick frame. Smashing his head on the luggage compartment (which these days inexplicably can hardly hold any actual pieces of luggage) in the process. A new pain shooting through the base of his brain, joining the more profuse but widespread neck pain he experienced from sleeping crack-necked for the first five hours of the flight.

In his haste to stand, Ledgerman knocks the overhead light on above his seat. An accident, one that temporarily blinds him, leaving a residue of lighted spots floating around his eyes. He fumbles back to turn the lights off. Something much easier said than done.

"Excuse me," someone says from the row of seats in front of him, cringing and pulling away from Ledgerman's general direction. He knows himself to be an intimidating figure at times—often one look can be all it takes to convince a person their sudden concern is no longer relevant.

"Sorry ma'am," he says back, holding up a hand in a small show of peace.

She turns away from him with a look of either bitter disdain or quiet disgust. Either one perfectly fine with Ledgerman, so long as he doesn't have to deal with her anymore. He doesn't mind fraternizing with the general public, as he calls them. But once his watch vibrates, it becomes an operational hazard for him to do so.

Ledgerman is not a clumsy man. He is actually frighteningly precise with his physical movements. A fact that many who have been caught in his preordained path came to find out the hard way.

But there is something about the past few minutes that's turned him into one, apparently. And he's pretty sure he isn't going senile yet.

Was it his unremembered dream, the afterimage of which is imprinted onto the inside of his eyelids? The fading vision of it only visible for a fleeting second when he closes them? He can't be sure. Can't even remember the damn thing to evaluate whether it was the cause or not.

He closes his eyes for a second, inhaling in a deep breath through his nose to center himself. He hears the laughter of ten, twelve people as if they are still sitting next to him. Warmth in their hearts. They are close, though he can't see them. The laughter is there. So, so close.

The laughter rises, falls, crescendos. It's ten, twelve different laughs all come together as one.

Until it's gone.

Not faded away.

Muted.

He opens his eyes, the laughter echoing in his memory.

What the hell was that?

Ledgerman feels off today—tonight, whenever the hell it is—on this plane.

Which is very unfortunate for his current state.

Because the main thing Ledgerman's watch does not tell him about the person it identifies is which decision he must make regarding that individual's future.

To kill them or save them.

Those are the only two options. And it's up to him to figure out the right one for this situation.

TWO

The trick is how to find Kylie Rudd on an airplane in six minutes or less.

Step one. The most direct, but not always the easiest. Ledgerman sometimes looks up from his watch into the smiling face of his subject. Sometimes he needs to smoke them out of a hiding spot.

Looking around the dark cabin, with exactly three lights turned on above random seats between him and the back of the plane, Ledgerman thinks finding Kylie might be a difficult task. He sees people zipped up in hoodies, beneath blankets, even wearing eye masks. He can't make out many faces.

Not going to be easy at all to find Kylie Rudd. Much less determine which of the two conclusions she deserves.

Ledgerman doesn't have much of an issue being judge, jury, and executioner (or exonerator) in these situations. He isn't sure exactly how long he's been doing this work, for he can't remember a time before doing it. There *was* a time before, however. Of this he is certain. His memory only stretches back so far. He doesn't remember school, parents, his first job. All of that is as dark and distant as the world he falls into as he dreams each night.

Though he still can't get past the feeling that he's missing something from that time earlier—something big, the feeling sitting in his chest and stomach like dread embodied.

He isn't a jittery man. He detests unsteadiness in people and would never tolerate it in himself. Yet the weight of unfulfilled dismay hangs heavy around his neck. He can't understand this feeling, simply has no mechanism even for comparison.

Ledgerman believes, deep down, that he wears the watch because of his reliability and steadfastness at completing the tasks that come to him. He is a man capable of improvisation. Of calm amidst the chaos.

He can't stand the fact that the inner chaos of a dream has gotten to him. That some unremembered darkness has got him shook.

He shakes himself free of the thoughts. Or tries to, at least. With only five minutes left, Ledgerman doesn't have the luxury of time anymore. He needs to get moving now.

He starts off for the back of the plane, having already gotten a sense from his earlier bathroom trip that Kylie wasn't in the first twelve rows of the plane. As a matter of habit, he scanned through those passengers already. He would have noticed her, even if she was zipped up tight in one of those hoodies that, for some reason, can be closed over your face.

"Sir," a stewardess asks, placing a small hand on Ledgerman's considerable shoulder.

He spins, quick and precise. The type of movement that most people who sneak up on him see just before drifting into their own land of darkness and dreams.

As quickly as he engages, though, he can slam the brakes, avoiding what would have been a horrific mistake. Thus far, Ledgerman has avoided the long arm of law enforcement when completing his missions. No matter how skilled or tough he is, getting off this plane in anything but handcuffs seems unlikely if you get violent with the staff.

Laying a hand on a flight attendant would surely land him in federal prison.

Knocking her out cold on her feet for placing a gentle hand on his shoulder would have put him there for quite some time.

She senses something, though it's clear she can't quite fathom what that is. He can relate, his own sense of some foreboding event on the horizon making him uncomfortable. She leans back, eyes focusing first on his chest and shoulders and then on his hands.

The human mind is a terrific judge of danger. Often, with people who find themselves injured or in need of saving from some horrible event, they can point back to a thought or feeling in their mind that should have clued them in to reassess the situation. A gut instinct, a smell, a *vision*. All ways the human mind strips away the infinite kaleidoscope of sensory inputs around us when a certain few of them need to be focused on.

It's only when people talk themselves out of the need to listen that they wind up in the wrong place at the wrong time.

The flight attendant takes several seconds assessing Ledgerman's chest, arms, and shoulder for danger, which is smart. Those are the places most likely to do her harm. But, seeing a lack of danger and harm, her eyes rise up to greet his face.

When they do, Ledgerman feels a sweat forming on his lower back. The haze in his mind dissipates, if only slightly. His eyes open wider, as if they could somehow take in more of the beauty in front of him.

These days, it wasn't common to see an attractive woman as a flight attendant. A thing which he figures shouldn't be voiced aloud, like so many of his thoughts. He can't actually remember a time when it was common, though a not-so-careful rewatching of *Catch Me If You Can* tells him that, at some point, this custom was an honored part of airline travel.

Now, of course, the honor seemed to be found in how miserable a particular airline could make its customers.

This attendant, however, was something out of the vintage catalog.

Brunette, flowing hair cut stylishly to her shoulders. Big, almond-shaped eyes with flecks of blue sky mixed in with the green.

Thick, pouty lips.

A uniform that fit in all the right places.

Ledgerman notices all of these things immediately, pleasure centers bombarded with information-carrying neurons like Iraqi air force bases back in '91.

Under normal circumstances, this flood of hormonal and evolutionary information might signal to him that it was his lucky day—that he might be pressing the call button a few extra times to get the chance to talk to her a bit more.

Instead, Ledgerman tries to wrestle his dry tongue from the back of his mouth, the dry air leaching every last bit of its moisture.

The flight attendant standing in front of him is an exact replica of the woman in the picture on his watch. Her green eyes beam out at him, the same color as a field of clovers.

Kylie Rudd.

"Sir?"

Ledgerman's pulse slows down to its normal resting rate of fifty-two beats per minute. He knows the watch tracks this (he even will check it on occasion), one of the few useful things he actually does with the watch besides taking its messages and plying his craft on those it says for him to.

His eyes dart down to the flight attendant's name tag, which reads: KYLIE RUDD.

This confirms it.

"Sir, is there anything I can help you with?"

Ledgerman thinks, takes what seems like forever to acknowledge her and form a cogent response through the surprise of stumbling on her like this.

It takes him an extra second to actually produce this cogent response from his dry mouth, an internal warning sign that does not go unnoticed by Ledgerman.

A master of improvisation, he is not today.

"I think maybe there is, actually."

THREE

Kylie's beautiful green eyes open expectantly, waiting for Ledgerman to reveal whatever it is he needs from her. In the dark and cramped aisle, with only the faint light from around the cabin and peeking in from two lowered window shades, she looks like a sultry dream.

Now that she doesn't fear for her safety, she takes him in, her eyes drawing a circuitous path from his broad shoulders, down the front of his wool button-down shirt, and then back up to his face.

Maybe she likes him.

Maybe he likes her, too.

She opens the angle of her body to him, her perfume enveloping him in a mix of sandalwood and cool lavender, replacing the stale, filtered plane air in his nostrils.

No one around them stirs, everyone either asleep in the darkness or hunched over phones or glowing tablets that light up rapt faces. Such concentration tells Ledgerman they are effectively alone. Most of these people are so deep into a binge, they might not even notice if the plane started to go down.

Beyond Kylie, in the forward area where the first class attendants prepare fancy beverages for their fancier passengers, no one looms.

Kylie, it seems, might be the attendant responsible for the front of the plane.

"I think we might know someone in common," Ledgerman says, the words tumbling out of his dry mouth faster than he can consider them, or the overarching plan they may or may not suggest. One thing about having your back against the wall that has always worked for Ledgerman, though, is to get your conscious mind out of the way and let your instincts simply go to work.

The human soul has an amazing penchant for surviving and thriving in uncertain situations, one that predates any single living organism today by hundreds of thousands of years of evolution.

He watches Kylie's face as the words register over the constant hum of the plane's engines. What might, on some people, read as a straightforward mixture of surprise and delight at this news instead reads as concern—or maybe fear?—masked with the veneer of delight. What could the reason be for that?

It seems Kylie is hiding something.

"Oh? And who is that?"

Good question, Ledgerman thinks. "I fear that telling you outright might ruin the surprise." He says this with a coy, flirty smile.

Kylie is familiar with this game. Male passenger, above a certain age. Alone on a cross-country flight, unable to get his mind off what all men have on their minds 24/7. And she, the perfect embodiment of it.

She smiles, one that touches the edges of her eyes. Almost looks genuine. Probably a thousand guys before him have gotten this same one.

"I see. So it's a game, then?"

Ledgerman nods. "I suppose it is."

Kylie giggles, more nerves than actual enjoyment. She looks back over the cabin behind her, confirming there isn't anything pressing that requires her attention.

This is part of the game. The naughty feeling of doing something you shouldn't in a place you shouldn't, and (for her) during a time you definitely shouldn't.

Satisfied that no one requires her attention, she turns back to

Ledgerman and nestles in closer to him. Once again, her perfume overpowers him, its warmth and sweet lavender wrapping him in the warmth and luxury of femininity. Say what you will about women. They smell damn good to a man.

Ledgerman fights to keep his composure. The scent itself isn't familiar to him. But the *feeling* of it is. Finding himself tied up in it like bedsheets on a lazy morning. The warmth of another right next to you.

Kylie's hand brushes against his.

Skin-to-skin contact.

How long has it been for Ledgerman since he's felt that? Too long.

He uses his other hand to steady himself against the seat, the feeling of having a beautiful woman so intimately close with him going to his head like a few glasses of gulped-down champagne.

His face reddens, not with excitement or nerves, but with the enshrouding fog of the forgotten dream that he experienced earlier.

His mind reels, sliding toward the cliff-edge of confusion. Is this sensation a memory? And if so, a memory of what? And when? He perfectly remembers everything that's happened to him since he started on his calling, this unholy alliance between himself and whatever entity delivers him messages through the smartwatch.

He remembers nothing from the time before. If there even was one (though, there must have been, right?).

"You from New York or L.A.?" Kylie asks, flipping her hair over her shoulder.

"I'm not really from anywhere," he says, catching himself from tumbling over the cliff of confusion. Holding on for dear life as he tries to navigate through the fog suddenly enshrouding him. She has no idea how difficult of a question it is for him to answer.

Kylie smiles mischievously. "How mysterious. A real man of the road, huh?"

"I guess you could say that. Where are you based out of? L.A., I'll bet."

"How'd you guess?"

Ledgerman has no idea. "You're tan. Hard to do in New York in midwinter."

Kylie laughs. "A regular Sherlock Holmes, this one."

Were Ledgerman trying to pick Kylie up, this conversation would be well on its way to promising. He has, however, only four more minutes to determine if Kylie is going to live or die. And if she is to live, he must determine how he's supposed to save her when the time comes. There is no clear threat present. He wishes it was as simple as just shadowing her, though that, even by itself, is difficult to pull off without being a total creep. Especially on an airplane.

Besides, if killing is the way it has to go down, it has to be done at the appointed time.

And saving her life needs to be done before he can rule out murder.

It's just then she gives him an idea.

The same hand that brushed against his hand before now reaches up, squeezes his bicep. "And not the book version, neither. I'd say you're at least the Robert Downey, Jr. one." After another squeeze, Kylie says, "Maybe even in better shape than that."

Ledgerman gives her his best half-aw-shucks, half-devious smile.

"Say, I'm thirsty. Got anything to drink in the back there?"

Kylie smiles, licking her pouty upper lip as she does so.

"I thought you'd never ask."

FOUR

Kylie expertly opens a drawer about the size of a shoebox and slips a manicured hand inside. Out come two airplane bottles of vodka—Tito's, Ledgerman is pleased to see. She grabs two plastic cups and loads them with a scoop of ice from another drawer.

"Straight?" she asks.

"Yes, I am."

She hoots with laughter, putting a hand over her mouth to keep herself quiet, but unable to stop the giggles. She peers around the corner, looking to see if she woke anybody. Then she slaps him playfully on the arm.

"You're bad."

"Can't help myself," he says, surprised this flirty strategy is actually working. He makes a mental note to try this more often, especially when the woman he's flirting with might *not* be dead three minutes from now (by his hand, no less).

Kylie pops both caps off as if by magic and pours the vodka into each glass at the same time. She sticks her chest out a little as she does so, which Ledgerman pretends—rather poorly—not to notice.

They tap cups and both take a swig. The ice does very little to soothe the burn of vodka, though on balance, Tito's isn't bad. Of course, a little time spent with ice in a shaker would be a huge improvement. But they were throttling through the air twenty-five thousand feet above the earth, after all. So beggars can't be choosers.

He must have winced after taking a sip because she says, "I thought you could handle the burn, baby. What's a matter? You don't like it too hot?"

Ledgerman takes another sip, careful not to wince at all this time.

He grabs Kylie's ass and pulls her closer. "I like it hot just fine. How about you?"

Her neck arches back, her weight held up by his arm, which he's still got wrapped around her. She doesn't know that this move, aside from being generally pleasurable for him and totally in character for the situation, is also designed to find anything on her that might be pointy or staby, if it comes down to him needing to kill her.

Luckily for him (in more ways than one), it's all flesh and bones. Plenty taut, for sure. But that never hurt anybody.

Not too bad, at least.

Her scent rises up, chokes him (in a good way). The movement pulls her undershirt beneath her blazer down just enough to give him a peek at the top of her breasts.

A fine, fine peek.

Then she snaps back up like a stripper at the end of her song. Leans into him, all soft hair and warmth.

"Let me freshen up, Mr. Wanderer."

She slips into the front bathroom behind her, the same one he used earlier.

Ledgerman finishes his vodka, the third sip going down easier than the first. His face is flushed, the remnants of his unremembered dream and brain fog still stubbornly clinging to his skull like an early afternoon fog in San Francisco. But the burn clears his head a bit.

Probably the increased blood flow helps, too.

He checks his watch. 5:00 p.m. on the dot.

Three minutes left until he needs to decide if Kylie deserves to live or die.

FIVE

Ledgerman looks around the kitchen area. It's nothing but plug-and-play drawers and cabinets. Like those houses of people obsessed with keeping all their possessions hidden away in secret compartments, as if they don't really live there.

Not interesting, really. Except for the drawer with the booze in it.

But also not useful.

Behind him is the plane's emergency exit door. In front of him is the other one, the exit door that they would also deplane from. To the right of that is the bathroom Kylie is in. And farther right of that is the cockpit.

Not a lot of space to find answers here. Which doesn't bode well for Kylie's chances of walking off this flight.

Ledgerman doesn't fly much, but he remembers seeing something that might be worth checking out when he entered the plane. The short bald man in front of him had a head like Mr. Clean and a body like Mr. Magoo. Carried himself the same way, wore a big heavy coat with a fur shawl collar that looked as expensive as it was ostentatious, especially on a plane to California. This was a man who hadn't a care in the world. He strutted down the jet bridge like he was in slow motion.

Upon entering, one of the stewardesses (not Kylie) took his coat and placed it in a closet right inside the emergency exit doorway in front of him. Ledgerman never saw the guy's face, but he was sure it had a look of smug satisfaction on it the entire time.

Now, he would never allow someone to take his coat (in this case, Ledgerman wasn't wearing one) but the person behind him tried to give their coat to the same stewardess. They were denied. Only first class passengers can use the closet, apparently.

Ledgerman crosses the kitchen area. A glance into the first class section tells him that everyone is either asleep or has their head down. No sign of struts-with-the-shawl-collar, but the darkness throughout the cabin makes it hard to see anyone.

At least, if Ledgerman needs to end Kylie, nobody seems to be paying much attention.

He opens the closet—like everything else, about one-fifth the size of normal, human size and tucked away like the hidden piece required to finish a damn puzzle. Inside, three coats hang on hangers, one of which is Mr. Magoo's. Seven additional hangers—all empty—remind Ledgerman that air travel is perhaps the last bastion in modern life where it is acceptable to blatantly discriminate against people because of how much less they have.

Well, that and the lines to get into sporting events.

Everywhere else it's considered bad taste. The airlines seem to have made it their business model.

Aside from the coats, Ledgerman has to squint to see what he's really looking for. Another factor of planes he didn't even realize he hated. They're too dark when trying to investigate someone.

A purse about the size of a binder. And not just any purse—this one is faux cheetah fur lined with black lace and fringe.

A purse he immediately pegs as Kylie's taste.

He unzips the top, has to practically cover his nose to lessen the heavy perfume scent pouring out the top. Holding his breath, crouched down in the tight space inside the kitchen, he flicks through the contents of the purse: a thin brown leather wallet (cheap), a thicker alligator skin wallet (expensive), and two books—*The Divine Secrets of the Ya-Ya Sister-*

hood and a battered copy of *Pride and Prejudice* (if you can square those two). Beneath that is a one-quart plastic bag full of an astonishing amount of over-the-counter medications—Tylenol, Advil, Tums, etc.—band aids, tampons, an inhaler, and at least three kinds of cough drops of various colors. Ledgerman's fingers unearth a keychain with keys from three different kinds of cars, various unmarked house keys, and an electronic fob that might open a garage or the front door to an apartment building.

The rest of the items aren't much—makeup, a travel-sized hair spray.

Nothing at all to suggest foul play is afoot.

Ledgerman checks his watch. 5:01 p.m.

Unsure what to do next, Ledgerman almost puts down the purse before another flight attendant emerges from the aisle and sees that he's got it in his hand.

"What are you doing?" he says, startled by the man hidden in the shadows of the dark plane.

Ledgerman is wondering the same thing.

SIX

Ledgerman is never tongue tied.

    Mainly because when he doesn't know what to say, he just shuts the hell up. Too many times he's been on the other end of a person trying to make something up on the fly. Usually, you practically have to duck out of the way of their verbal diarrhea. But he gets it—people get nervous (especially around him). They babble.

    The flight attendant doesn't say anything either, just steps back, instinctively putting distance between himself and Ledgerman. Sensing—much like Kylie did before—that danger lies here in the dark.

    Ledgerman means him no harm, of course. But his instincts aren't wrong. Harm may very well come to him if he interferes with Ledgerman's task here.

    The entity who provides Ledgerman guidance has never explicitly told him this (or anything, really), but he *knows* it to be true: there can be no failure to perform the task in question, no matter the collateral damage.

    Ledgerman tries to keep this damage to a minimum, never using more force than is absolutely necessary.

    But he isn't afraid to use it, either.

It comes as very little surprise to Ledgerman (who must often stereotype in split-second moments of indecision) that the attendant is not a physically imposing man. He's never seen one who was. He stands a lean (not mean) five foot ten, buck sixty-five at the most (maybe on a day when he's bloated *and* soaking wet). White-blonde hair, almost albino. Chalky skin to match. His shoulders are straight, the posture of a dancer or equestrian. Not someone, though, who is going to physically harm Ledgerman.

But harm can come in many different ways.

"Excuse me, sir. I said, 'what are you doing?'" The attendant's (do they call them stewards?) voice rises an octave, discomfort creeping in like Jack Torrance entering a locked bedroom. His eyes dart between Ledgerman, the closet, and the rest of the airplane like a pinball.

There isn't much time for Ledgerman to explain. Not that he could. *Why, I'm snooping through a stranger's purse, hoping to find incriminating evidence that can be used as the justification to kill her,* doesn't seem like a response that would go over well here. *Oh, what's that? Yes, I understand killing is wrong. Sometimes. But you see, I have this special smartwatch that says it's all ok...*

Yeah, Ledgerman isn't sure that will fly at all.

On the other hand, he doesn't want this pipsqueak making too much noise in the next ninety seconds before doing what needs to be done.

Whether Kylie lives or dies, Ledgerman doesn't yet know (though if he can't find any reason for her to live...).

"Sir, please answer me."

The shrill tone of voice tells Ledgerman that this is close to the breaking point. A point that normal people reach once they are truly pushed to the limits of their comfort. While this might not seem an extreme example of being made uncomfortable, Ledgerman can appreciate that a flight attendant—a *steward*, he's decided, is the appropriate term—carries additional emotional baggage in their place of work. People are already dumb and rude enough before they get on a plane. Combine their nature with the third-world confines of "Economy" travel and you have a recipe for disaster. Add in all the associated security concerns, and the fact that perhaps the first priority of a flight attendant is to keep everyone on board as docile as possible (lest they think about the reality of the situation—shooting through the sky at hundreds of miles per hour, thousands of feet above the ground)?

Being a steward was damn near miracle work.

This steward—nametag reads: Alex—though, seems intent on causing trouble for Ledgerman (not that he has any hard feelings about it, hard to blame the guy for doing his job).

Unfortunately, trouble for Ledgerman also means trouble for Alex. Much more trouble than his pasty little body can handle.

Alex grabs the white plastic phone next to him but doesn't put it to his ear.

"Sir, please put the purse down and your hands in the air where I can see them."

This is not good. Ledgerman must put an end to this.

"Listen," he says, trying to keep his voice calm and non-threatening, which is tough to do when you need to yell over the hum of the jet engines.

Alex puts a hand up to stop him. "Sir, please do as I say."

"Just put the phone down, Alex. Let me explain. It's not what you think."

Alex hesitates.

"Just getting something for Kylie. No nefarious activity. Promise." Ledgerman gives Alex a big wide smile. Knows the name drop probably buys him a few extra seconds.

"Where is Kylie?" Alex asks.

That's a good question, Ledgerman thinks.

SEVEN

Alex says, "Something's not right here."

And he's right.

Ledgerman needs him to put down the phone, though. Even through the hum from the plane, he hears someone's voice on the line.

Ledgerman senses the tension returning to the man's actions and mannerisms. He's falling prey to the tight quarters of the kitchen area, the increased pressure on his ears as the plane lowers in altitude, the relative smallness of himself compared to the strange, dangerous man standing across from him.

"She's in the bathroom," Ledgerman says. No sense lying about it.

She'll be back out in a second. He checks his watch.

Been in there ninety seconds already. And now he's up against time.

Ninety seconds left before he needs to do something.

And all signs point to her dying once that time limit is up. Which is going to prove tricky, now with Alex in the mix.

Would be tricky anyway, though, on a damn plane.

He never questions the watch. It pings him with information as it sees fit. And he knows deep down that it can somehow see all things. Trusts deep in his gut that when it identifies an instance where he needs to get involved—whether by killing or saving—that it does so from some all-knowing source of fairness and equanimity.

Alex holds the phone in limbo.

If he doesn't put it down, Ledgerman will have to kick it out of his hand.

Or just kick him in general.

That would get ugly.

Luckily, he doesn't have to make that determination.

A thud against the bathroom door. Unmistakable, even over the thrum of the engines:

Dead weight.

EIGHT

Ledgerman doesn't hesitate, slams a right fist against the bathroom door to his left.

Doesn't budge. Not even a little.

He could probably hit it harder, but based on his first try he doesn't think that will do anything different. Airplane bathroom doors don't operate like normal ones. Normal ones, he has no problem knocking off the hinges.

He's never had to do that with an airplane bathroom.

Isn't even sure it's possible. After all, they fold by design.

"What was that?" Alex asks, a little slow on the uptake.

Ledgerman steps away from the door, into Alex's circle of trust. He pulls the steward close to him, so their noses almost touch. He smells the residue of Wrigley's Double Mint Gum—which tells Ledgerman the man he is dealing with might very well be mentally unstable. Only a psychopath would chew that gum, which loses its flavor within ten chews. Alex's cologne is of indeterminate brand, and Ledgerman has been standing here long enough to know that at least it lasts longer than the steward's choice of gum.

Alex tries to back up. Ledgerman's hold on his arm ensures he doesn't go anywhere.

"Hey! What the heck?"

"Quiet. Don't move."

Alex obeys, as if Ledgerman just deployed a magic spell.

Ledgerman grabs the phone from his hand and hangs it up. Then he stares Alex in the eye for a long moment, making sure the steward feels something of the gravity of what's going on, even if he doesn't actually know what that is.

Eighty seconds left before the deadline.

Content that Alex will not cause him anymore trouble, Ledgerman turns back to the bathroom door.

NINE

"Kylie?" Ledgerman says, speaking loud enough for his voice to penetrate through the folding door.

No answer.

Ledgerman presses against the door, which should fold up and in when pressed from the outside. But the indicator is turned red, meaning it's locked. And he can feel from his hand against it that the dead weight on the other end of things is too much of a counterweight to make any progress.

At least not without crushing Kylie in the process.

"Do you have any sort of special key for this thing?" Ledgerman asks Alex.

The steward shakes his head. "There isn't even a keyhole."

He's got a point there. The locking mechanism is all on the inside of the door. Outside is just the wheel that spins to tell you not to try to enter. Someone else is already doing their business in there.

Sixty seconds left.

And Ledgerman doesn't have the faintest idea how he's going to complete his mission.

TEN

Behind them, a few passengers are leaning out of their seats and into the aisle. It's clear—probably from Alex's body language—that something is wrong up here.

And these days, that gets people's attention on an airplane.

"I need to call up to the pilot," Alex says.

"Don't. I might need your help. He's got better things to do anyway, like make sure we don't crash."

Alex seems to take this into consideration. Nods in agreement.

"There's no key to open this thing..." Ledgerman says, hoping his words will lead his mind toward the conclusion. The fog he experienced earlier hasn't fully lifted, but the adrenaline of the last two minutes is doing its best to push it offshore upstairs, "...so let's open it ourselves, shall we?"

"How are you going to do that?"

Ledgerman pokes a finger at the spinning indicator on the door, which shows red for OCCUPIED. It moves a little.

He punches it twice, the hard metal pieces sending shooting pains up through his knuckles and into his elbows. Probably there is cut skin, blood. But there will be time for that later. Probably. He's never failed a mission before. Isn't sure what the penalty is, or even if there is one. He has seen the justice the watch metes out, though, and doesn't want to find out.

Reaching two fingers into the space that he just punched loose on the lock's outer indicator, Ledgerman finds a hard and sharp metal environment that doesn't seem willing to budge. It bites him, leaving behind a small trail of blood.

Luckily, he isn't dissuaded so easily.

Thirty seconds left.

Ledgerman turns around, scanning the LEGO block structure of the kitchen. So little metal, airlines afraid of too much opportunity for stab-y behavior.

The closet.

He pushed past Alex, reaches into the closet, and grabs one of the empty hangers. Silently thanks the stewardess earlier who turned away the first plebe requesting his jacket be hung up. It would have triggered others to want their own. And that would have made for a bunch of hangers full of coats.

Ledgerman moves with an economy of motion that scares Alex. Probably it scares anyone leaning out of their seats and looking toward the kitchen, too.

He rips the hanger apart with his hands, removing the wood from the wire frame. Straightens the wire hook as if it were a pipe cleaner, then takes this newly developed shank and jams it into the loose locking mechanism he's punched some daylight into.

Three, four violent jerks of this jerry-rigged lock pick and the mechanism breaks free from the door, bouncing off the floor.

Nothing happens. The door doesn't open, doesn't loosen. Kylie doesn't stumble out of the bathroom.

"Shit."

Twenty seconds left.

"Oh gosh, you broke the door," Alex says helpfully.

Ledgerman ignores him, doesn't have the time to deal with him right now.

Ledgerman pushes against the door, finds it much more amenable to moving than it was before. Pushes a little further, gets daylight.

Kylie's dead weight still pushes back against the door, a surprisingly strong counterweight to Ledgerman's efforts. Physics can be a real bitch sometimes.

But he has daylight.

He reaches his arm through the opening he's created in the doorway. Holds the opening with his other arm, making sure not to let go, lest he crush his arm with the door in the process.

With the free hand, he open-palms Kylie on the shoulder and pushes her back away from the door. Toward the back of the bathroom.

The rest of the door opens, Ledgerman first catching himself from falling into the bathroom.

Then, catching Kylie as he tumbles out through the space where the door had just been closed.

He lays her slowly to the ground. It becomes clear to him, now with less than fifteen seconds left until he needs to complete his task, that Kylie doesn't need to be killed.

She needs to be saved. Only not from someone else. She needs to be saved from Death himself.

Her face is white and blue, like how Alex's would look if Ledgerman needed to knock him around a bit. She feels cold—scary, since it's only been seventy seconds since she went dead weight against the door.

"Oh, gosh, oh, golly, what in the world is wrong with her?" Alex says. He's got his hands up on his face like an old maid who just found out Aunt Maude died.

And how should Ledgerman know what's wrong with her? Despite the flirt show he put on, it isn't exactly like she opened up about all the ways she'd be susceptible to an early death today.

Ledgerman looks at her, practically feels the seconds ticking off his watch (though it doesn't tick, it's a digital), and doesn't know how he's going to pull this one off.

Ten seconds left.

Nine, eight, seven...

ELEVEN

Ledgerman turns around. Lunges across the small kitchen space.
　Grabs for Kylie's purse inside the closet.
　Rifles through her things, pulls out the big plastic bag full of random medicine.
　Thanks to whatever force allows him to remember things.
　Finds the inhaler. The one he'd glossed over before.
　Turns back around, puts it to her blue, Rigor mortis lips like the elixir of life.
　Five seconds left.
　Depresses the inhaler's button.
　Holds his own breath.

TWELVE

Ledgerman's watch beeps, the shrill alarm sound cutting through the kitchen area, through the thrum of the engines.

Alex is horrified, his eyes hardly moving, some unknown movie playing behind his eyes acting as his only true interface with the outside world. Shadowed faces behind him in the dark part of the plane emerge from their strange slumbers like wraiths in the aether.

The darkness of the plane's cabin seems to expand, inky blackness diffusing, leaking out and blurring the edges of Ledgerman's vision like a broken film projector.

Did he fail his task?

Kylie coughs. Once, twice. Launches into a full-bodied cough that emanates from her stomach, the muscles in her neck contracting tight against the effort.

But she develops a hue of rouge around the neck and cheeks. Color returns to her lips slowly.

Ledgerman feels a massive sense of relief, knowing that he has once again completed his task, that the smartwatch he so slavishly obeys has put him in the right place and time to positively affect the world again. He has, just in the nick of time, fulfilled his responsibility to the universe.

And avoided the unknown fate that exists were he to fail.

Kylie regains her breathing. Slowly, though Ledgerman is in no rush now. Her eyes open, wide and thirsty for the kaleidoscope of colors that life offers. True understanding now of what was so close to being lost fills her green eyes, which shine through, even despite the fear.

The emerald orbs find him, though they don't yet recognize him as the flirtatious man who shared a drink with her a few minutes earlier. Instead, they see him as the beacon upon which her new life can count its blessings—the lighthouse that guided her back to shore through stormy seas.

For his part, Ledgerman feels a constriction in his chest. Kylie isn't a bad looking woman, even after being medically choked-out for a minute and a half.

As he always does, Ledgerman never tries to steer the person he saves in the minutes after he saves them. Often, they have seen him inflict mortal damage upon others. He's happy that wasn't the case here, that Alex didn't become collateral damage. That overall, this experience was one that only had good outcomes.

That isn't always the case.

Watching people in these moments, though, gives Ledgerman an interesting glimpse into the human psyche. Into how people process the traumas of their lives. Despite being human himself, he often feels a step or two removed from truly *belonging* to the greater community of mankind. While he can sit in a restaurant and conduct a conversation, something about his unique journey also sets him apart from the crowd. He supposes this is mainly due to his own unique focus, one not shared by many. Probably not shared by any. He has no attachments, no true home, none of the obligations that make up a *normal* life, like family or friends. No real memories to speak of. No idea what may have come *before*.

He has only the calling. And it often puts him at odds with people.

Though in times like these, it also brings him closer. Within arm's reach, at least.

Two minutes after he saves her life, Kylie speaks.

"What happened?"

Ledgerman looks at the inhaler in his hands. "Whatever you need this for seems to have caught up with you. I'm guessing you fainted in there before you knew what hit you, couldn't get out."

Kylie puts a hand to her collarbone, similar to the damsel in distress in an old-timey movie.

"Gosh...that's never happened to me before. My asthma is usually under control."

Ledgerman says nothing.

"But I guess you just never know when your time might be up, huh?"

THIRTEEN

Three minutes after he saves her life, Ledgerman helps Kylie up to a seated position. Alex the steward and a number of people in the first few rows watch stunned, their journeys in the sky momentarily interrupted. Their eyes make him uncomfortable, but he's unconcerned. If he needed to kill Kylie, eyes on him would be an issue.

As it stands, he can just take whatever credit and attention from his act of heroism, minimize it as much as possible, and then disappear back into the anonymity of life and continue on his journey.

But there is still one thing left to do.

Now Kylie is ready for it.

He puts a hand on her shoulder. "Listen to me," soft at first to get her attention. Then with more gusto. "You've been given a second chance, have received a gift of sorts."

"I don't understand," she says.

They never do.

"You don't have to. Not yet. I just need you to understand that you've been given a unique gift. An extension of life that otherwise would never be available to you. And now that it *has* been made available, I want you to keep it in the back of your mind for the rest of your days. To never think of it directly, but never let it flit away too far from your mind, either."

Kylie stares at him blankly, emerald eyes wide and uncomprehending.

"Live your life. But don't hesitate to pay this back when you think you can. Little here, little there. Pass it along, huh?"

Kylie nods agreeably. Alex does too, though nobody expects him to make a damn difference in the world after this.

Ledgerman leaves Kylie with that message in the quiet and the two sit next to each other in the dark of the front kitchen area as the rest of the flight proceeds normally.

Several minutes later, the pilot comes on the intercom and says, "OK, folks, we had a bit of a medical scare up here in the front of the plane, but everything is handled now. Sorry for any confusion or fear we caused. But we are getting ready to settle in for landing. So thank you again for flying with us and hope to see you again."

"Thank *you*," Kylie says to him. "Seriously, thank you so much for saving me."

"It's nothing. Same thing anybody in this situation would have done."

Not exactly true, of course. Nobody else would be in this situation.

"What you did..." she says again, still replaying whatever memory of it she has.

"...was nothing. Seriously." Nothing she would understand, at least.

Kylie goes quiet then and leans a head against his shoulder. They sit like that as the air pressure grows and the jet engines scream out in preparation for landing.

FOURTEEN

As the plane's door opens, Ledgerman steps back and away from the medical team who comes in to take Kylie's vitals. By now the passengers are up, reaching overhead in the miniature luggage bins, ready to move about with their day.

Kylie is talking to the first EMT on the scene, a thirty-something guy with muscles like an ex-linebacker. Hopefully she can continue some of their flirty banter with him—Ledgerman will sure miss the feeling. He's grateful for the reminder of how fun it can be to enjoy the company of another. Especially another of the opposite sex.

He just knows it won't be something he gets *too* familiar with. His calling will take him away from here, a wandering divining rod of extrajudicial equilibrium.

This brings him neither joy nor self-pity. Not exactly. Instead, he finds himself...longing, perhaps, is the right word for it. A deep and depressed sense of gnawing inside. A new emotion, certainly, in a man who hasn't a need for that side of himself.

All in all, it's been a strange day, he must admit.

As the passengers start to deplane, Ledgerman slips into their exiting stream like a ghost. No goodbye. No fanfare. Simply blows away on the back of the wind.

The narrow, cramped jet bridge feels like it's a million-mile pilgrimage, him just a single pilgrim trying to make his way to the end of it.

The air is hot but not humid. Smooth Southern California charm. He notices—quite late given his usual vigilance, the last sleepy wisps of fog still stubbornly clinging to the shores of him mind—the man in front of him. The same one who'd hung his heavy, shawl-collared coat in the front closet when he got on the plane. A strange coincidence, seeing him again. And not the first Ledgerman ever experienced during his time "in the field," so to speak.

As they emerge from the jet bridge the man turns his head, as if he's forgotten something on the plane and just remembered.

Ledgerman freezes.

In profile, this man's face sends a lightning bolt of vague premonition through Ledgerman. He's never seen the man before today, he's sure. Even seeing him earlier on the plane hadn't given him any strange notions like this one.

So, what is this?

Ledgerman isn't sure, wracks his mind and condensed memories to place the man. But simply can't.

Though he occasionally experiences the odd coincidences like seeing a man who factored into the task he's called upon to perform, Ledgerman does not believe in any higher power—at least not like most people do. Instead, he believes in an ideal—a disembodied sentient communications device that he wears on his wrist.

As strange as it sounds, he knows this constant companion to be the only thing he believes in that can't be explained by science.

But he wonders now if perhaps something has shifted. If his perspective changed—or if it needs to.

Outside of the plane, in the open spaces of the terminal, the fog of his earlier dream has finally cleared. With it, Ledgerman feels like the man's image in profile has floated away with it. Turned to atmosphere. He doesn't know exactly why he associates the two with one another, but he does nonetheless.

The man turns back away from Ledgerman. Continues walking. If he has forgotten something on the plane, he just decided it wasn't worth the trouble to go back for.

Ledgerman keeps walking, deliberately and at a slower pace, to stay behind the man, his eyes following him, hoping for an epiphany as to why he looks so oddly familiar.

None comes.

Instead, the man peels off into the airport men's room.

Ledgerman, eager to put this whole strangeness behind him, decides not to wait. To simply continue on his way, waiting for the next moment that his watch vibrates.

In the meantime, he would get something to eat.

He is starving.

BURN OFF

INTRO

This story is a special one to me. It was my first attempt at writing something Crichton-esque. Taking an interesting science-related story and trying to turn it into a live-wire suspense story.

The original draft of this story was a lot longer–and I wonder (though as a writer, it is literally impossible to ever evaluate objectively) which version was "better." I say "better," of course, because that status is impossible to determine. A group of three people might read three stories and each one would give you a different "better." Not to mention that any person I gave the two versions of this story to–the one you now hold and the original, longer one–would always be biased toward the one they read first. Because while the two stories differed in length, they all go to the same place.

And in a story like this one, where I tried to keep the pressure on the main characters all the way through, I think brevity tends to serve better than expansion.

There's less to burn off with the former versus the latter.

And so I hope you find everything in this story that I attempted to plant here. A thrill ride, of sorts, through terrain so rugged and solitary that it plays its own little role in the story.

WRITERS OF THE FUTURE AWARD FINALIST

NIZ THOMAS

BURN OFF

AN ORIGINAL CRIME STORY

ONE

The road back from Jackson rattled Gideon's nearly thirty-year-old 1989 Ford F-250 pickup the same way a grizzly bear might handle a lame jack rabbit that limped into the wrong den once spring had sprung.

He grimaced against mounting pain in his hands, wrists, and forearms. Knowing for certain it would spread and get worse. Knowing that even as bad as it was, knocking him out of the damn workforce a little over a month ago, it wasn't nothing compared to life's true pains.

Gideon checked the clock on the dash. About the only part of the F-250 that worked properly, even though it was twelve minutes fast, showing a reading of four fifty-eight in the afternoon, meaning it was actually about quarter-'til five. Meaning they'd be cutting it close to arrive by nightfall. It wasn't a dealbreaker, but this truck didn't generate much from the headlights to guide their work should it have to happen too long after the sun went down.

He tried to do some simple calculations as he gazed through the speckled glass windshield onto the desolate, open land ahead: they were near the southern portion of the Gros Ventre Wilderness now, a place so pristine that it served a constant reminder that a more God-touched area did not exist in this world. Heading south away from it. Forty miles left to go. Good, clear conditions, nothing around to slow their route except for Angus and Hereford cattle that dotted the landscape and the fact his truck was near old enough to file for Social Security. The grass on either side of them was the same color as the Mountain Dew label (not the toxic sludge in the bottle) and stretched off in all directions until the silver sagebrush took over, then gave way to bur oak, then to dense copses of quaking aspens and thick, dark-green pine trees that seemed to blot out the last of the light on the western skyline. Off to the southeast, out his driver's side window, the Wind Rivers loomed in their dark grey countenance, still a ways off in the distance.

Whack. Whack. Whack. Each of the bones in his arms getting an aftershock from the road below like it was San Fran, 1906.

Gideon had modded the pleather steering wheel covering with hockey tape snagged from one of his nephews about eight years back—one strip wrapped at ten, another at two, both faded from white to "aged" (if one were kind with the descriptors). Family really was everything around these parts where the weather could be harsh, the wilderness unforgiving, at times cruel, and the work available to a man was rougher than anywhere else on land (if at sea, maybe they could talk).

So right then, as the rattling car went south down the solitary two-lane Route 191, Gideon was happy to have benefited from little Gabe's kindness to his uncle all those years ago. But the tension inside Gideon made it so he was gripping the wheel the way his grandfather gripped hold of the life raft in the waters off the Marshall Islands once the sharks started to circle and the wake started to rise and fall with approaching storms. Maybe that tension had never left his line ever since that moment. Maybe it had always been there to start.

Family really was everything around these parts. For better, for worse.

Driving now back from Jackson, the light of afternoon just beginning to fade to dusk as the bottom of the sun dropped behind the tips of the Tetons on his right, he recognized his truck was ready to be put out to pasture.

The deep ache had already settled into the places up his arm that he knew from experience would take days to fade. But he just tried to focus on their destination: the abandoned spot south of Pinedale where natural gas bloomed out of the ground like pollen from a dandelion in a spring wind. Gideon silently cursed himself. These bum arms and hands were the whole reason he was in this mess to begin with. And if he wasn't careful, they'd be the thing preventing him from getting out of it.

Assuming, of course, a way out existed. That remained to be seen.

Gideon's eyes cut to the rearview, to the bed of his truck.

A seismic quake of a jolt from a three-inch deep pothole the size of a manhole cover brought his attention directly back to the road.

At times on this drive back, he felt like he was back on the job, working his six-ton NPK hydraulic hammer attached to the long arm of his excavator, opening the earth below looking for pockets where natural gas flowed. He'd always been sensitive to what the subtle changes in vibration coming off his hammer told him about the land and the potential treasures below. A rise in the frequency meant harder rock, maybe shale–Cody or Mowry. When the vibration lessened, maybe rhyolite that gave the Wind Rivers their ghost-like color. Or just some soft sediment that had too much water from a nearby underground source. They had fancy radar on the computers these days that could identify that stuff, too. But he'd always done it by feel.

"Maybe try a straight line, 'hon," Trish said from the seat next to him. She had her seat pushed all the way forward, the upper part reclined so far back it was almost to bedding (much as you could get out of this pickup anyway, even with the extra cab room). Two long, toned legs caught his eye (mercy–always had). Two bare feet out the open window already with a light dusting of road grime, and they were only thirty-five minutes outside town headed home.

Gideon didn't catch her face but he could tell her eyes were closed. Resting. He'd never seen anybody able to rest in conditions like this. Not even back in the service (though to be fair, he'd been part of the generation of plant eaters who served after the Gulf War and checked out before round two in the sandbox). Her chair had even less padding in it than his, and if it weren't for the pounding his arms and hands were taking, his back would be making itself better known right now.

Something behind him, beneath the bed of the truck (he guessed, though he was practiced at diagnosing the truck's problems by sound alone), was loose. It whistled with the high whine of ungreased metal against metal. Gideon's eyes once again fluttered to the rearview, toward their cargo: a rectangular metal frame about three feet long by one-and-a-half feet wide and tall, four long, rolled-up rubber hoses, and three loose connector wires affixed to ... what had the dweeb in Jackson called it ... a *mother*board? It was the green status light Gideon keyed in on, though. It was how he knew the rig–what was basically a computer attached to a homemade generator with some very specific modifications–was still operational. As long as that light stayed green, they had a chance.

Well, as long as it stayed green *and* they got back in time.

The truck's left tire jerked. The whine now taking physical form. Felt like someone put a cue ball in a sock and slapped him with it. *This* was the pain that had caused him to start missing work.

"Like I said, 'hon. Straight is the way to do it."

Gideon grunted. Very funny. She always had been. Beautiful with those long legs, smart as a whip, funny as all get out. That's where Brett got it from, no doubt (except the beautiful part. The kid was cute going on boyish-handsome, but no son of Gideon's would ever be *beautiful* in the way Trish was).

Gideon checked the rearview again.

"It'll be fine, Gid. Thing is made of machined metal as thick as my tibia. And you sure spent enough time tying it down."

"Kid like that," he started, trying to find the words.

"Kids like that are sending people to the moon, old timer. I think he can make a generator and a computer work together just fine."

Gideon grunted. He'd spent years working with roughnecks out on the high plains drilling for natural gas. Guys that were one bad decision away from prison. Plenty who already belonged there, but they were able to skate by with work in remote places where cops didn't feel a need to visit much. Some good men, too, like Gideon. Stable. Sober. Fellas who worked a hard job in a hard way, kept themselves and others safe as they could.

Ain't a single one of those men looked like the dweeb kid from Jackson. David, was his name. Sat half-slouched in his chair with clothes that were bewilderingly tight around his crotch. A sweatshirt big enough to take up into the Tetons to camp with, maybe fly it down the side of the mountain when he was done. Like those X-treme athletes in the squirrel suits. Didn't look like any man Gideon had ever worked with, ever trusted. Certainly not one that had ever manufactured a piece of useful equipment.

But Trish said to trust the kid–he knew computers, knew a way to turn something Gideon and Trish could get into cash.

When Trish looked him dead straight in the eyes and says, "Trust," Gideon did exactly that. That was family. That was bond.

It would all work out. Had to. Assuming, of course, they could make it back before true dark. And before David the Dweeb's vague deadline was up. "Before the other guys ..." was all he'd said.

"You're setting back your jaw like a pit bull got whiff of chicken fried steak," Trish said. "What is it?"

The pain didn't help none. But Gideon said nothing. Cut his eyes at the rearview again. David the Dweeb's equipment was still back there fine. Green light switched on.

The road was otherwise empty again. Not even a distant headlight around.

He wondered whether the kid was bluffing about the others.

Trish wasn't thinking about that, apparently. Wasn't like her to leave something alone to fester. And true to form, she didn't. "You don't agree with the plan, say something. It's awfully late to do so, but it ain't *too* late."

The plan could work. He could admit that. But it needed to go off without a hitch. He'd never experience a plan like that before. Plans were freaking hitch magnets.

"Not the plan you disagree with, huh?" Gideon knew without

looking that his wife's one eye was open now. Watching him. Waiting for a reaction.

Or about to create one.

"It's the *kid*, isn't it? Not the plan. It's the kid you don't agree with."

Honestly, everything was the problem at this point. Pain was the one at the forefront of his mind, though. It was enough to make winning the lottery a grim event in his life right this second. Inside him, somewhere deep in his soul, he hurt even worse. Brett, their poor son, at home. Injured. No. Paralyzed. Didn't help none to pretend otherwise. Fell off a rock outcropping one day playing out back behind the house. With Gideon unable to work and the roughneck who replaced him falling asleep on the job and damn-near decapitating one of the other fellas on the crew, the small drilling company he worked for went under. Scary to think how thin of a margin so much survived on in this life. But that was the way it went for roughnecks in a rough place. Wyoming sure ain't New York or Miami Beach.

So this plan was born from Trish's internet research. Contacted David the Dweeb, kid who apparently had pioneered some technology that used flare gas to power computers to mine something called *cryptocurrency*. Gideon didn't know a thing about it, but it seemed lucrative given how much David was willing to pay. Flare gas was something the drilling companies needed to burn off when they found gas somewhere that didn't have a pipeline close to it. It was essentially waste product, which was not only dangerous, but also a bit like burning piles of cash all day, every day. Now that the company had gone under, the burn off was done for. Nobody to maintain it. And the site was abandoned.

Meaning the flare gas was free for the taking.

"Well, Gid, say *something*, would you? Heck, say the first thing enters your mind."

They'd played this game before. It felt to Gideon like shaking up a bottle of pop for thirty, forty years and then cracking the top.

Gideon exploded. Smacked at the dash and instantly regretted it. A lightning strike of pain shot through every nerve ending in his arms. He saw yellow spots at the edges of his vision.

Trish sat up. The half-rolled passenger window beside her knocked against its track inside the door.

She touched his arm, gently rubbing it like she had so many nights. Only thing kept him from the bottle or the pills or (like so many others around) the crank. Her, those touches, and Brett.

"Ah, 'hon, c'mon. You know once this is–"

Gideon turned his head toward his wife, so sudden did she stop speaking.

Trish's eyes were straight ahead. "Watch out!"

Right in front of the windshield: a massive crow. Nearly as big as a baby fawn. Hovering there as if suspended in time and space.

Gideon slammed the brake.

The truck, bless its weary, Tin Man heart, didn't just come apart at each and every seam in the old beast. But it seemed to come as close as possible under the circumstances.

Luckily, the dust settled atop the roadway wasn't so thick and the brakes (Lord mercy what was left of them, anyhow) bit, sliding the car to a stop. Safe.

The crow, unfortunately, wasn't so lucky.

TWO

It probably wasn't more than a minute.

A full sixty seconds.

Gideon sat there in the driver's seat of his raggedy F-250, the quiet of the valley completely blotted out by the pulse in his ears.

The windshield was spider-webbed with crimson. It felt like both he and Trish sat there for a long night of the soul, considering their complicity in the act which had just befallen them.

Gideon stepped down from the truck and surveyed the damage.

It was mostly the windshield, though the damage there was significant enough that it would require some finesse before driving further. Finesse, in this instance, wouldn't be so hard to come by–he had a tire iron somewhere in the back, he could use that to bash out the windshield and they could ride home getting bugs stuck in their teeth if need be.

From the outside of the truck, it appeared as if the crow had somehow collided first with the windshield before denting the hood of the truck in several areas. A trail of blood marked the way. Nothing critical, especially to an old beast like the F-250, but curious nonetheless.

About twenty feet away, the crow lay motionless, glass-eyed, its feathers ashen with the slick oily texture of a Louisiana bayou. Part of it seemed to have exploded out, but he was happy to find it was the part facing opposite where he now stood.

Whether they could drive the truck home was an open question, though one he was certain would be yes.

But he was more interested right now in the generator.

"Bad omen, to be sure," Trish said.

He and Trish were all alone out here now. Nothing new there. Ever since he had to stop working because of his hands, it had been them against the world. They had enough squirreled away to survive on for quite a while if things went off without a hitch.

They just never worked out like that for Gideon.

Without Gideon being able to work, his health benefits would run out soon.

Once Brett got injured, the razor's edge got sharper. At first, they thought the paralysis was temporary. Would clear up. Maybe. It only bonded Gideon and Trish closer, being there for their son. In a way, him being off work was a blessing. He got to be there for everybody, physically, emotionally.

But the money was tight. Getting on some government plan would be their next best option, but that just made their margin for error even tighter.

Then things got noose tight once the doctors changed their story. Long-term care. Rehabilitation. Specialists. The numbers the social worker at the hospital had been quoting them seemed made up to him. Game show numbers. Christ, he cloned himself three times over with good, strong hands he couldn't afford those bills.

So to David the Dweeb they'd gone, once Gideon told Trish about the company going under.

"Thank God," Gideon said, leaning over the truck bed so he could see the generator. "Still operational."

Wouldn't be but a few minutes until purple dark arrived, setting their valley to the darkness, to the night.

"Now we gotta get back," Trish said.

As if on cue, the hitch in the plan emerged right then.

The back left side of the truck dropped about six inches lower with a crash of scraping metal. It didn't pop out the back left tire so much as it crushed it down beneath the weight of the truck. Whatever part of the truck he'd heard rattling around before had finally given up holding on. Gideon rushed up and into the truck bed, grabbed the jack, and got the back of the bed up off the ground so the tire didn't give out fully. The road underneath the jack was, of course, cracked and potholed, so the jack's hold on the truck seemed precarious at best, but it was the best he could do with what was at hand.

They wouldn't be driving the truck any further. Bad omen, for sure.

"No service here, I bet," he said, wasting no time now complaining about what had just happened.

Trish leaned across the driver's seat and grabbed her phone. "Bingo. Probably not for a few more miles."

"That figures." This was a known dead zone. Perfect place to get your car pelted with crows.

"Uh huh."

To Gideon's right, a flash of light caught his attention. "Well, would you look at that." A car was coming from off in the distance, same way as they had. If that wasn't something like good fortune, he wouldn't know what was.

"I'll flag 'em," Trish said. "You might want to hide, old man. Wouldn't want to scare any of these nice folks off, eh?"

Gideon smirked. He'd never been what you might consider intimidating, but he couldn't argue with the logic of Trish flagging down a car instead of him. Heck, she was beautiful enough to flag down an airplane.

He watched as the truck slowed a few hundred yards up the road, as if only now just seeing them stuck there. For a second of panic, he thought maybe they'd been spooked. Like they looked ahead up the road and saw danger. A trap. Please Lord, show some mercy.

He held his breath. Please don't turn back around.

The truck picked up speed again, red-lit dust kicking up behind it from taillights just turned on. Gideon and Trish would have a chance at a ride, it seemed. A tow was probably out of the question with the tire. But a ride they could do.

"Looks like some kind of utility truck," Trish said. "Big enough bed in the back to house that thing."

"You think we're getting a ride back, cargo in tow?"

Trish smiled and winked and it about exploded Gideon's heart. He loved this woman. He couldn't imagine being in this situation with anybody else. Where he was weak, she was strength. With any luck, they'd live out the rest of their days without her recognizing his deficiencies with what he brought to the table. Her face still visible as the last fingers of sun stretched through the tops of the mountains off in the distance, she said, "If we do, we can ride the four-wheeler out to the site. Hook this thing up, confirm it works, then David said he'd wire the money straightaway."

Wire the money. Gideon had never even heard of such a thing prior to their meeting. Trish had been prepared, of course. Had given David the Dweeb all the details, the kid nodding and tapping away at his computer like he was playing piano.

"Could have this whole thing behind us here shortly. Brett'll be getting the care he needs by week's end." She made it sound so easy.

The utility truck pulled up beside them. New truck. An interesting one, too. Municipal electricity in Pinedale, according to the logo on the passenger's side door. But it also had a U.S Postal Service decal stuck along the truck's bed, which was covered by a hardtop camper shell. This truck did double duty, as some did out this way. And it seemed the driver was pulling in two clean incomes, too, as very few did out this way.

"Carl Lyle. Is that you?" Trish asked as the truck's passenger side window rolled about halfway down. Inside the cab was dark, the light in the sky so faint now that it didn't provide any illumination inside.

Carl Lyle. Gideon breathed a sigh of relief. It seemed fortunate smiled upon them, indeed. Trish wouldn't have to flex too much charm for them to get a ride back. He didn't know Carl much, but he knew Denny, Carl's older brother, from working together. Denny was a roughneck all the way through. Both the good qualities and the bad. One of those fellas who lived at the edge of the prisoner line. But smart, too. More so than most. Denny knew some things about the world. How he learned them was anybody's guess. But he had enough smarts to make something of himself in the world. Why it was such a shame he hadn't. Or wouldn't.

Carl was the good egg of the family. Would know Gideon's name, even if he didn't remember meeting him once or twice at one of the local bars.

"How do you know him?" he said to Trish.

"He delivers our mail."

That made sense, what with the Postal Service decal and everything.

"Howdy, Trish. Gideon." Carl's voice boomed from inside the cab.

Rather than get out or roll the window all the way down, he reversed the truck and did a wide circle around so that his truck's back end came up close to the back end of the F-250.

The driver's side door of the utility truck opened. Out stepped Carl– a thickset man with fiercely black hair, dressed in jeans, work boots, and an olive-green fishing shirt.

"What in the world happened here?"

"Attack of the crow," Trish said, flashing her warm smile. Even in the approaching darkness, it was a megawatt smile.

"Something else, huh?" In that moment, Gideon tracked something odd about Carl.

A second appraisal called more into question. Though he had always been a thickset fella, his face was now thin. Almost gaunt in the deepening shadows of dusk. Eyes seemed a bit sunken, though they were alive with an energy that scared Gideon in that moment. He realized, too, that the clothes were made for a thicket fella, but a thickset fella wasn't wearing them.

Standing before them was a fella who used to be thickset.

And around these parts, a sudden weight loss isn't usually a good thing.

In fact, it almost only ever happens when the person losing the weight starts using.

Trish's back went straight. Like hackles on a cat.

Something was wrong here.

The passenger door opened.

Out stepped Denny Lyle. Looking for all the world like he was here to cause wreak havoc.

Gideon's heart started hammering in his ears, the pain in his arms receding only slightly due to adrenaline but reminding Gideon that his arms weren't strong enough to take on Carl or Denny Lyle, let alone both of them.

Family really was everything out there.

THREE

Carl took another step closer to Trish, his movements twitchy.

Gideon reacted, closing the distance between himself and his wife so that he could at least get between Carl and Denny and Trish. He got a feeling he might need to fight these boys, and he already knew that wouldn't end well. Besides both being a head taller than Gideon, he wasn't sure he could hold tight on a fist at the moment.

David the Dweeb's words came bounding back like a shout from Zeus at the top of the mountain. "Before the other guys ..."

Now Gideon realized what it was about that statement that struck him so cold.

There was competition for David the Dweeb's money.

Out here, money wasn't an especially easy thing to come by.

Especially not the sums David had thrown around.

Had Gideon thought more about it, it would've made sense the competition was from someone familiar. This wasn't a big place. Industry here wasn't like in the big cities, millions of people buzzing about like bees. Here you could fit the population of all the oil producing counties into a New York City apartment, probably. Gideon might not have chosen Carl and Denny as the first competitors, but they were as likely as anybody else. David the Dweeb was here, after all, in Wyoming. If he had someone interested in West Texas, likelier than not he'd have gone there.

"No need to make a big scene," Carl said with a tight jaw, waving Trish away from where she stood. "Two of you just stand right there so I can see you both close. This'll be quick, don't worry."

Trish stepped backward until she was about even with Gideon. She put an arm around him and pulled herself closer to him. Protected. Though what that meant with a gun pulled on you was anybody's guess.

Gideon tried to pull her tighter against his body, but he flat couldn't. He wondered if she noticed. Her husband was about as strong right now as a babe.

"How'd you find out?" Trish asked.

Carl smiled something dark and mischievous. "Noticed the bills first. Thought you all were either flush with cash or needing some pretty quick. Overheard you one day babbling about it on the phone. About setting a meeting in town, how you had access to a pocket of natural gas, how it wasn't even being used right now but your fella was the one to find it. So, we followed ya."

Denny stepped up to Gideon. "Help me put that thing in the truck. Or are you too weak even to do that?"

"Might be, Denny. Honest. I could barely hold the wheel."

Denny's eyes blazed with the fire of the lost soul. "I wasn't planning on killing ya. Don't make me change my mind."

For some reason, that comment actually made Gideon feel lighter. Denny knew Trish and Gideon couldn't go to the cops once the generator got taken. What they were trying to do wasn't exactly legal, so there'd be no crime Gideon could call up the sheriff and pin on Denny. Not without implicating himself. And Denny knew Gideon well enough. The old driller wasn't the criminal kind–current situation notwithstanding. Some of the roughnecks they knew, those old boys would string you up if you even thought of robbing 'em.

Gideon simply would not retaliate in that sort of way.

Denny knew it. Nothing Gideon could say or do here to make him think any different.

And that, too, pained Gideon. Meant he'd once again let down his wife and his boy.

Meant they were back where they started. Unable to care for the kid who so needed them right now.

"You're not taking that generator, Denny. You neither, Carl. Kill me if you need to. But we ain't leaving here without it."

Denny smiled. Almost like he relished the thought. "You go that route, we ain't gonna just kill you."

That sent a shiver through Gideon.

"Please, Denny. The money ain't for us. It's for our boy."

Carl cut his eyes over to his brother. Denny didn't flinch. Told you something. Even through whatever hardships had fallen on Carl to make him find the dirty path that so many around these parts walked on, he still had some humanity in him.

Denny apparently didn't share that.

Gideon stepped closer to Denny. Gun be damned. Maybe Carl wouldn't pull the trigger.

Denny stepped to Gideon. "You want me to show you how it's going to be?"

Anger welled up in Gideon. And just like the company was doing with the blooming natural gas pocket, it burned off. In its place was only despair. "I got no choice, Denny. Please."

Denny got close enough so Gideon could smell the wintergreen chew tucked inside Denny's mouth. Probably the cleanest vice the roughneck had. "And what makes you think I do?"

Gideon looked straight into the man's eyes. All he saw there was a deep, empty well of nothing.

"Get your ass to the truck and help me carry that generator," Denny said, knocking his shoulder into Gideon and pushing past toward the back of the F-250.

Carl kept the gun on Gideon. His eyes went colder and he nodded for Gideon to follow his brother.

Without anything else to do, Gideon turned back. As he went to his truck, he couldn't bear to meet Trish's eyes.

Gideon went to the opposite side from Denny, the side where the truck had dropped lower, twisting the metal of the underside into a mangled mess.

Denny smiled. "Something loose on that side of the truck?"

Gideon understood. The Lyles made it so the F-250 was never making the full trip back to Pinedale. They were always going to take this generator, presumably leave Trish and Gideon stranded on the side of the road. That just pissed him off more.

Denny hopped into the bed and unlatched the numerous ways Gideon had secured the generator in place. "Ain't got all day," Denny said. He hopped down and held one side of the generator. Gideon tried to ball a fist around the other side but the effort shot daggers up and down his forearm. Instead, he just kept an open palm around one of the pieces of metal framing, matching where Denny had grabbed on the other side.

They pulled the generator off the back of the truck.

Before he took a second step, Gideon dropped his side, unable to stand the pain and unable to fully close his fingers around the metal framing. The generator wasn't particularly heavy, but it was awkwardly-shaped.

Denny got in Gideon's face. "What the hell, man. I need to have my brother put you and your bitch wife in a ditch or something?"

Gideon's face flushed hot.

"Get over here, Carl. They ain't doing nothing to stop us."

Carl came over and took Denny's place so the larger Lyle brother could now hold one side of the generator and still keep eyes on Gideon and Trish, both standing frozen now beside the F-250.

Denny bent down to pick up the side Gideon had dropped. "You weak little pus—"

Gideon snapped his foot out like he was kicking a hundred-and-fifty-yard-long field goal attempt. His work boot knocked Denny straight across the jaw, whipping the roughneck's head around with a kinetic snap that turned Gideon's stomach. He was no pansy, had seen plenty of fights around the job sites. Been in a few scrapes with fellas who deserved it. But this brush with violence was both surprising to him and unsettling.

Carl stood there in shock, unable to process what had just happened.

When he finally did, he looked bug-eyed at Gideon, as if he was processing in slow motion from an instruction manual of what to do next.

Gideon saw the light behind his eyes go out.

Carl raised the gun toward Gideon.

Trish came out of nowhere and slammed her body into Carl's side, knocking him off-balance and coloring the Lyle brother more than a little confused. Carl tripped over the edge of the generator and fell to the ground, the pistol knocking out of his hand and skittering a foot away from his outstretched hand, coming to a stop just beyond the place where the F-250's back tire was bent at its weird angle on the car.

Carl hit the ground with a grunt but didn't seem shocked anymore.

He army crawled for the gun, reaching his hand out to grab it.

Gideon put his work boot onto the back left bumper of the truck and pressed against it with all his weight. Trying to knock the truck's jack out of place.

It gave, but not all the way.

Trish ran in beside Gideon and lent her weight to the effort.

Gideon heard metal against concrete. Carl's hand and the gun.

The truck–bless its dinky heart–finally gave way, the unsteadiness of the jack working in their favor. As the F-250's weight slammed back toward Earth, the sound that erupted from beneath them was haunting. A thousand lemons all crushed by the world's biggest lemon squeezer. Trish screamed out. Gideon, in too much shock, simply swallowed back against the rising bile in his throat.

As darkness finally fell over the mountains, the scene went once again silent.

And it was just Trish and Gideon and the generator, whose green status light now glowed.

FOUR

Five minutes of excruciating pain later, Trish eased the utility truck in a loping circle back in the direction of Pinedale. Toward their forgotten pocket of natural gas.

Gideon sat in the plush leather passenger seat, sweating, the pain from helping Trish move the generator into the covered back of the utility truck's bed now engulfing so much more than just his hands, wrists, and forearms. He had to close his eyes and breathe deeply against the new throbbing rolling in waves into his shoulders and upper back.

The adrenaline was fading, but he still felt jolted to attention with what all had happened.

Trish said, "So what was the deal with that crow?"

Gideon thought about that. Thought about Denny's unconscious form as Trish dragged him out of the road and onto the shoulder. Thought of Carl's head going water balloon pop beneath the F-250's weight. Gideon shuddered.

"I guess it was like you said. Bad omen. Just not for us."

They were both silent for a while.

Eventually, Gideon was able to open his eyes. The pain receded, only slightly, but under the conditions, it felt like a great reprieve. Trish flipped on the utility truck's brights. "Should be enough light to see us through," she said. "Seems they've come a long way in the lights department in the past thirty years. I can actually see out the window."

Gideon smiled even despite the pain. "Smooth ride, too."

"From here on out, let's hope."

Gideon doubted it would be. Though they might not have competition, they still needed to get the generator working. They would need to deal with the fallout from the Lyle brothers, one of whom's death would be difficult to explain. And even then, assuming they got past that and Denny didn't come out seeking revenge, Brett had an uphill battle to climb, though the specialists had been optimistic about everything except Gideon and Trish's ability to pay for the necessary care.

But whatever might be ahead for them, Gideon knew the woman seated beside him would make it survivable.

They couldn't afford to fail.

And Trish wouldn't let them.

EXCLUSIVE SNEAK PEEK

Keep reading for a look at the forthcoming crime suspense novel from Niz Thomas.

For more exclusive content, sign up for Niz's newsletter at: nizthomas.com/newsletter

AFTERWORD

If you've made it this far, then there isn't much more I can than say thank you.

Then again, being as I *am* a writer, I can dig deep and find a little something else extra to mention.

First–if you've made it this far *and* haven't thrown down this book in frustration at any point (perhaps even if you've felt the tension, the fear, the breathless grip of these pages), then I hope you'll check out the next volume of *Nizpatches*. Depending on when you're reading this, it will either be a short wait, or a wait only as long as it takes to get to your nearest e-tailer, where *Nizpatches: Volume Two - Twisted Crime* is surely waiting for you.

If you enjoyed any of the series stories–*The Omega Diner* (Ledgerman series), *Thin Air* (Ledgerman series), or *Call Me Betsy* (True Name series), I hope you'll find the rest of the series at your preferred e-tailer as well. You can also sign up for my newsletter at nizthomas.com/newsletter, where you'll hear first about when new releases are coming out, along with a bunch of other cool stuff.

Second–I love to hear from readers! Please drop me a note at niz@nizthomas.com. You've already read through plenty of what I have to say, so I'm interested to hear what you've got to say for yourselves, too.

Third—I guess I already mentioned the newsletter, but know that by signing up, I always go to that list of fans first with cool stuff—exclusive stories not published elsewhere, the occasional FREE story, limited edition art, information about sales and book discounts, contests, and notifications about stories in progress and stories forthcoming, recommendations about the books I'm reading that I think readers will LOVE. The newsletter is just getting going, so there is bound to be a whole lot more in the future, too. Sign up at nizthomas.com/newsletter (and don't worry, if you end up wanting to remove yourself from the list, it's easy to do so).

Fourth (remember when I said there wasn't much more I can say?)—if there's anything in these pages (or any other pages of mine you read), please pass along the word. In the writing business, word of mouth tends to be the most effective form of marketing, which is the bedrock upon which I can build a sustainable business that allows me to continue doing what I love (and, if you love it, too, for you to keep getting more of what you love). I thank you in advance for putting in a good word with others.

But mostly, thank you for being willing to take a chance on a collection of short stories—little "dispatches"—from the strange primordial soup that is my mind.

It means the world to me.

And I hope it brought you some crime-riddled enjoyment during these turbulent times in which we find ourselves.

Niz Thomas
January, 2024

FAMILY TREE

A SUSPENSE NOVEL

WRITERS OF THE FUTURE AWARD FINALIST

NIZ THOMAS

FAMILY TREE

A NOVEL

by Niz Thomas

EXCLUSIVE SNEAK PEEK

ONE

Joe Parry woke up with a jolt, like he'd just been struck with a cattle prod. His eyes shot open but it took him a second to register where he was. His heart was pounding against his chest like it was trying to escape. Or explode. For a brief second he wasn't sure it had a preference, though his would have been for whichever did the job faster.

He saw a single salmon-pink splotch of paint on the bedroom wall, peeking out from under what was otherwise a complete cover-up job. His daughter, Samantha, must have missed the spot last month when she sponge-painted the entire wall charcoal grey, part of a number of recent changes that Joe wasn't completely comfortable with. He didn't need another look at the nude art posters she'd hung above the eave of her desk for a reminder of that fact.

Joe tried to catch his breath. He'd been dreaming of something dark and ambiguous, a heavy weight of a feeling, like impending doom. Or an anvil on his chest. Unfortunately, he knew the feeling well. He'd had plenty of nights like it in recent years, though this one felt somehow different for him. Worse, sure, but also like the end of something that he hadn't known had started yet.

Turning his neck — which he realized, with some discomfort, hadn't managed to find a pillow in the night — and he felt his heart rate slow a bit, knowing he was at least in his own house. He took a long, deep breath to reacquaint himself with the land of the living and inhaled the orange and lavender scent from the candle he'd bought Samantha two months earlier, and given to her last week for her eighteenth birthday. He felt ashamed now that he'd bought it so far in advance and upon giving it to her, it couldn't have seemed any stranger of a gift.

Even unlit, the smell was so potent it crept through his nostrils and settled deep in his throat, constricting his windpipe just enough to make him cough. Like a feminine version of chloroform.

That scent, and the thought of every moment since he'd first smelled it at the mall, hurt him more than any cattle prod could have. He could see now that two months could move mountains in a teenager's world. Even the two weeks since Samantha had turned eighteen had felt to him more like wrangling cattle than being one. Things started happening much faster and he felt like they needed to be contained.

He could never quite get his hands around the situation though.

Joe put his feet on the floor and slowly pulled himself up. His neck cried out something fierce at the effort and he felt a few muscles down his back and ribcage light up with their own protests, too. He let himself sit there, on his daughter's empty bed, the realization of her not coming home another night made it feel like he just woke up from a car wreck.

Five nights. Five of the longest nights he'd ever had — and that was saying a lot. He wondered if Samantha had ever sat up at night as a kid, waiting in vain for him to come home. He put that thought aside as quickly as he could muster in the cold of the empty room and the darkness of a fall morning. Talk about the shoe being on the other foot.

Sitting there, he picked up the cordless phone next to Samantha's bed. He'd brought it in from his room, just in case she called. It was the only phone in the house and he'd thought about getting rid of it for the last few years but never cared enough to do so. He checked the caller ID but saw there had been no missed calls. He put the phone back on the side table.

He became aware of the tick, tick, tick of his wristwatch. The rest of the house was silent. A far cry from the city sounds he'd spent most of his life cocooned in. There wasn't a single car horn or emergency siren to be heard. The sticks — as he referred to them, but in reality, what most people would call the suburbs — were far too quiet for him. It gave all the thoughts inside him more amplification than he liked.

He always could have used more of a chance to think before he acted. But sitting in silence, thinking about the worst? Well, that just wouldn't do for him.

Even after two years living in the sticks — a northern New Jersey town called Mendham — he didn't feel adjusted to the quiet. The town wasn't far from where he grew up in Newark, but it might as well have been in another country. The biggest commonality was that people breathed oxygen in both places. Most of Newark was rundown now, but it hadn't been so bad when he grew up there. It was a city of immigrants back then — Italians, mostly. By contrast, the houses in Mendham consisted of a few historic sites built by militia men during the Revolutionary War surrounded by lawyers' and bankers' mansions built sometime after the last bull market. The legacy was still alive, Joe supposed, but the reality was that, despite the fact that just a few miles away George Washington and his army camped during the winter of 1779, the only thing that still remained from that era was the quiet.

And sitting alone in the house his then-wife convinced him would be the salve on half-a-lifetime of putting the badge first, the silence of this place felt personal. Like it was made specifically to torture him. He wondered if any of those militia men had felt that, too.

He got up and smoothed out the bed's comforter, wanting the room to feel exactly how Samantha left it whenever she decided to come back home. Then he went to the threshold of the doorway and turned once more back to the room, wondering if he was being too naïve. If the thought of her coming back to him and this house wasn't more than a pipe dream.

The room looked so different now. Grey and black color had replaced the pinks and pastels from only a few months ago. But that felt like another lifetime at this point. Samantha's closet, neater than any kid's he ever knew, was more of the same color palette. Black and grey jeans and long tees replaced the rainbow colors of dresses and blouses. And a growing collection of nude art posters.

He closed the door and went downstairs.

In the kitchen, he set up the coffee. Samantha had taught him how to use the thing when she bought it for him a year earlier. It was one of those machines with more levers than it seemed to need — like Rube Goldberg's idea of a coffee maker. At the time, Samantha had been going through a "coffee phase" and he was pretty sure the gift had been more for her than for him. Either way, he had to agree with her. It tasted better than the watered-down version his old drip machine produced.

Joe opened the cabinet above the machine and reached past the decaf and lighter roasts for a brand called Unleaded Java. It was that type of morning. After loading the beans into the dispenser, he switched the machine on and it went to work grinding them up. It couldn't finish the cup fast enough for him.

He reached for the stereo remote and hit play, not sure what would come on. It had sat silent for the past five days. Since his wife left them, Samantha had always worked the stereo for him. While her taste in music didn't really match his, he felt it was something that brought them together. Especially before she decided coffee wasn't for her anymore, due to the injustices involved with making the beans, or whatever the issue of the day was.

The song that started up was faint at first, almost mechanical in its introduction. There was no singing or words yet, just a low humming sound mixed with the timbre of a factory — grinding metal and power tools. Definitely not the type of music that Samantha would have played six months earlier, but he guessed those days were long gone. At the moment, he didn't care about the music. He just wanted the noise. The song had an eerie quality mixed with the grinding of the coffee machine. It hearkened back to the days when people like him would have been working the factory floor, not much more to worry about than what the wife was making for dinner that night. But then, he guessed those days were long gone now, too.

Joe stood there, eyes closed, letting the sounds wash over him. For a moment, he fell into a trance, thankful for the brief respite from his own mind.

Once the machine was done, Joe took a big sip of the coffee, the bitter smell and taste bringing back the closed throat feel from the candle in Samantha's room. He hardly noticed, though, desperate to wake up. The song kept playing, growing in intensity, leading him toward something dark and mysterious. He felt like he was moving toward the end of a hallway in a horror movie.

His phone buzzed on his hip, making him jump and almost spill, and pulling him up and out of the trance-like state the music created. He lifted the remote and turned it off.

"Parry."

"Joe, it's Shea," the voice said. Shea Walters. With the music and the fog from a shit night of sleep on his mind, he'd forgotten she said she'd get back to him today. She was a private investigator who used to work undercover with him. A good, reliable cop, though she'd had a bit of a fall from grace in recent months, from his understanding of things. He knew the feeling well enough — his move out to the sticks wasn't *exactly* a selfless move — and he also knew a cop like Shea wouldn't let it get to her. He'd asked her to pull in a favor with a contact she had.

"Hey Shea, you got something for me?"

"Yeah, I'm doing great, Joe. Happy to help a friend in need."

"Sorry. My mind's a little fucked right now. She hasn't come home in five days. I'm just worried."

"Yeah, well, when kids turn legal, sometimes they rebel. My parents would have killed for me to just slip out of the house for a week. They still, to this day, don't believe I was a cop. I didn't have the heart to show them the newspaper clippings after I got canned, just to prove it to them. Try not to take it personal, Joe. It's probably more about her own thing than anything you did."

Joe wished that were true. He took another sip of the coffee, finally feeling it working on his cobwebbed brain, and went over to the sliding glass doors off the kitchen. Growing up, Joe could never have pictured himself living in a place like this. It was too green, too wholesome. He'd worked narcotics and then homicide for a bit in his hometown. The only green he saw was the money they took off the dope dealers when they popped them. The setting out here was more like something out of a Stepford brochure. Not even the dealers wanted to score big and live like this. He doubted they even had the imagination. And these were the same sort of people who started sculpting fake toys made out of cocaine to avoid detection.

He took another swig of the coffee, having a sudden hankering for a shot of Jameson in it. He stared out at his manicured backyard, the showcase piece of which was a twenty-five-foot tall chestnut tree that sprawled at least as wide, canopying the flowers and hedges planted in mulch on the back end of the property. A single rope swing hung from the tree's thickest branch, an addition he'd made on Samantha's fifteenth birthday. He could practically hear her laughter from that afternoon echoing through the quiet of the house.

It was thought to be one of the last surviving chestnut trees in the whole northeast. It was basically the reason they chose the house in the first place.

"You there, Joe?" Shea asked.

"Yeah, sorry. Just trying to stay positive, that she took off with a friend or something."

"I'm sure that's what it is, bud. I wish I had something to help ease your mind. Unfortunately, my contact came up empty. The phone's been off since Tuesday night."

An icy fear rose up in the pit of his stomach. That was the last night he'd seen Samantha. The night of her birthday. He wasn't all that surprised that she hadn't turned it back on yet — other than being a teenager and have the phone practically be a third appendage.

"I figured as much."

"How's that?"

"The night she left. We had a fight. It got kind of ugly, the mudslinging back and forth. I would have left it at that, but she decided to fling the phone, too. It got busted up, though I thought they made those things out of titanium these days, so I was hoping it didn't break all the way. Or that she'd gotten it fixed if it had. I know she took it with her because it wasn't on the floor when I came back downstairs. She's got pretty good aim, Shea. If I hadn't ducked, that trace would have led you straight between my eyes."

He could hear Shea laugh on the other end. "A girl that takes after my own heart," she said. "Or my dad's, at least. You think he didn't want a son with a golden left arm, you'd be dead wrong."

Joe watched a squirrel bounding through the grass, into the mulch, and up the front of the tree. It worked itself around to the backside and disappeared from his view. He had a sudden urge to tell Shea the rest of what happened that night with Samantha.

"Well, the Amazin's sure could use one right now," he said, ignoring the urge.

"Yeah, every day since '76."

"So what do you think I should do, Shea? I figured she might replace the thing, turn it back on. Your search would have caught that?"

"Yeah. Even if she used a different SIM card or a new phone. My guy is at the company. He checked it all. And what should you do? Shit, it's hard to say. You call around to her friends?"

He had, though Samantha had recently changed more about herself than just her favorite colors and taste for coffee. A few months back, she started hanging out with a different crowd at school. Artists, mostly. At least that's what she'd told Joe they were. He hadn't pressed her because, well, he didn't think she was preparing to run out on him. And because after so many years working the streets of Newark, the kids out here wouldn't have alarmed him unless they started leaving IEDs along the side of the town's lone main road.

He'd need to do a better job digging them up.

"Listen, Joe, I've got another call. One other thing you might try? Her phone is listed under your account. Check who she'd been talking to recently, see if any patterns emerge or any numbers that might clue you in. Gotta run, though. Let me know if you need anything else, alright?"

"Sure. Thanks, Shea. And let me know how I can pay back the favor."

They hung up.

Joe finished his coffee, but by now it was lukewarm and the bitterness tasted like stomach acid fighting its way up into his throat. He'd spent a few days assuming Samantha was just blowing off steam. Then a few days telling himself not to overreact. But now he felt the cold instinct that something was wrong creeping up the base of his spine.

Outside, a gust of wind blew through the backyard, swaying the rope swing as if a ghost were sitting in the seat.

His little girl was missing.

And maybe not of her own volition.

JOIN THE MAILING LIST

Did you like this story? How about another one for FREE?

Join Niz Thomas' mailing list for a FREE copy of the short story *The Omega Diner*, which placed Honorable Mention in the prestigious *Writers of the Future* Contest.

Join now to also get:
MEMBER DEALS & DISCOUNTS
FIRST LOOK ACCESS
AUTHOR INTERVIEWS
LIMITED EDITIONS
AND MORE

Join the newsletter here: nizthomas.com/newsletter

ALSO BY NIZ THOMAS

For a full list and links to purchase, visit: nizthomas.com/books

Nizpatches
Volume One: Crime Stories

Volume Two: Twisted Crime

---

the Ledgerman series
The Omega Diner: A Ledgerman Story

Razor's Edge: A Ledgerman Novel

Thin Air: A Ledgerman Story

Last Ride: A Ledgerman Novel

---

the True Name series
Call Me Betsy

Call Me Gertrude

Call Me Aileen

Novels
Family Tree

Door Number Five at the Memory Motel

And The Moon Is Full And Bright

Election Day

Short Stories

A Refraction of Kind Light

A Void of Ascendant Light

Becalm This Mighty Sea

Burn Off

Burn Together

Cheers

Elder Hunger

Fiona's Mercy

First Light of Every Morning

How to Commune with a Futurist

Lady Death

Lane Change

My Bleeding Kansas

No Control

Paint It Thrice

Rail Music

Ray-Ray's Stoop

Recidivist History

Red Tempest

Ships in the Night

Songbird

The Bad Guy

The Climb and The Glory

The Forever-ish Flame War

The Imminent Fire

The Impassable Way

The Light Alone

The Two O'Clock Killer

The Voice of Rage and Ruin

Upon Your Dreams They Prey: A Lullaby

Vanguard

Vida's Sixth Trip Around the Sun

When Sheds Talk

ABOUT THE AUTHOR

Join the mailing list for a FREE short story
website: nizthomas.com/newsletter
email: niz@nizthomas.com

Niz Thomas grew up a fan of *The Silence of the Lambs*, heist movies, and 007. Not surprisingly, as a kid he wanted to be an FBI agent, a cat burglar, and a spy. He decided to go to college instead and has regretted it every day since.

Niz is an eleven-time honoree in the *Writers of the Future* contest, receiving a Finalist designation for his short story *Vida's Sixth Trip Around the Sun* and several Silver Honorable Mention awards. He is also the author of over thirty short stories and several forthcoming novels, including the highly anticipated horror novella *And The Moon Is Full And Bright*, the dark suspense novel *Family Tree*, and the near-future political cat-and-mouse novella, *Election Day*.

Join his mailing list for limited edition story art, early access to new releases, and periodic FREE short stories.

Join the mailing list: nizthomas.com/newsletter

Made in the USA
Middletown, DE
23 January 2025